Resisting the Doctor

Resisting the Doctor

A Marietta Medical Romance

Patricia W. Fischer

TULE
PUBLISHING

Chapter One

"SINGLE CAR MVA. Starred the windshield. Awake and—"

"Get me the hell off this thing!"

"Combative."

Dr. Lucy Davidson's valiant attempt to stay upbeat in the last thirty minutes of her twenty-four hour shift had almost lost its potency, but the chaos of a new trauma patient immediately revived her exhausted body like she'd mainlined a double espresso.

"No loss of consciousness," Paramedic Amanda Carter continued as Lucy ran with paramedics Amanda and Kyle Cavasos, along Officer Brett Adams toward a trauma room.

A quick scan of the patient told her if there were any immediate signs of distress.

ABC-Airway. Breathing. Circulation.

"I hate these backboards. I need to sit up! My face hurts. Give me something, *stat!*" The patient rolled his shoulders in an attempt to get out from underneath the backboard's Velcro straps that kept him solidly in place. He tried to pull the bandage taped to his forehead off. "Why is this crap on my face?"

Lucy pushed his hand away. "Leave it."

"Why?"

"Leave it." As they rolled into room one, Lucy patted her pocket to make sure her favorite stethoscope was with her.

Got it.

"It's a bandage for the blood, sir," Amanda explained as they positioned the EMS stretcher next to the bed.

Immediately, scribe Ethan Flynn, Nurse Shelly Westbrook, and nurse's aide Poppy Henderson surrounded the bed. Along with the first responders, each grabbed a handle of the backboard.

Lucy donned a pair of gloves and nodded. "Okay, on three. One. Two. Three."

Easily, the group lifted the patient and quickly went to work disconnecting him from the EMS monitors.

Lucy jumped into the fray, adrenaline coursing through her veins. With swift efficiency, she palpated his arms, legs, and his abdomen. When the patient didn't grimace and she didn't feel any obvious fractures, she breathed a small sign of relief. "Can you feel your legs and arms, sir?"

"I can feel you grabbing me. Kind of like it."

"Let's logroll him off the board." Ignoring the patient's comment, she helped the members to peel back the Velcro straps and turn the patient to his side.

Lucy ran her hand up and down his spine. "Anything hurt, sir?"

"Nope, but keep rubbin' my back there, sweetie. Been a long time since I had a good back rub."

Her teeth clenched at his sexist commentary. *There's one*

in every town.

"He's a real smooth talker." Amanda gave Lucy a sideways glance.

They rolled the patient to his back and Lucy verified the C-collar placement.

Shelly and Poppy reattached the bedside EKG leads to the chest stickers and the pulse oximeter to his finger as Ethan typed everything each medical team member called out.

"I need to sit up," the man demanded. "I need to sit up now."

"Work with me, first. Can you tell me your name? Where you are?" Standing at the head of the bed, Lucy grabbed her purple penlight and checked his eyes. "Pupils equal and reactive to light."

"Got it." Ethan's fingers sailed across the keyboard as Kyle pushed the collapsible stretcher out of the room.

The patient turned his head as much as the hard cervical, or C-collar, would allow. "Quit shining that shit in my face."

Before Lucy could respond, the hard smell of stale alcohol, dried blood, and nicotine slapped her in the nose.

Without warning, the burn of anger danced in her chest, momentarily derailing her momentum. Tears pricked the backs of her eyelids and she turned away, pushing the wicked memories to the far corners of her brain.

Where did that come from?

"You okay, Dr. Davidson?" Ethan asked.

Focus, Lucy. Focus. "Yes. Sorry, thought I was going to sneeze."

"He does smell like he washes with nicotine." Brett wrote on his clipboard.

Kyle reentered and added, "The back of the ambulance smells like a morning-after frat party."

"That's one way to start a Monday." Turning back towards the patient and staff, she nodded. "Who did you bring us this morning?"

"This guy was going about forty miles per hour. Icy road. Hit a tree. No other passengers in the car." Amanda's voice dripped with exhaustion as she hung a half full bag of fluids on the IV pole. "He was standing outside his car, smoking a cigarette and texting when we got there."

Brett stood at the end of the stretcher, his police badge hooked to his belt. "When I arrived on the scene, he complained of neck pain and immediately lost the ability to stand."

"It wazzzzn't my faullllffff." The patient slurred, then laughed. "I'm kidding. I'm slurrin' on purpose."

Lucy's jaw clenched at the man's flippant attitude of driving while intoxicated. The bulky, blood-soaked bandages on his forehead covered up part of his unshaven face. "I'm sure that tree jumped right out in front of your car. Happens all the time."

"Screw you."

Just what I wanted. A lying, drunk jerk at the end of my shift.

"Have some respect." Kyle growled as he handed three vials of blood over to Shelly. "Here you go."

"Thank you, Kyle. You always bring the most thoughtful

gifts." Shelly held it up and Ethan nodded, but when she turned the bag upside down, all the blood fell in clumps in the vials. "Ugh, these have coagulated."

Kyle let out an aggravated sigh before picking up his metal clipboard. "Sorry. It's freezing out there. It took a while to get him secured on the backboard. He wouldn't cooperate."

A wicked cackle escaped from the man. "I'm cooperative. I'm cooperative all damned day."

"Please draw another round, Mrs. Westbrook." Lucy added, as she pulled out her stethoscope and listened to the patient's lungs. "CBC, chemistry series, recreational levels."

"You can't get my alcohol level unless I say you can." The patient smirked as if he'd been through this before.

"Sir, we draw vials of blood in the field to get a baseline at the scene." Kyle shook his head in disgust. "The doc decides what tests to run when we get here."

Draping her stethoscope around her neck, Lucy smiled sweetly, "If you want anything for pain, I have to know what you've already got in your system. Otherwise, you'll cold turkey it. Either way, I'm gonna get my job done. Lungs clear."

He swallowed hard. "I'll sue."

Without losing a bit of sweetness in her voice, Lucy responded, "Cold turkey it is then."

Yeah, I can play that litigious game too, buddy.

The man gritted his teeth. "When you see I'm clean, you'll give me morphine."

How she hated liars, especially ones who endangered the

lives of others. "Clean? You smell like a distillery."

"So what? I had a few beers."

"And?" Anger simmered under her skin at his arrogance.

"A few shots of whiskey."

"And?"

His lips went thin.

Checkmate. "Clean indeed."

Lucy looked at Ethan, relieved to see he typed as he appeared to watch her and the patient's interaction. Having a scribe had been a game changer. It freed Lucy up to take care of patients without being weighed down by documentation after the fact. Quoting the patient in real time would help if he came back later insisting something else had occurred. Especially a patient who would certainly alter the truth.

Brett shuddered and rubbed his hands together. "Wish I could take Duke with us on runs like this. He would have gotten this guy in line much faster than we did."

Lucy had met Brett's large German shepherd, Duke, a few different times when she visited the Main Street Diner. Brett would often park in front and run inside to get a to-go order and say hi to his sister, Casey, who worked there.

"Duke is always a happy guy." Lucy slowed down the rate of the IV as the patient's heart rate held a steady tempo on the monitor. "When he sees me, he presses his wet nose against the window of your truck and barks."

"He's a sucker for smart women."

Brett's subtle flirtation made the corner of Lucy's mouth curl up. "Well, thank you, Duke. I thought German shepherds could easily handle the weather like this. I slowed the

IV rate down. Site appears patent."

"Duke does okay for short sprints, but with the slush and ice, he'll run around until his paws are soaked, frostbitten, and bleeding."

"What about booties?" Ethan asked as he furiously documented.

Brett laughed. "I tried that and he ate two of them. I ended up having to give him laxatives until he got rid of them."

"Gross." Ethan grimaced, yet his fingers never broke tempo.

"What's the temp outside?" Even as Lucy counted the minutes to the end of her shift, she dreaded walking out into the frigid air of the Montana morning. A hard change from Jupiter, Florida in spring.

I miss the beach.

"It's seventeen degrees before wind chill. Too cold for Duke to be out for as long as we have to be." Brett's twenty-four hour shadow was more obvious under the fluorescent lights of the ER than it had been when they ran in.

He must have been working since yesterday too.

Lucy peeled back the bandage on the patient's head, revealing a large bruise and multiple small cuts. "His forehead is even. No obvious fractures, but a lot of small lacerations and a large hematoma. Nothing sutureable. No obvious foreign bodies. You said he starred the windshield?"

"Looks like. No one else appeared to be in the car." Amanda nodded and yawned before sitting behind the central desk and picking up the phone. "No footprints going away from the vehicle. Just his around his car. Gonna call in to Betty, tell her we've given y'all a report."

The patient's eyes went wide as though he'd just processed their previous conversation. "You keep your shit eatin' dog away from me Adams. Last time, he bit me in the ass."

Lucy stifled a laugh while she pulled out her stethoscope checked the patient's lungs again. "Glad to know you and Officer Adams are already acquainted." *And that you're about ten seconds behind the rest of us.*

"Looks familiar, but I can't place him. Always hard to identify people when they're beat up and don't have any ID." Brett narrowed his eyes. "Or won't tell you who they are."

"Quit yer yappin'." The patient yanked on the C-collar, a thick, silver ring with jagged edges sparkled on his finger. "I hate these plastic contraptions. Gonna break someone's face if you don't let me up!"

Lucy rolled her eyes. "You can try, but you won't get very far."

"You think you can take me, *little girl?*"

What a total jerk. "Well, I haven't used my black belt since I've been here. If you want to go there, I'm game if you are."

Everyone in the room gave a lighthearted laugh as though none of them believed her, but the man's lips went thin when he looked up at her.

She raised an eyebrow. "You wanna do this, we can do this."

He clenched his jaw as though her words caused him to

think again.

"Need me to get Dr. McAvoy?" Nurse Shelly Westbrook leaned toward the doorway.

"No, Mrs. Westbrook. I don't *need* Dr. McAvoy." No matter where she'd worked, this always happened the first time Lucy got an obnoxious patient. Immediately, the staff would assume because of her size or gender or whatever, she needed backup and that always hit Lucy the wrong way.

If they knew what I'd already fought, they wouldn't be so quick to assume.

Shelly held her hands up in surrender. "Yes, ma'am."

Well, that came out harsher than I intended. "Sorry, Mrs. Westbrook. Let me do my assessment. Trust me. Things will be okay. Besides, Officer Adams is here."

A look of cautious understanding washed across Shelly's face. "Sounds fair."

"I ain't afraid of Adams." The patient attempted to turn his head, but the hard neck brace kept him from moving more than an inch. Apparently, he'd finally processed who she was. "You're my doctor? What are you, twelve?"

If any of the male physicians walked in here, he wouldn't be so disrespectful.

"No, sir. I'm more than old enough to take care of you. Don't move." Lucy opened the c-collar and palpated the man's neck, gently moving her fingers along his spine. "Am I hurting you?"

A look of bliss replaced anger and he let out a long, over-zealous groan. "You can hurt me like that all day, sweet cheeks."

What a gross individual. "I'm Dr. Davidson, if you please."

Poppy rolled her eyes. "Ugh, I might know who that is."

"No step-offs in the spine. Okay, sir, I'm going to move your head from side to side. Let me do this. Don't move." Cupping his head in her hands, Lucy gently turned his head to the right. "Please tell me if anything hurts when *I* move you."

She hadn't turned it two inches when he dramatically grimaced. "That hurts. It hurts soooooooooo bad."

I'm dubbing you Mr. Obnioxious.

"This stays on, then." She rested his head to center and reapplied the C-collar. "I need a spinal series."

Ethan nodded and tapped the screen. "Ordering."

Mr. Obnoxious's eyes went wide. "What? No. No wait, I mean it hurts so *good.*"

"I'm not going to play this game with you. You hit the windshield. Were you even wearing your seatbelt?"

"Don't like them."

"Spinal series it is." Lucy stepped away and stood next to Ethan to get a few breaths of non-alcohol filled air. "If you do that same crap when I check your belly, you're ending up with a CT scan and potentially an I and O catheter to check for blood in your urine."

"Whatever...wait. No catheter."

Amanda gave Lucy a thumbs-up as she spoke on the phone.

He snapped his fingers as he gave her the side eye. "I meant you hurt me so good. Do it again."

"No." Reviewing what the best course of action would be for her mental toddler of a patient, Lucy dreaded examining his abdomen. He'd already made gross sexual innuendo, but if he had a liver or splenic laceration, she had to know.

"Shit. Can I have a drink of water?"

"No."

"Why not?"

"Because if you've got any internal bleeding, you'll need to go to surgery and you need an empty belly." Lucy answered without a hint of compassion.

"This sucks."

"Be grateful it only sucks for you." As she pressed on his stomach, she said a silent thank you when he didn't even flinch with her examination.

The flippant demeanor of her patient had been one thing, but knowing he made light of driving intoxicated sent a burning sensation up and down her esophagus. "You could have killed someone tonight."

The patient rolled his eyes, but the rest of the staff's faces fell in shocked surprise, making Lucy realize how fiercely the words had escaped her. Embarrassment warmed her cheeks, but she refused to apologize. Instead, she focused on the bedside monitor and how stable the man had been since his arrival.

Lucky bastard.

Shelly pulled a tourniquet out of her pocket and wrapped it around the patient's arm.

"What are you doing?" He growled as he attempted to crane his neck, but got nowhere.

"The last blood clotted. I need another sample."

He began to pull away. "I don't want my blood—"

"Cold. Turkey." Without looking at him, Lucy replied with the compassion of a school marm, but caught him throwing daggers at her with his eyes.

The room remained silent except for Ethan's typing, Kyle writing on his clipboard, and Amanda on the phone.

Brett leaned against the desk and appeared to be documenting as well.

From needle insertion to applying the Band-Aid took Shelly less than a minute. "I'll get these processed."

"Thank you. The croupy kid in room five, okay?"

"Last I checked, but I'll peek in on him."

"I'd appreciate that, Mrs. Westbrook." Lucy stripped the gloves off, washed her hands, and took out her stethoscope to listen to the man's belly. "Bowel sounds active. No guarding on abdominal exam. No distention."

Before she left the room, Shelly nodded to Kyle. "Tell Gabby we said hi."

Despite the bags under his eyes, a wide grin spread across Kyle's face. "I sure will."

"She making any of that orange cinnamon bread today? Freddie and Tia were hoping I could bring some home. They eat it for breakfast."

"I hope so. I could use a good meal." As Lucy backed away to rescan the patient for subtle and obvious signs of guarding or fractures, her stomach growled at the mention of food, especially anything from the Main Street Diner. "Been basically living there for the past six weeks."

"They still don't have your furniture here, Dr. Davidson?" Amanda asked as she handed Poppy something off her clipboard.

"No, ma'am, they don't. My furniture is somewhere in Michigan right now." She rubbed her neck, hoping to work some of the kinks out from her twenty-three hour, forty-five-minute shift.

Kyle pointed. "Is that why you've been there so much?"

"I like the bread." With lungs now full of non-alcohol fumed air, Lucy grabbed a clean pair of gloves as she approached the stretcher again.

"Not that I'm complaining. Gabby's loving having someone to talk to in Spanish."

"It's nice to keep my skills up. I took every Spanish class I could to get that fluent. I'd sure hate to lose it. Sir, I'm feeling your skin for obvious pieces of your windshield." Running her fingers tenderly across the patient's forehead, around his face, and his neck. She felt nothing but a few scratches and dried blood. "I feel a couple of bumps here, but looks like, so far, you didn't fare too badly."

"Hey, assholes. Quit talking about bread. I'm hurtin'." The guy slowly snapped his grubby fingers before laughing at his own joke.

"Guess he's paying attention even though he's about ten seconds behind us. Concussion it is." Lucy ran down her mental checklist again as the hard scent of cheap whiskey and cigarettes hovered in the air around him like a cloud.

The bitter taste of anger coated the back of Lucy's tongue.

Another selfish drunk driver.

Without thinking, she tapped the scar at the base of her neck, making her flinch. The want to let her hair out of the clip to cover the spot hit her unexpectedly hard, but she pushed the idea away.

Despite time having faded the wound, right now, it felt as raw as the day she got it.

And her life changed forever.

Chapter Two

*F*OCUS, *LUCE. FOCUS.*

To avoid being strangled by the potency of his liquored-laced breath and her sad memories, Lucy inhaled through her mouth as she pressed on the man's stomach. "Okay, Mr. Patient. I need to ask you some basic questions."

"No. Fix me first! I ain't answering anything you stupid—"

"That's enough. I've been more than patient with you." Lucy slammed her hands next him, making the bed momentarily shake. "If you're going to be jerk about it then we'll just let Marietta's finest take it from here. Officer Adams?"

"I told you, I ain't scared of Adams."

Brett smirked. "Fair enough. I guess I could call—"

"D-d-don't call Tate. Or Shaw." As cocky as the man had been, his demeanor immediately turned one-eighty as he played with the shiny ring on his finger.

The staff members' eyes widened with amusement.

"Guess he has met Marietta's finest." Brett handed paperwork over to Poppy, who paused and glanced at the patient again. "Said he swerved to miss an elk and hit a tree. No ID. No car registration."

"Because that doesn't scream illegal activity at all." Poppy rolled her eyes.

"There was an elk I tell you. Huge! Ginormous." Mr. Obnoxious snarked, "I'm pretty sure there was an elk. Or maybe it was a rabbit. Could have been a snowman."

He sang the off tune version of the holiday favorite, "Frosty the Snowman", moving his arms randomly along with the song, a new layer of aromas floated off him. The hard stench of *sweetened* nicotine and dried blood mixed with the booze and sweat.

The wicked combination hit Lucy in the face, making her stomach twist and threaten to protest.

"You okay, Dr. Davidson?" Ethan's forehead furrowed. "You look a little green."

She waved her hand in the air in front of her while she struggled to keep her fury at bay. The quicker she was out of here, the less chance she'd say something to ruin her chances of keeping this job during her first ninety-day probationary period. "I'm good. He's not guarding or grimacing. Let's get back to that elk, sir."

"What elk?" The patient yawned. His yellowed teeth sat slightly crooked.

She ran her finger along his chin and bottom teeth. "Doesn't appear to have any loose, cracked, or missing teeth. The animal you swerved to avoid hitting, sir."

He held his hands wide. "Right. Elk. Maybe a beaver. It was a big ole son o' bitch."

"Patient freely and purposely moves his arms without difficulty or guarding. Chest moves evenly, no step-offs. No difficulty with work of breathing." She pulled her purple stethoscope out of her pocket again, reassessing his lungs and then his abdomen. "Lungs clear, no crackles, rubs, or crepitus. Bowel sounds are normal. I'm sure the animal in question was enormous, sir."

Ethan's fingers flew across the keyboard. "Got it."

After she pulled away, a mischievous twinkle flashed in the patient's eyes as a sly smirk spread across his bloodied face. He slid his hand over his crotch and cupped. "That's not the only thing that's enormous, sweet cheeks."

The sexism gets old. "You should write greeting cards."

A snicker from Poppy, Amanda, and Ethan helped lessen her annoyance, but the man's arrogance sliced at her already exhausted, raw nerves.

If I had a dollar for every gross sexual comment that's been made to me over the years, I wouldn't need to work as a doctor.

She looked at the wall clock. Six-fifty.

Is Dr. Clark my replacement? I can't remember.

"What'd I miss?" The deep voice of Dr. Thomas McAvoy tickled her ears before she noticed him.

When she turned, he smiled at her, making her stomach feel as though it had been filled with anxious butterflies.

He looked fresh shaven and bright-eyed.

How does he even look that good? He's been here since yesterday.

Suddenly, Lucy became very aware that she hadn't brushed her teeth in the past several hours. She reached into her lab coat pocket and said a silent thank you when cellophane crinkled between her fingers. "Dr. McAvoy, we were just getting acquainted with our new patient here. Can you tell me your name, sir?"

"Only if you tell me yours first, ohhhhhhh, foxy lady." He attempted to play Jimi Hendrix air guitar as he sang off key, to one of the musician's signature tunes.

"No one told me there would be a rock concert." Dr. McAvoy threw up a few fist pumps.

"I know exactly who that is." Poppy snapped her fingers and returned to the central desk. "Let me double-check."

"When you know, let me know." Brett's shoulder walkie-talkie went off and he stepped out to take the call.

Thomas leaned over and got within inches of the patient's face. "You'll have some respect. That's *Dr. Davidson* and she's here to save your ass."

As much as Lucy appreciated the chivalry, she always hated the immediacy of it. No matter where she worked, before ever getting to know her, no other male doctors gave her the chance to defend herself. More times than she could remember, she'd explained repeatedly over the past month, how she earned a second-degree black belt in Kung Fu before completing her extremely busy ER residency. As of yet, she'd made little way convincing any of the staff of her full physical capabilities.

For some reason, Dr. McAvoy seemed not to totally trust her the most and she'd yet to figure out why.

What's his story?

She cleared her throat, hoping to get his attention. "Thank you, Dr. McAvoy, I can take it from here if you want to start on another patient."

"I'll stay since I'm going to watch him after you leave."
As Thomas slowly moved away, his jaw clenched. "I'm here
until noon."

"When did you come in?" A subtle smell of spicy citrus
floated around him.

"Seven last night." He shook Kyle's hand, who stood
near the central desk.

How can you possibly smell like you just showered?

"Amanda and I are finishing a twenty-four." Kyle
stretched. "Ready to go home."

"Jade sure has the doctors on weird schedules." Nurse
Dave Fletcher entered with an iPad in hand.

"She sure does. Insanely long hours." Shelly tapped the
bedside monitor. The low hum of the blood pressure cuff
inflating filled the room. "I don't see how either of you are
standing. After a good twelve hours, I'm done."

Lucy's lips thinned. "We don't need to do it. We've all
served our times in residency and school for ridiculous
clinical hours. We can make this work without beating
ourselves up."

"Good luck getting her to listen to you."

"I've taken over that duty as of yesterday. Hopefully
schedules will align more efficiently here soon and we'll hire
a few more physicians to help with the load."

"Does Jade know about that?" Dave raised an eyebrow, a
sly look of amusement on his face.

Not that Lucy looked forward to the conversation. Since
Lucy's arrival, Jade Phillips had made it very clear she'd run
the ER without anyone's help, thank-you-very-much.

Despite Jade being a strong nurse practitioner, she had been put in charge of the doctors when the last ER director, Dr. McMasters, gave her a blank check his last couple of months before retirement. "I realize she stepped up quite a bit when the last director decided not to, but she's got plenty of obligations without needing to worry about scheduling the doctors."

"Battles are ugly when women get into it," Ethan mumbled.

A beep momentarily pulled Lucy away from her angst about dealing with the territorial employee. "Vitals normal."

"Got them," Ethan replied, his fingers dancing across the computer keys.

Jade handing off duties to Lucy had gone about as smoothly as the ocean in a category five hurricane. "It'll all work out. I promise."

But the uncertainty in Lucy's voice didn't even convince herself.

Dave shrugged. "It's your funeral."

"Speaking of Jade, isn't she supposed to be here?"

"I'm Jade today." Dave raised his hand.

"Jade, you look rather mannish today," Amanda replied.

"Thank you. Yeah, Jade called me an hour ago, saying she had an emergency."

"Did she say what kind of emergency?" Thomas's brow furrowed as Dave shrugged.

"No clue."

Thomas's inquire about Jade irritated Lucy. *I wonder what the deal is between those two.*

Then she mentally berated herself for even caring. *That's not the issue here. Focus!*

There had been multiple discussions among the staff about how Thomas had come to Marietta to help Jade. That he owed her a favor as he stayed at her house despite his locum tenens company offering to pay for his housing.

When the two were together, the lack of romantic chemistry caught Lucy's attention more than once. Either they were both incredibly good at hiding their feelings at work or there was nothing intimate going on. They acted more like siblings than lovers, past or present.

Why are you concerned about this? She pulled herself away from the discussion and tried to appear busy. *You're supposed to be the ER Director. Act like it.*

Dave tapped the iPad and held it up for Thomas. "The next patient in line. Told her to let us know when she needs to pee."

"A woman with abdominal pain for six hours. This won't be complicated at all." Thomas sighed and shook his head.

Annoyance bubbled in her stomach at his sarcasm. "Not up to the challenge of a female belly pain, Dr. McAvoy?"

"I'm up to the challenge, just fine, Dr. Davidson." He calmly answered without missing a beat. "More things to consider, that's all."

Crap. I didn't mean to say that out loud. "About one hundred more."

Because of basic anatomy, the source of the cause of abdominal pain was always more complicated in women. All during training, Lucy had heard her share of sexist commentary from coworkers and attending physicians about a women's *faulty* anatomy. How women always had to make things more complicated than they needed to be.

Yet, since working as the new ER Director at Marietta Regional, Lucy had yet to hear one disparaging thing from the staff about male versus female patients. Other than nurse practitioner Jade Phillips's general dislike for Lucy for unknown reasons, her initial weeks here had been professionally pleasant.

Her personal life had been nonexistent, but the incredible respect amongst the staff, regardless of gender, had been a wonderfully refreshing change. One Lucy was still getting used to.

The only wrinkle in her world since arriving had been trying to stay professional when thinking about Dr. McAvoy. For whatever reason, he'd been more than a distraction in her perfectly planned agenda of success.

I have to make this job work. Prove everyone back home wrong.

Thomas McAvoy had proven to be a charming variable she hadn't planned.

As Thomas's eyes scanned the iPad screen, Lucy reminded herself that, presently, her simmering annoyance had nothing to do with the man standing across from her, but at the drunken man on the stretcher.

Well, maybe a little of her frustration could be because of the guy standing across from her. The good doctor had shown his competence more than a few times since his arrival in Marietta. He had a calm and cool demeanor when dealing with difficult patients and their families, to the point of being downright charming.

Not that he needed help gaining appreciative looks. His hazel eyes and naturally dark sun-kissed skin, along with his amazing arms did that all on their own.

But Lucy *thought* she knew his type all too well.

Beautiful. Arrogant. Chauvinistic, but damn if Dr. McAvoy had proven her wrong.

So far.

Why does he have to be so unpredictable?

For some unexplained reason, that annoyed her.

A lot.

Maybe because she'd let her guard down one too many times around men like him and ended up with professional and personal heartache.

Besides, Dr. McAvoy mentioned he'd taken three locum tenenses assignments a year for the past five years and had no intentions of stopping his travels anytime soon.

His stay would be temporary so no reason to get her hopes up about him.

Plus, Jade whispered more than once Thomas had been considered for the ER director job, should Lucy fail.

I can't fail.

She couldn't let him earn this job over her. Lucy desperately had to prove she was more than the girl who survived the horrible crash years before. She was more than her famous medical siblings and local celebrity stepfather.

More than a feel-good headline.

Here, in Marietta, she could make her own world, her

own footprint, her own name, but she had to focus and not allow complications to derail her success.

Complications like the tall drink of water in front of her.

Momentarily lost in her thoughts, she jerked herself out of them, only to find him looking at her. The corner of his mouth curled into a perfectly adorable smirk that sent her ovaries into a round of happy backflips.

Ugh, focus. You need sleep. Not sex.

Without taking his eyes off her, Thomas asked, "Mr. Dave, has the patient complained of any guarding, fever, intermittent pain for the past six hours, unusual weight gain?"

Dave shook his head. "Yes, nope, not that she mentioned. I'd be surprised if she were pregnant."

"Why's that?"

"Because she's a lesbian."

Thomas's eyes narrowed on the screen. "Sure enough. She put that on her medical history. Well, good for her."

An unexpected laugh escaped Lucy, interrupting her silent lust. "That's the best explanation for not being pregnant I've ever heard."

"Let's go with the obvious stuff first. Since she hasn't had a hysterectomy, run a HCG anyway." Thomas tapped the screen several times before handing the iPad back. "I added a couple of things there if you could get that rolling."

Crap. All of that was right on the money practical.

Even his approach to the patient's pregnancy possibilities.

As she refocused back on her patient, she berated herself

for running out of reasons to, at least professionally, appreciate her handsome colleague's knowledge base.

"Got it. Thanks, Dr. McAvoy." Dave quickly filed the iPad on the counter of the central ER desk before disappearing around the corner.

"I'm gonna go check on my other patients really quick," Shelly stated and left the room.

"Go ahead, Mrs. Westbrook." Despite being bone-deep exhausted, Lucy never hated a day working in the ER. The ability to change a person's health and get them on their way as fast as possible had been her motivation for going into medicine.

Someone did the same for me.

Every day, the scars on her body reminded her of that. How life could change in a second.

And there aren't any seconds to waste.

She smiled sweetly while standing at the patient's bedside. "Go ahead and get your first assessment on your belly pain, Dr. McAvoy. We're good here."

Thomas crossed his arms and stood firm. "Don't worry about it. You want to give me a report so you can get out of here?"

As much as she'd love to leave and start a long nap, Lucy didn't completely believe he'd only come in to get a report and let her go home. *No one wants an annoying drunk as a patient.*

A wash of worry blinked in his eyes before he rotated his left shoulder a few times and grimaced.

She didn't know whether to find Thomas's behavior endearing or insulting.

Lucy lifted the patient's blood-crusted forehead bandages. "You sure?"

The man snored so loudly he woke himself. "Wha'd I miss?"

"I'm sure." Thomas stepped near her, his gaze appeared laser-focused on the patient.

Interesting. "Let me finish a couple of things and he's all yours."

"Fair enough." His words were tense. His usually jovial demeanor, muted.

Very interesting. "Sir. Can you tell me where you are?"

Mr. Obnoxious narrowed his eyes at her. "You're still here buggin' the shit out of me. I'm in the ER."

"What year is it?"

"Why are you asking me this crap? I need drugs, stat."

"Stat, huh?" She looked up at Thomas, who smirked. "You hit your head. I need to know if you know what year it is."

"The Olympics happened last month. That Chloe chick snowboarded."

"Yes, but what year is it?"

Tapping his ring on the bedrail, he clenched his jaw. "Damn, you're demanding. You're not gonna let this go, are you?"

"It's part of the job description." Lucy raised an eyebrow. "Tell me the year and I'll consider some acetaminophen."

"2018," the man blurted. "Where's my pills?"

Lucy pointed at the scribe. "Please order six hundred and

fifty of Tylenol."

"Tylenol?" He began to sit up but Lucy shook her head. Immediately, he let himself plop back down again, but kept a white-knuckle grip on the siderails.

"That's what I offered."

"That's all I get?"

"It's that or nothing."

"This sucks." He pouted.

Good to know he can carry on a constructive argument.

Ethan tapped the computer monitor. "Done. What else?"

"Patient awakens easily, knows date, place, and recognizes staff. Sir, wiggle your toes." Lucy waited.

Silence.

"Sir!" Lucy tapped the man's shoulder.

"Shit! What?" He snorted and groaned.

"Wiggle your toes."

"Why?"

"I want to see if you can follow directions and can move your toes." The buckle on his brand spankin' new Prada loafers sparkled. Those along with that jagged ring on his finger were stark contrasts to the grungy jeans and local band t-shirt.

I wonder where he got those fancy pieces and if anyone's missing them.

To her right, his steady heartbeat and perfect oxygen level showed the patient continued to appear stable.

He shook his feet, then tapped the toes together before individually throwing his legs up like an intoxicated dancer.

"See, I'm fine. New York. Neeeeeeew Yoooooooork!"

"Sir! Sir."

Thomas leapt forward and grabbed the man's legs before lowering them to the bed. "Come on, man. Calm down."

Kyle jumped in to help and Amanda ran around the desk.

As Lucy moved toward them, Thomas held his hand up. "We've got this."

Stop it! I didn't ask for your help.

"Get off me!" Mr. Patient kicked his feet like a spoiled toddler.

"Calm down first." Thomas growled before inhaling. When the patient's knee made hard contact with Thomas's shoulder, he cringed, but he didn't lessen his hold. "What have you been smoking?"

"None of your business." Suddenly, the patient went flaccid like a balloon that had been instantly deflated.

After a few moments, Kyle and Thomas slowly backed away.

"He was this argumentative at the scene. We'd fight him and he'd calm down. He has the endurance of a tomato." Amanda rubbed the bridge of her nose. "His car is totaled."

"He's got a bruised forehead, a few scratches, but no major lacerations and nothing is actively bleeding." Lucy pulled back the forehead bandages as the rapid tapping on the computer keyboard played in the background. "The airbag didn't deploy?"

"Much older car. No airbag."

"Before 1999, then," Thomas murmured as he rubbed his shoulder.

"1998." Lucy responded without thought.

"What?"

Lucy repeated, "It was 1998 when airbags were required."

Thomas looked around, "Dr. Davidson. It was 1999 when airbags were required."

"No, it wasn't." Her hands clenched at her sides.

"Why are you arguing with me?"

It had rarely bothered Lucy about being incorrect, but it always chapped her ass when someone told her she was wrong when she damn sure wasn't. "I'm not arguing. I'm correcting you."

"That would be fine if I were wrong."

His arrogance wiped out the last of her patience. She had no fuel left to fight her own anger. "It was September 1, 1998."

"What was?" Thomas's forehead furrowed and he looked around as though someone else would answer his question.

Tears threatened to fall, but she squared her shoulders before she answered, "The Intermodal Surface Transportation Efficiency Act of 1991 went into effect on September 1, 1998. It cited that every truck and car sold in the US had to have airbags in front of the driver and front seat passenger."

Except for the patient, everyone in the room stood slack-jawed, staring at her.

Kyle typed in something on his phone then held it up. "How did you know that?"

Because they would've changed my entire childhood and saved my father's life.

Chapter Three

LUCY SWALLOWED HARD as her eyes went wide. "I knew that because it's important. I-i-it was a test question on my ER boards."

No, it wasn't. No one I talked to has ever had to answer that question. "You must have had a different exam than I did."

"Probably. Seems they have several different versions." With her chin tilted slightly up, Lucy had the presence of JJ Watt about to take the field on a fall Sunday. A stark contradiction to her true size.

Why is it so important to be right about a damned airbag?

"Okay, Dr. Davidson." Thomas smirked. "1998 it is."

"Thank you, Dr. McAvoy." Lucy appeared to slowly exhale her frustrations as a hint of appreciation twinkled in her eyes.

"You're welcome, Dr. Davidson."

"Get a room." The patient crossed his legs at the ankles and yanked on the collar. "And get me the hell out of this thing."

"Here comes radiology," Poppy called from the desk.

"I'm giving you two minutes, then I'm taking this thing

off myself," the patient demanded, pointing his grease stained fingers randomly in the air.

Lucy shook her head. "No, you're going to stay there until we get you cleared, otherwise I call Shaw."

Brett reentered and smiled. "I won't take that personally."

"Ahhhhhh!" Slamming his fists on the bed, the man mumbled, but he made no attempt to remove the C-collar as they wheeled him out of the room.

Every hair on Thomas's neck stood straight up when the patient began insulting her. Lucy standing within an arm's reach of the jerk didn't alleviate any of Thomas's concerns.

This guy is bad news. I can feel it.

Thomas ignored that instinct before and it almost cost him his life. He wouldn't brush his worry off again, especially not where others were concerned.

Especially not when Lucy stood so close to trouble personified.

He breathed a sigh of relief when the patient headed to radiology and far away from her.

With the patient gone, the staff cleaned up the room, Amanda and Kyle returned to the ambulance, Brett called into dispatch, and Lucy and Ethan reviewed the documentation.

Thomas began to leave the room, but stopped short, his angst on high alert. "Please let me know when he gets back, Dr. Davidson,"

Without looking at him, Lucy replied, "Dr. McAvoy, I've got this."

"Lucy, please, let me know."

For a moment, he didn't think she'd heard him, but when she turned, her eyes sparkled with curiosity. "Okay, Dr. McAvoy, I'll make sure you're here when Mr. Obnoxious returns."

"Thank you." Swallowing hard, Thomas gave her a quick nod and quickly checked on his other two patients, discharging one and heading back to trauma room one.

Ever since his arrival in Marietta a month ago, Thomas McAvoy wondered about the sweet, walking encyclopedia that was Lucy Davidson. Her endless knowledge of medications, research studies, and even pop culture made it difficult to outsmart or even help most of the time. She'd been an intriguing challenge to figure out, but her being near this idiot triggered a protective instinct in Thomas he didn't know he had.

Not that she can't handle herself.

Other than his friend, Jade, every staff member mentioned how constantly chipper Lucy stayed. Each shift in the ER, she never lost her sweet, calm demeanor and the patients always responded positively to her, even during differences of opinions.

She'd been more than respectful to the staff and her professionalism couldn't be more textbook.

Until today, when he unknowingly challenged her about an airbag and she practically shot fire out of her nose.

What's your story, Lucy Davidson? I'd like to know.

Not that he should be asking himself that. He'd only come to Marietta to repay a debt. Help Jade get her father's rundown house ready to sell, get some good mountain air in his lungs, and a nice paycheck in his bank account. Then he'd be on his way. Move on to the next adventure, just like he'd done pretty much his entire life.

Rubbing the bridge of his nose to stifle a yawn, he attempted to refocus on completing the rest of the shift instead of the throbbing pain in his shoulder.

For the past four weeks, if he wasn't working ridiculously long hours in the ER, he had a hammer, screwdriver, or gloves in his hand, trying to fix the unfixable. Although he'd made this promise to help Jade after she'd saved his life two years ago, he wished he'd known what kind of money pit her father's house had been. Otherwise, he would have sent her the money for a bulldozer and called it even.

"Still helping on the house, Dr. McAvoy?" Ethan asked as Lucy helped pick up a few pieces of trash before she stood at the desk with Poppy and Shelly.

"It's a money pit, Ethan." He dug his fingers into the sore muscles of his scapula, alleviating the tension for a few seconds. A sharp pinch of pain at his rib made him grimace.

"That's what I hear. Her dad let it go close to ruin those last few years. I don't know how he even had the money to pay the light bill."

"Jade probably paid it like she's paid for everything else." Thomas wondered how much his friend would be willing to lose before she realized how far gone her father's house had fallen.

Ethan leaned against the counter and popped his knuckles. "I know a couple of people who might be interested in the land, but would want to start over with building a place."

"That's what I keep telling her, but she's insistent the house needs to be fixed before she'll even consider selling. She won't sell to anyone who's gonna tear things down." Thomas rotated his arm in a circle, stretching the tight muscles of his shoulder. He needed a long run, workout, and hot shower and he wouldn't get any of that staying at Jade's place. Not when there was too much to fix.

"Why save a shack and a few storage buildings?"

"No, idea Ethan." Thomas had given up trying to figure out Jade's reasons for saving her father's house. "But I promised her I'd help and I keep my promises."

"You always keep your promises, Dr. McAvoy?" Poppy asked coyly.

"I do."

"Good to know." Lucy smirked before the melodious complaining of the patient echoed into the ER.

Every muscle in Thomas's body clenched. His brain sat on high alert.

"Give me my shit and I'll be out of your hair," the man demanded as they wheeled him back into the room.

"Speaking of hair"—Lucy put on a new pair of gloves— "Dr. McAvoy, you wanna check his films and I'll check if there's any glass in his scalp?"

Mr. Obnixious smiled as if he'd won the lottery. "Come on, pretty lady. Rub my *head*."

Before she could reach the stretcher, Thomas rested his hand on Lucy's shoulder, stopping her. "Why don't you look at the x-rays before you do that?"

She turned and blinked at him for a moment, before nodding. "Guess I must be tired. You'd think I would have thought of that first."

Mr. Obnoxious pouted. "What? I'm not gonna get checked?"

"Well, he heard that fine," Lucy mumbled.

Ethan clicked a few things with his mouse and brought up the x-rays.

A quick scan of them showed nothing of concern. Thomas pointed to the monitor. "See anything?"

Leaning forward, the subtle smell of flowered citrus danced around her. "No, I don't see anything. Neck looks good too."

The hard rip of Velcro yanked their attention to the patient, who'd removed his cervical collar and thrown it across the room.

It landed with a hard slap, making Poppy jump and Thomas's heart rate hit the roof.

Lucy's eyebrows hit her hairline as she spun around. "What are you doing?"

Grabbing the siderail, the awkwardly sat up as he, barked, "Give me my scripts and I'm out of here. Shit. My head!"

"That's not what we're doing here."

With his anger simmering just below the surface, Thomas stepped forward, placing his body partially between Lucy and Mr. Obnoxious. "Dr. Davidson, why don't you let me finish this?"

The patient tapped his ring on the bedrail; his eyes leered

at Lucy, scanning from shoes to the top of her head. "I want the chick to finish me."

For a moment, Lucy stood silently. Thomas could see the wheels turning in her head.

Walk away. Walk away.

She blew out a long breath and stepped back, her hands up in surrender. "I'm done. He's all yours, Dr. McAvoy."

Thomas locked his arms across his chest. "Get some sleep, Dr. Davidson."

"Thank you." Her hand gently patted Thomas's arm, making his skin tingle. "Thank you."

"Hey, hey where you goin'?" The patient attempted to snap his fingers. "Where's she going? I need another neck rub."

"You need a ride." Moving to the end of the bed, Thomas's eyes narrowed on the patient, but his brain was still back on Lucy's touch. "Who can come get you?"

Like a stubborn child, the patient shook his head then cringed. "Don't need no one. I can get home by myself. Why's the room spinning?"

"That's the concussion. I need someone else to give instructions to."

From the other side of the desk, Amanda's shoulder radio went off. She called over her shoulder, "Kyle, Brett, we gotta go. Accident on Highway 87."

"Thank you, everyone. Be safe." Standing next to Ethan, Lucy and he reviewed something on the monitor.

The whoosh of the emergency room doors and a wall of cold swept in as quick footsteps faded and the doors closed.

A chill still drifted around the unit, making several people shudder.

To avoid the cold, Thomas wandered over, leaning against the counter of the room's sink, opposite side of the room from Lucy and Ethan. "I thought you were leaving, Dr. Davidson."

"I am, but wanted to review this." When Lucy rubbed the curve of her elegant neck and closed her eyes, Thomas's mouth went dry.

The image of him passionately kissing up that supple skin to her delicate earlobe flashed in his mind.

What the hell?

Shifting his feet, he shook his head as if trying to shake such a preposterous idea out of his brain.

"You too, huh?" the patient murmured.

The oily commentary caused Thomas's blood pressure to soar. "What did you say?"

"I see you lookin' at her." Dropping his legs over the side of the bed, he lowered his voice as he replied, "You gonna tap that ass, aren't ya?"

If Thomas could have gotten away with it, he would have his hands around this guy's neck and squeezed the last ounce of air out of him. "Do you have a ride or not?"

With a satisfied grin, Mr. Obnoxious shrugged. "Not talking to you. I wanna talk to her."

"No. You talk to me. I'm your doctor, now."

Silence.

"It's fine." Standing at Thomas's side, Lucy rested her fingertips on Thomas's arm, whispering, "Calm down. You look like you're about to blow an artery."

Breathe, Thomas. Breathe.

When her hand slid down to cover his wrist, his anger immediately decreased to a strong simmer. He pulled away as though her touched burned him.

"Sir, who can come get you?" Lucy coaxed.

"Need my phone. Don't know her number."

"Fine, where's your phone?"

The man scooted down the stretcher toward Lucy, a look of lewd determination in his eyes. When he got within a foot of her, his gaze darted from his pants to her. "It's in my pocket."

With her feet planted, Lucy pushed her shoulders back and locked her arms across her chest. "And?"

A thick silence filled the room. Thomas's heart pounded in his ears.

Laying his hand on the small of her back, he stepped in. "That's enough. You have a ride or not?"

"Sure I do. It's on my phone. In my pocket." He chuckled.

"Come on. Get your phone." Lucy tilted her chin up. "Enough of this."

"What's wrong, sugar tits. Worried you might like it?"

"That's. Enough." Thomas growled and gently moved Lucy back a couple of feet.

"He's all yours, Dr. McAvoy."

But as she turned to leave, Mr. Obnoxious leapt at her. "Hey, where the hell you going?"

Thomas stepped in his way and all hell broke loose.

The patient began swinging and connected to Thomas's jaw. A blinding pain swept through his teeth and Thomas stumbled backwards.

"Thomas!" Lucy yelled, but a sickening shriek pierced Thomas's brain.

"Call Deputy Tate!" Ethan yelled as he continued to type at lightning speed. "911!"

"Already done," Poppy replied as she held up her phone, possibly filming everything. "Get him, Dr. McAvoy! Help Dr. Davidson!"

Regaining his focus, he saw Mr. Obnixious with a handful of Lucy's hair, his lecherous eyes scanning her. "Now it's just you and me, sugar tits."

"Somebody help Dr. Davidson." The young scribe moved from the computer and frantically looked around as though he had no idea what he should do.

Quick footsteps approached as Thomas advanced, his anger beyond measure.

"I told you—my name is Dr. Davidson." Reaching up, she pinned the patient's hand to her head and turned to face him. With quick movements, repeatedly slammed her heel on the end of his shoes, crushing his toes until he let go.

"Son of a bitch!" When his fingers loosened, she pushed his hand away, grabbed him by the shoulders and kicked him in the nuts twice before slamming his nose to her knee.

He crumbled to the floor and curled up in a ball.

Thomas blinked twice to process what had happened.

It happened so fast, everyone, patients and staff, went dead silent.

Dr. Gavin Clark appeared at the desk, standing next to Poppy. "What'd I miss?"

"Apparently, Dr. Davidson's a ninja warrior," Poppy mumbled.

The only thing Thomas could hear was the pounding of his heart until Ethan proclaimed, "And though she may be little, she is fierce."

"One of my favorite Shakespearian quotes, Mr. Flynn." Lucy panted as she looked around the room. When she locked eyes with Thomas, her forehead furrowed. "You're bleeding."

It took a few seconds for Thomas to realize she'd spoken to him.

The salty taste of blood coated his tongue as a warm line dripped off his chin, soiling his scrub top. He dabbed his face with the back of his hand and flinched as sharp pain caused his teeth to ache. "Dammit. He caught me off guard."

Lucy gave him a sympathetic smile as she snatched a few clean four-by-four gauze pads before inspecting the deep gash in Thomas's lip and chin. "I think his ring got you."

"How did you kick me so hard, Doc? You're a girl. Uncool! Uncool!" Mr. Obnoxious howled as he writhed.

"No, she's not a girl," Thomas whispered. "She's a woman."

Chapter Four

*D*ID I SAY *that out loud?*

When Lucy's chocolate brown eyes went wide with surprise and when she began to step back, Thomas realized he'd let the words slip from his brain and out for the world to hear. Thankfully, no one else said anything, but Lucy had obviously heard him.

Thomas McAvoy had always admired strong women, but Dr. Lucy Davidson held a class all her own, as illustrated by her recent display of defending him against a patient who'd gotten the upper hand.

And the multiple times over the past month he'd seen her take control of chaotic situations on busy nights with the charisma of a Super Bowl sports commentator.

Thomas silently cursed himself for being taken by surprise.

I should have seen it coming. I should have been ready.

She pressed the gauze against his face. "I told you I could handle this guy."

Regardless of what Dr. Lucy thought, he hadn't come in here to be the heavy in the room. She could handle herself just fine, but an unruly and drunk patient was a helluva way to end a twenty-four shift. Loads of paperwork not to mention the crap the patients throw at the staff.

Sometimes literally.

But something about this guy had Thomas off center.

Figured the moment he'd tried to do something gallant, like let her go home early, Thomas had gotten punched in the face and let his stupid mouth run wild.

No, she's a woman? What the hell, dude?

Poppy yelled, her fist in the air. "Whoop! Whoop! Wondah Woman!"

More like a force of nature.

Heavy footsteps approached as the steady jingle of metal against metal sang in the air.

"Somebody call me?" asked a low voice with a hint of amusement.

Pounding the floor with his fist, the patient growled. "Shit! Why'd y'all have to go and call the pigs?"

Deputy Logan Tate extended his hand to help Mr. Patient off the floor. "Good to see you too, Junior."

He hesitated before taking it, but guarded his nuts as he stood. "That chick slammed me in the balls."

"That *chick* is Dr. Davidson to you, Junior. Just for being damned disrespectful, she should have kicked you in the balls."

"That's assault. I'm calling my sister about this."

"Since you haven't talked to her in a year, I'm sure she's sitting by the phone, waiting for your call." Tate replied without a hint of irony. "Sit your ass down until we get this figured out."

Like a scolded child, Junior made it back to the stretcher and curled up on it. "I wanna blanket and a pillow and something to drink."

"You'll get nothing and like it." Tate's forehead furrowed when he noticed Lucy tending to Thomas's lip. "You okay, Doc?"

"Yep," Lucy and Thomas replied in unison as she dabbed his mouth.

"Mrs. Westbrook, we have an empty exam room?" Lucy asked.

"Room five just opened up." Shelly sprayed bleach on the pool of blood under the stretcher.

"Room five. Who sent the croupy baby home?" Lucy grabbed Thomas's hand and placed it on the gauze. "Hold that there."

"I did." Thomas couldn't have been more thankful she gave him something to do. He hooked his other thumb onto the waistband of his scrubs. He'd already spoken his mind out loud. With her standing so close, the natural thing would have been for him to place his free hand on her curvy hip as she kept him from bleeding more all over his scrub top and the floor.

Frustration stirred in his gut, but he couldn't decide if it was due to admiration for her for taking care of business or annoyance at her for not letting him take care of business.

"You sure that little boy was ready to go home?" Lucy stripped her gloves off and washed her hands.

"The croupy kid? He looked good. Sent him on his way, but told them to come back for any concerns."

"I hope they understood what you told them."

His fist balled at his side at her critical commentary. "Dr. Davidson, I think I know if a croupy kid's cleared to go home."

"I'm sorry. I'm tired. I'm not saying this well." Without looking at him, she started typing on the counter computer. "You misunderstand. Dad speaks broken English. Mom, who wasn't here today, only speaks Spanish. They are migrant workers. Here to pick cherries next month. Staying with family for now. I wanted to give instructions in both languages so there would be no question to what they were supposed to do."

Way to go, asshole. She's only trying to be thorough. "You worried if they understood my English only discharge instructions."

"*Claro.*" She tapped her finger to her nose.

"Right." Pain in his lip pulsated, but he couldn't decide if his mouth or pride hurt more.

Pointing, she motioned for him to go. "I'll meet you in room five. Mr. Fletcher, can you get me set up for suturing?"

"You're gonna sew me up?"

"Lucy, I can do it. Go home. You've been here for twenty-four hours." Gavin tapped his watch, but as soon as he motioned for Thomas to head to the room, a call came in from dispatch.

"Inbound with a sixty-five year old male complaining of chest pain, shortness of breath. History of diabetes."

Thomas's heart kicked in a bit, knowing Lucy would stay a bit longer.

"I'll get him stitched up, Gavin. Don't worry." Lucy patted Thomas's arm. "You have any patients you need to see really quick before I take care of you?"

He dabbed his lip. "Nope. I discharged one and the other is still getting hydrated. Stomach flu."

"Hey! What about me, Doc?" Junior whined.

Without missing a beat, Lucy shrugged. "Dr. McAvoy's waiting for your test results to come back."

"Who the hell is that?"

"The guy you just punched."

A wicked smirk spread across his face. "I said you couldn't—"

"And I told you I was going to get my job done whether you consented to a blood alcohol level draw or not." Lucy approached Junior with the confidence of a general.

"I don't like you anymore."

"Take a number."

Thomas couldn't help but smirk, only aggravating his lip.

The deputy put his feet on the end of the stretcher. "When he's cleared, Dr. Davidson, I'll take custody."

"Sounds good to me." She began to walk away, but turned a one-eighty on her heels. "And you should be damned thankful you didn't hurt anyone tonight. Or worse. Do you hear me?"

"Yeah, yeah, I hear you." Junior rolled his eyes.

"Your selfishness could have wiped out an entire family."

Her words dripped in fierceness as she berated Mr. Obnoxious's behavior.

Thomas had seen his share of car accidents due to DUI, but something about the force of her words made him wonder how many she had seen.

Or if she'd lost anyone special because of it.

Her hands balled at her sides. "If I ever catch you in my ER again doing this, I'll run every invasive test on you that's legally and ethically at my disposal."

Junior's eyebrows hit his hairline. "Geez, lady. Calm dow—"

"That's Dr. Davidson to you. It's not foxy lady or sugar tits or whatever disgusting nickname you think I want to be called."

The rapid clicking of fingers to the keyboard continued as Ethan typed away, documenting every word spoken.

"If I hear any other name but Dr. Davidson come out of your mouth when addressing me, I will order an I and O to get urine on you with the biggest catheter we have in the ER."

"What's an I and O?" Mr. Patient's lip curled up in confusion.

"Because you've potentially had hard impact to your abdomen due to not wearing a seatbelt, I could order a test where we insert a large rubber tube up your—"

"Okay, okay. I won't call you sugar tits anymore."

"And you still have to pee before we discharge you." She pointed behind her at Thomas. "That man right there helps people. Everyday he's in here taking care of patients and working ridiculously long hours, which is more than I can say for you."

Thomas moved the gauze to cover his painful smile.

"Sit down, be quiet, and wait until I'm done fixing the mess you've made."

"Yes, ma'am." The man slouched like a sullen teen.

"Yes, ma'am, what?"

A mask of darkness washed over his face. "Yes, ma'am, Dr. Davidson."

Deputy Tate's shoulders bobbed as he laughed silently.

The rest of the staff became very interested in the pens in their pockets or the ceiling, but Poppy gave a thumbs-up. "You're such a badass, Dr. Lucy."

Shakespeare had it right. She is fierce.

When he first worked with Lucy, he figured her to be the touchy feely type of female doctor who would slow down the pace of the ER, like so many he'd worked with over the last five years. He expected her to have long-winded, feel-good discussions with patients. After one shift, he discovered her compassion was only matched by her efficiency. Most of the time all of them were trying to keep up with her and he wavered between finding her provocative and a major pain in his ass.

Thomas pressed the gauze on his lip and flinched as sharp pain shot through the bruised tissue. "Dammit."

The whoosh of the ambulance entrance doors pulled Gavin away from the desk.

Amanda, Kyle, and Brett were back, Kyle rattling off report as they wheeled into the room next door.

"Sixty-five year old, complaining of chest pain during his drive to work this morning. He swerved into a snowbank..."

Lucy placed her stethoscope on the counter behind the desk. "Dr. McAvoy, I can sew that lip up. You don't have to wait for Dr. Clark to do it."

Grimacing, Thomas dabbed at the wound again. A fat glob of blood fell on his shirt. "Shit."

Taking his hand, she placed her fingers over the gauze and gently pressed. "You know you have to hold pressure to get it to stop bleeding. Stop being so impatient."

The softness of her touch almost outweighed his annoyance towards her.

Damn the woman was stubborn. And appealing.

"Ready?" She motioned for him to follow as he walked towards room five.

A subtle scent of citrus danced in the air behind her. He guessed it was her shampoo.

How does she still smell that good after twenty-four hours? I had to run down to the call room, take a five-minute shower around two this morning so I wouldn't clear out rooms when I entered.

Nurse Dave pulled the suture kit out from a top cabinet before he grabbed the bottle of one percent lidocaine, setting them both on an instrument tray next to the bed.

Thomas's heart flip-flopped at the familiarity of the situation. "You sure we can't do this with some Dermabond and some steri-strips?"

Lucy shook her head and pointed to the mirror over the standalone sink after she pulled the curtain around the bed. "It's through the vermilion border. It needs sutures if you want good results, otherwise it's just going to pop open again or you're going to have a big lump in your lip. Besides, you know Dermabond doesn't do well on lips. Take a look and see."

Not that he didn't trust her, but the thought of having another shot in his lip made his mouth dry. Plus, having stitches would be more than annoying. It would be another sign he'd let his guard down.

Again.

Leaning forward, he inspected his mouth. There, a two-inch gash in his lower lip just to the right of his front teeth. "Shit. He got me good, didn't he?"

"He got you off guard, that's all. I have no doubt you could cause enough damage with one punch for that guy to need a head CT. At the least an orthodontist."

Her confidence in his fighting skills stroked his ego.

I'll let her keep thinking that.

The deep aches in his muscles taunted him, reminding him of when he'd let an enemy get the upper hand.

The sickening sweet smell of whatever Junior had been smoking sat in Thomas's nostrils. He blew his nose hard to clear the smoke. The room spun and he braced himself against the sink as he took deep breaths through his mouth to regroup.

"You okay, Dr. McAvoy?" Dave's forehead furrowed.

"All good." Thomas waved off the nurse's concern as he splashed cold water in his face.

The chill of the water burned his wound and he silently cursed himself. Then a flash of red caught his attention. A long blob of blood decorated his scrub top. "I forgot I had blood all over this."

"Here's a gown," Lucy tossed him one. "We'll work on getting you another scrub top for the rest of your shift. When do you get off?"

"Noon. Came in at seven last night." When he first graduated from medical school, sixteen-hour shifts were a walk in the park, especially after working thirty-six during his second and third years of residency. Now, his body begged for sleep after twelve hours and it took a solid day to recover.

Lucy rolled her head from side to side. "I don't know what Jade was thinking when she scheduled these long, weird shifts, but I'm hoping to change it so no one works more than twelve hours."

"You won't find any arguments from me on that. I paid my dues in residency." Stripping his top off, he tossed it in the laundry bin and slid on the faded blue-grey hospital gown with too many snaps to navigate. He pinched a snap on either side of his neck and loosely tied it in the back as he approached the stretcher. The gown, about two sizes too big, had a scooped neck collar that revealed a good portion of his chest. "How do patients figure this out?"

"That's why you have us, Dr. McAvoy." Dave raised the head of the bed and adjusted the light on Thomas's face after he settled in. The gown fell off Thomas's shoulder, revealing the scar from his last fight with a patient. He tried to move the gown up, but each time he adjusted, it fell off his shoulder again.

He quit trying after the third attempt.

"It's just a flesh wound." He laughed at his own humor.

Lucy slid on the gloves before filling the syringe with a large bore needle. "Junior got the upper hand on you for sure, but patients like him are sneaky. Just when you think they're going to do one thing, they do something else."

His eyes stayed on the tip of the needle as she pulled up the medication. His anticipation of the numbing medication sent his heart racing higher.

Even ER docs hate needles when they were on the receiving side of them.

She glanced at Dave as she changed out the larger needle for a much smaller one. "Thank you, Mr. Fletcher, but if they need you on the floor, I've got it covered."

"We're good out there. I'm here to help." He gave her a nod and peeled back the outer wrapper of the suture kit. "What size gloves do you need?"

"Seven. Now hold still. This is going to burn." Lucy gently laid her forearm across his forehead to stabilize his head. She turned her wrist so her arm blocked his view and laid her hand along his jaw. "I'm going to walk you through this."

"I'm not a child, Lucy." He moved her arm away, but as soon as he did, his eyes met hers. His mouth went dry at her intent stare. "I don't need you to treat me like one."

"I'm well aware you're not a child, Dr. McAvoy, but your eyes are about the size of dinner plates right now. It's obvious you don't like the idea of a being sewn up." Moving the syringe behind her, she leaned forward, the faint smell of peppermint on her breath. Her eyes darted to his shoulder and back to his eyes. "Want to tell me why because I can see you've had stitches before and not that long ago."

"No." Panic wrapped around his chest and squeezed the breath out of him. Subtly gripping the side of the bed, he silently counted until he could breathe without the smothering fear that had paralyzed him before.

Her forehead furrowed and she laid her hand on his scarred shoulder. "Dr. McAvoy? You okay?"

"Don't like the idea of having a needle in my lip." *Come on. Get a grip.*

"Fair enough, but this can't get done any other way."

"Give me a sec."

"Okay."

But the memories were too strong, too fresh for Thomas to shove aside. His bone-deep exhaustion spent his reserve. He couldn't fight it.

The words. The confrontation. The knife.

His shoulder twitched under her fingers when he replayed the scene in his head.

His body felt like an unpopped popcorn kernel simmering in hot oil.

Moving her hand, she laid her slender fingers on his sternum, half of which was uncovered. "Dr. McAvoy. Would you feel more comfortable if Dr. Clark—"

"No, no." His hand covered hers, keeping her in place. Even with gloves on, he could feel the warmth of her touch.

"That's quite a grip, Dr. McAvoy." Concern laced her words.

"Sorry." He released her fingers, but kept his hand in place. "I hate needles."

"I get it." Her kindness slowly brought his angst down to tolerable levels. "When being on the receiving end, I'm not much of a fan either."

"Good to know." He let out a long breath.

"There you go. Your heart rate is decreasing." Shifting her weight, she stood and brought the syringe into his line of sight. "Okay, let's get this—"

Without thinking, he turned his head.

Dave raised an eyebrow. "Seriously, Dr. McAvoy?"

Lucy's sweet voice coaxed, "Come on, Doctor. I have popsicles in the freezer. I'll get you one when we're done."

"I don't want a popsicle." *Breathe, Thomas. Breathe.*

She spread out her fingers over his chest. "Goodness, your heart rate just jumped up about ten points.

"Sorry." He hated feeling this vulnerable, this out of control of something in the past. *Come on, man. Get your head right.*

"It's gonna be okay, Thomas."

The sound of his name floating over her lips felt like a warm hug. Looking at her again, her kind eyes, her touch made his anxiety plummet and for a moment, he could relax.

"Can I play you a song? Calm you down. I like Rascal Flatts." Dave pushed a few spots on his phone screen. "Shuffle RF playlist."

"Music might be a good idea. How about it?" Lucy nodded.

The upbeat guitar rhythm sent his frustration up again, but he liked the song "Life is a Highway" and tried to focus on the lyrics as they blared in his ear. "That's a good one but it's too loud, Dave."

"Glad to help." He adjusted the volume and put his phone on a spare instrument tray.

Lucy smiled. "Stay still and when I'm done, you can have the two peppermints I have in my pocket."

"Come on, Lucy. Don't patronize me." Even with one of his favorite tunes for distraction, his frustration was back to feeling like a bat to a hornet's nest.

A mischievous twinkle sparkled in her eye. "What about a lollipop? I'm sure I could find one."

"I don't want a lollipop."

"Stickers?"

"No stickers." Thomas attempted to relax, but as soon as he felt angst leave his body, it hit him hard as though it had rebounded off the wall. He sat up and swung his legs over the side of the bed. "Nope. Nope. I'll steri-strip it."

"Please don't. You want a good result."

"Dr. McAvoy, calm down, dude." Dave encouraged. "We'll be out of here before you know it. Dr. Lucy is da bomb when it comes to sewing people up."

"Hear that. I'm da bomb." Lucy playfully shrugged and wagged her eyebrows. "Da. Bomb."

Sweat poured from his brow and he couldn't take his mind off the needle he knew she had behind her back. "I'm done. It's fine."

"Wait. Wait. What about this?" Holding her hands up to keep him from sitting up, she blurted out, "I'll take you to get a hot chocolate at Sage's."

"What?"

"Seriously?" Dave's lips went thin.

"Yes, yes, I'll take you to get a hot chocolate if you will let me sew up your lip."

"Are you asking me on a date, Dr. Davidson?"

"Um… I… um…"

Suddenly, Dave opened one of the cabinets. "Where did I put that thing?"

She swallowed hard. "N-n-no. I just want to get you… you know, with a nicely sewn lip."

"I see." The confidence she'd exuded waned and Thomas couldn't believe he could fluster her so quickly.

Dave kept looking in the cabinet.

She twisted a lock of hair around her gloved finger before looking at her hand and rolling her eyes as she stopped. "Seems it would be a sad thing, your lip not lining up like it should."

"Really? And why's that?"

By now, Lucy's cheeks had flushed a healthy shade of crimson. "Because, because they lined up nicely before."

Never had Thomas heard a more sexy reason to get stitches. "Sold."

"What?" Now her eyes went wide as though he'd surprised her with his reply. "A hot chocolate sounds great."

"Awesome." Dave closed the cabinet door and turned around with nothing in his hands.

Lucy nodded. "Yes. You let me sew your lip and I'll take you to Copper Mountain Chocolates."

"Deal." He held out his hand.

The cool, calm, and collected Dr. Lucy responded in

kind, her hand shaking. "H-h-h-ot chocolate it is."

The overwhelming fear that strangled Thomas not moments before dissipated as he stared into her kind eyes.

Lying back on the stretcher, Thomas took a slow, deep breath in and exhaled.

Shelly poked her head in around the curtain. "Dr. Davidson. Can I borrow Dave? We need his pediatric IV expertise for a minute."

"Absolutely." Lucy waved the nurse on. "Go do your magic, sir. I'm fine here."

Yes, you are fine.

Dave saluted both and headed out the door as another Rascal Flatts song with an intricate piano introduction began. This one spoke about a broken road.

Dabbing his wound with gauze again, Lucy pursed her lips. "And, Dr. McAvoy?"

"Yes?"

"What you said about me being a woman."

Damn. I'd hoped she hadn't heard it. "Yes?"

"I didn't think that it was appropriate." She cleared her throat and whispered, "Still, I appreciate your lovely intent."

Chapter Five

P INCHING JUST BELOW the base of his wound with her fingers, Lucy silently counted to three before popping in the needle. "You're going to feel some pressure and a burn."

"The needle in… yep, there it is." Thomas white-knuckled the bedrail as she gently shook his lip to help with the pain and medication distribution.

Besides, her nervous fingers couldn't help but shake with Dr. McAvoy around.

What are you doing?

Offering to take him on a date?

And in front of staff, no less. You are so unprofessional.

She mentally berated herself for being so flustered.

And then you twisted your hair like some sort of sex kitten? What's wrong with you? No one is going to take you seriously when you do that.

When he realized he'd needed stitches, his reaction was nothing short of panic. Lucy wondered what sort of trauma he had in his life to garner such fear. She remembered all too well the gut-wrenching terror and uncertainty of being in an ER, cut up, broken, and beaten.

If it hadn't been for the kindness and patience of the

medical personnel, that tragic day would have emotionally crippled her.

And if it weren't for their fast thinking, she wouldn't be here today.

The muscle at the base of her neck fluttered, a gentle reminder of those angels that saved her and treated her siblings and their mother.

Hence wanting to make Thomas's experience as gentle as it could possibly be and offering to take him to hot chocolate just fell out of her mouth.

Because that's what you offer to all your freaked-out patients who need sutures. A date.

She pulled the needle from his lip. "Okay, feeling that?"

He nodded and closed his eyes.

Watching him, Lucy couldn't deny the idea of getting to *know* Dr. McAvoy hadn't crossed her mind. This moment with him only encouraged her interest, despite it probably being the dumbest move she could make.

Concentrate on the task at hand.

"Now, I'm going to get a couple of other places." Within a minute she placed the syringe on the right of the suture tray. She held pressure with gauze for a few seconds before tossing the bloodied bandage in the trash. "That's the worst part. The area is going to be a little floppy."

He pushed his tongue against his bruised lower lip, sending a watery bloodied trail down his chin. "I can't really feel it."

"Stop it. You're making it ooze." She grabbed a four-by-four gauze pad and dabbed the wound until the bleeding stopped. "There. I think we can start. Close your eyes for a moment. I need to adjust the light."

While she moved the overhead light to shine just right, Rascal Flatts continued to sing about the many blessings a broken life can still have.

Don't I know it?

"You didn't say you 'ere a ninja." He gave her an awkward smirk, something that he had not had a few minutes ago.

Apparently, the medication had done its magic.

Cleaning up Thomas's wound with Betadine, Lucy joked, "Working in the ER, I've used several of the skills more than once. This is probably cold."

"I'd think that w-w-ould be a reason to hire you. Bleh, blah, blah. I can't feel my leep."

"It might have been." Her tired eyes narrowed as she mentally walked herself through the procedure. "I think you're gonna need about four to five stitches. No more than ten."

"No underneaf? Eeeenside."

"Nope, it didn't get to the orbicularis oris muscle. It looks like only external stitches are needed." She grabbed a couple of saline soaked gauze strips out of the tray, cleaned him up as she meticulously took in his wound. "Just cleaning you up here and checking the inside of your lip, making sure you don't have any lacerations in there. Decently straight cut despite his ring having a jagged edge."

The water dripped down his chin and on the bare skin above the collar of his gown. "Sorry, I spilled some of it."

Taking some more bandages, she dried the water line that ran down his more than impressive chest. His beautifully sculpted pectorals and deltoids made her mouth go dry. She wondered what it would be like to kiss his chiseled jaw and down his neck his chest and...

"Dr. Davidson," Thomas whispered. "I fink my shir-t is dwy."

Looking down, she realized she'd patted the same spot on his gown several times. "Right. Of course. Sorry, got lost in thought there."

Good grief. Get your head out of the clouds.

"Any-fing you wanna share?" He turned his head toward her and diluted blood dripped from his wound on his sculpted shoulder.

The peek of a scar on his deltoid caught her attention, but she quickly realized the scar was a good four to six inches long. She unthinkingly touched it.

"A 'atient."

"What? I didn't ask." Mentally tracing the beautifully sculpted line of muscle along his shoulder, her heart flip-flopped as her naughty thoughts did somersaults in her head.

He tilted his head toward his shoulder. "A p-p-patient did that. 'otatorh c'uff, 'ipped."

"Ripped rotator cuff? Ouch."

"b'oken 'ibs." He patted his left flank.

"He broke your ribs? How many?"

Thomas held up four fingers then pulled his gown up, uncovering his trunk revealing two long, thick scars along with two irregular circular spots that looked like puncture wounds. "A patient did all this?"

He held a thumbs-up.

"Good grief, who was this guy?"

"A d'unk 'atient. He tied to 'urt other 'eo'le."

A drunk patient. That's why he came into the room to help. "Sounds unhinged. Who or what stopped him?"

For the blink of an eye, fear flashed across his face before he held up his hand, mimicking a gun.

"Wow, someone shot him. How awful." Her eyes traced the wounds, trying to decipher what he'd been through. "Ripped rotator cuff. Broken ribs. You had to have a punctured lung."

A quick nod verified her statement.

Good God. What he'd been through. "You're doing okay in this cold air?"

"'ine." He flinched, as though the question bothered him.

"Fine, huh?" The slightly raised area to the left of his frenulum looked like it had been a relatively easy closure. She tapped it with her pinky. "Did the patient cause the scar over your lip as well?"

"Yef."

"Did they do Dermabond for this one?"

"Yes, but stee-ches here." He tapped the upper rim of the left side of his mouth and under his lip. "Eeenside."

"Can I ask how long ago all this happened?" Her finger traced along the repaired skin with her finger. "Where?"

He swallowed hard then shuddered. "Two years. San Diego. Nah 'ig deeel."

No big deal? The attacker sounds like a living nightmare.

The idea of him being attacked by someone he'd been trying to help boiled her blood, but what struck Lucy more had been his easy reaction to her unspoken inquiry.

Remembering her own journey through rehab, she could only guess the pain Thomas had pushed himself through. "Lung injuries are no picnic, but it looks like someone did a good job."

He nodded and closed his eyes.

The busy sounds of the ER continued behind the curtain, but there might as well have been no one else around. Being alone with him had her body buzzing like a triple espresso.

"Luceee," he whispered. "I fink myyyyy leep's asweep."

"What?" She blinked as his butchering of words registered. "Yes. Okay. Right. Let me wash my hands and we'll get started." She moved to the sink and stripped off her dirty gloves, tossing them in the biowaste container. Frantically, she washed, her hands shaking with nervous energy.

He's my colleague. He's my colleague. "Well, whomever sewed all that, did a great job."

"Yef. My leeep. Itsf no w-working."

"It's not supposed to." Drying her hands, she sat back down, donned her sterile gloves and picked up the hemostat. "Now be still and quiet and we'll get done super-fast."

The slow, sexy guitar melody of Rascal Flatt's hit, "I Melt", started on Dave's iPhone.

Seriously, Universe? Seriously?

Thomas chuckled. "This is a goo-d son-g."

"Yes." If she tried to turn it off, she'd have to reglove and if she asked him to mess with the iPhone, he might contaminate the sterile field and delay the procedure.

Hearing the lead singer, Gary Levox, croon about how looking at his lover is all he needs to do to get himself all riled up, didn't help her body stop buzzing. Observing the beautiful lines of the toned muscles of Thomas's upper body, her mind might as well have started singing *bow-chicka-bow-wow.*

Get your head out of the gutter. You've got work to do.

But after seeing him change his shirt, she swore her ovaries jumped and her mind simply wouldn't let go of that image. Nor did she want to.

"Why Kuuu-g-u?"

"Why Kung Fu?" Lucy pinched the base of the needle with the tip of the hemostat, getting it ready for sewing. "Because I can figure out how to use my opponent's momentum against them."

"You're goooo-d."

If he weren't incredibly ripped, she wouldn't have found his speech so stinkin' funny. She bit her lip to will her laugh away before answering. "If I can't fight someone off after fifteen years of Kung Fu, then I'm a pretty lousy student of the martial arts."

"'if-een years? Whenf di-d u staaa-r-t?"

"I was in middle school." *And in rehab.*

"Why?"

"Why did I take it? Bullies." The lie came so easily. Yet the words were right there on the tip of her tongue. For some reason, she wanted to tell him exactly why she had the ability to kick someone's ass, but opening the wound of the event of starting it all?

No. Fatigue had set in too deeply and taking care of a belligerent drunk unexpectedly unroofed too many sad memories. If she told the truth, she'd be nothing but a blubbering mess and the last thing she wanted to be here was the girl in the headlines.

"'ullies? Th-at sucks."

"Yes. Some kids had been mean to me, pulled my hair. You know, that sort of thing. Wanted to have a way to defend myself."

"Eaking of h-hat." Before she could insert the first stitch, he reached up and cupped her face.

Her heart rate jumped twenty points as she held her hands away from his body. "What are you doing?"

"Twust me."

"Twust you?"

Thomas gently tilted the top of her head towards him. "You okay? He u-ulled you 'retty hard."

A giggle escaped her at his attempt to be gallant, but sounding more like Elmer Fudd. "The lidocaine gave you a speech impediment."

"Dee he h-hur you?"

Butterflies danced in her chest at the endearing cadence of his voice. Lucy squeaked then cleared her throat. "I'm okay. Thank you."

When she tilted her head back, her breath hitched at the intensity of his gaze.

Oh, goodness.

The sexy rhythm of Rascal Flatts's chorus of their number one hit washed over her.

I could easily melt if he looked at me for too long.

"I gad," he fumbled. "Gad. G-l-ad u err ok-ay."

The screeching buzz of the EMS phone went off at the main desk, slapping her hard with reality.

She pulled away from his firm hands that made her skin tingle. She could feel the heat of a blush warm her cheeks.

What are you doing? Get your act together!

His eyes went wide and refocused like he'd been zoned out as well. Thomas held his hands away from her. "Sorry. W-w-wanted to 'ake sure you're—"

"Thank you, Dr. McAvoy. Now, that's enough stalling." With her heartbeat pounding, she exhaled a long breath before leaning forward.

"Tah-mas."

"What?" The needle was inches away from being inserted.

"It'sth Thom-as."

"Okay. Thomas." Drying around the laceration before starting the first stitch, she smiled. "Here we go."

"Ewe hab any sibbings?" He rolled his eyes. "I sound stooo-pit."

"Siblings?" Lucy placed her thumb on his chin to pull slight tension and her finger lay along his impressive jawline to steady her hand. "Please be still."

"Yefs. Sib-sib-sibbings." His eyes wide with anticipation of a suture he wouldn't feel.

She sat back as a smile threatened to break her stern look. "You know you can't talk while I'm doing this right?"

"Yepf."

"You're really going to make this difficult, aren't you?"

He gave her a lopsided smile. "Yepf."

"You're going to keep talking until I answer you, aren't you?"

"Yepf. I ne-ber ge 'o 'alk 'o juss you."

I didn't realize he wanted to talk to just me. "If you will be still and quiet for five minutes, I will tell you a little bit about me."

His eyebrow cocked. "And if I'm not still?"

Leaning in close, she replied sweetly, "Then I'll let the lidocaine wear off and sew you up without your lip being numb."

"You don' put up wif any-won's cap, do you?"

"You're right. I don't put up with anyone's crap." She whispered, "Be still and let me do my job."

Closing his eyes, he interlaced his hands on his stomach then placed them beside him and back to his stomach, interlacing them again.

The corner of her mouth twitched at his nervousness. She inserted the needle and threaded it through, pulled the suture until there was about two inches left of the line, triple tied it off and snipped the extra. "I have two brothers, one sister, all older."

"Namebs?"

"Peter, Susan, and Edmund."

"And you're Lucy." He held his finger up like he had an

eureka moment. "Nar-nee-a."

He knows the series. That raised his interesting level about ten points. She held the edges of the cut together before inserting the next stitch. "Yes. Another stitch."

"You nambes like the 'ook."

"Stop moving."

"Hab you read it?"

"Yes, please be still." A wayward lock of hair fell in her face. She blew it away before inserting the needle. She repeated the routine twice more. "I've read the books many times, but my favorite was always when my mom read it to us."

She could hear the sadness in her voice. As perceptive as he was, she had no doubt he'd hear it too.

"Moms hab a way of may-kin-g things 'agical."

"Yes, they do." She sniffled as she finished the last suture. "Did."

His forehead furrowed. "Sa-wry to hee 'at."

"It's been a few years since she passed away. She'd been in pain for a long time from a car accident years before." Lucy swallowed hard.

The pain of that day had never truly faded. This morning, it felt as raw as the day she lost her father. Holding her tears at bay, she willed the anger away.

Tears and suturing were never a good combination. "But we had a good run while she was here. You're done."

"Al-weady?" He sat up, but wobbled. He grabbed the bedrail and steadied himself.

"Al-weady. Take a look."

When Thomas made his way to the mirror, his gown gaped open and gave Lucy a clear view of his broad muscular back.

Is there anything wrong about this guy?

She paused.

He might be after your job.

"Grea' jo-b, Doc. L-looks goo-d." Thomas moved his jaw around as he looked in the mirror and shed his gown right as "Mayberry" kicked in on his phone.

Dave entered, carrying a set of scrubs. "Here you go, Dr. McAvoy. I got you large and extra-large. Sorry it took so long, Dr. Davidson. The kid was dehydrated from flu. Took me two tries."

"No worries. We're all done here."

"Oh, Dr. Sinclair and Dr. Watson are waiting for you at the desk."

"Okay, I'll get right—"

"They're waiting for Dr. McAvoy." Dave picked up his phone and hummed to the chorus.

Hearing her bosses wanted to talk to him set her on edge, but before annoyance could set in, Thomas shed his gown and tossed it in the laundry basket.

Attempting to stay as interested in cleaning up her instrument tray as possible, Lucy's eyes betrayed her when he stood shirtless before attempting to don a new scrub top.

Quit staring.

Thankfully, the first scrub top was too small, so he had to try again. When he turned she noticed his wounds again and mentally grimaced. The long-term lung damage he had to have from injuries like that made her wonder why he'd come to a place considerably higher above sea level than he'd been previously.

Those injuries were far more than a no big deal situation.

And that took his interesting level up about one hundred points as her annoyance at him slowly lost its grip.

Dammit.

Chapter Six

THE STEADY, HYPNOTIC beat of the windshield wipers almost put Thomas to sleep as he drove the quick fifteen-minute trip to the house just south of town. Driving in sleet after working sixteen hours wasn't among his favorite things, but a promise was a promise.

And he always kept his promise.

When he pulled up to the place, the muscles in his neck immediately tightened at the work ahead.

The bitter cold made his lungs clench. He coughed to loosen them, but to no avail. All the way out here, he'd fought to open his airways after sucking in that frigid wind as he walked to his car, but he'd made little progress.

"Dammit." Reaching into the glove box, he reluctantly pulled out the inhalers he'd been stuck with since his injuries. "I never thought I'd have to take these again."

As best he could with his floppy lip, he sucked in each puff of the medication and held his breath after each inhale. *This sucks. Thought I'd left my asthma days when I hit puberty.*

When he exhaled before the last puff, he sighed and touched his lip. A tingling radiated through his lower jaw and into his teeth. "Guess that's wearing off. Great. Fix one problem and get two more."

He gave himself the last inhale of medication and let his eyes focus on the monumental task at hand as he held his breath.

The ranch style home had seen better days. The brick exterior, faded from the multiple hard winters, needed a good scrubbing. The rotting boards along the roof and gutters should have been replaced years ago. Small flower gardens were nothing but frozen weeds now, their plastic borders broken and falling over.

Even the voluptuous garden gnomes were practically void of color.

At least the snow covered roof appeared in relatively good shape, but Thomas knew once the snow melted, leaks would certainly appear if they hadn't already.

The entire scene had his stomach twisted in one hard knot, knowing he'd sent Jade here more than fifteen years ago.

Please tell me the old man kept this place decent when she was a kid. Took good care of her.

His lungs began to relax and recover, bringing down his heart rate and lessening his misgivings.

Thomas never regretted making that phone call so long ago to CPS after seeing the abuse she'd suffered at the hands of her mother and her stepfather, but he'd lived with the responsibility of taking her away from everything she knew at the time.

Staring at the house, guilt slithered into his soul, giving him little comfort to what life had been like for her here in

Marietta.

When he'd ask her, she'd said little more than it was fine and Thomas knew women well enough to know that the words "it was fine" usually means anything but.

Leaning the seat back slightly, he closed his eyes and listened to the soft pats of sleet coming down on his car. He willed the kinks in his body to relax before he went inside to tackle another round of repairs and find something more to fix.

Wasn't that long ago, I could do a long shift and stay up afterwards, no problem. Since the attack two years ago, his endurance for chaos had waned and he hated how weak it made him feel. Although he'd passed physical therapy with flying colors, his body never felt the same energy it had for so many years.

His phone buzzed. A text popped up with Jade asking, *"You going to sit in your car all day, brother?"*

Her message made him smirk. After everything she'd been through, he sighed at his arrogance at being inconvenienced. Driving through some crappy weather to help repair an unrepairable house, was a small price to pay to the woman who saved his life back in San Diego.

The twenty-year-old heater barely kept the house in the sixties during the weeks prior. After struggling to stay warm a few nights ago, Thomas woke up exhausted and aching. Jade hadn't fared much better after he saw her that morning at the kitchen table.

Even though she'd grown up here, the bitter cold and a barely warm house easily stripped anyone of true rest, as shown by the bags under her eyes when he left for work yesterday evening.

He couldn't go on much longer like this. Maybe if he offered to pay for each of them to have a room at the Graff or Bramble House Bed and Breakfast, she would agree. That way they could come out to work on the place on days off, go back and truly rest.

Quit your bitching, get inside, and go to bed.

Cringing, he opened his car door and immediately a hard gust of frigid wind knocked the air from his lungs, burning his bruised lip.

The ice and snow crunched under his shoes as he quickly made his way to the front patio. He anticipated the thin wall of warmth that would hit him in the face when he walked in. Instead, only a slight shift in temperatures occurred.

"Jay-d?" He pressed his tongue to his floppy lip to warm it up. The entire way here, he practiced talking and made some progress. "R-r-roomie. Woomie. Dam-wit."

His foot came to a sudden halt as he rounded the corner, but his body continued, landing on his bags. "What the hell?"

"Sorry. The heat went out sometime early this morning," Jade called out.

Of course it did. "Why are my bags packed?" Thomas quickly got to his feet and walked into the kitchen.

At the table, Jade Phillips sat wearing a heavy coat, a ski cap, gloves, and snow boots. She wiped away tears as she spoke. "I figured you'd want to stay somewhere else than here. It'll be ridiculously cold without the heater."

"What about you?"

She pointed at the floor. "I've got these."

Peeking under the table, Thomas saw her sitting between two small space heaters. "Jade. You gonna sleep in that chair between those two things? You can't stay here. Let me get you a room in town."

"I can't leave Fred."

The hound mix poked his head out from underneath a pile of blankets on the couch, his happy tail made the corner of the blankets bob up and down.

"I'll call Brett. Maybe Fred can hang out with Duke. Or maybe Kyle. He has a backyard and Gabby's dog would play with Fred." The cracked linoleum floor creaked under Thomas's feet as the smell of caffeine drifted about the stripped kitchen.

"He'd have fun with Duke." She pulled her coat closer around her body and looked up at him. "I need to stay here—what happened to your face?"

"Got punched by an asshole patient. His stupid jagged ring split my lip." Thomas ran his tongue around his half numbed mouth. "Come on. Get packed."

Giving him a weak shrug, she sighed. "It's not that bad."

"It's twenty degrees *outside* before wind chill."

Jade's eyes went wide with surprise as she hopped to her feet and cupped Thomas's chin between her thumb and index finger. "Wow, whoever did it, did beautiful work. The edges are perfect."

Thomas had always been amazed at Jade's ability to turn a conversation on a dime, especially when discussions turned to something she had no intention of resolving.

"I guess hell froze over." The pressure of her fingers hurt his face. Thomas pulled his chin out of her touch.

"Why?"

"Because you said something nice about Lucy."

"She did that?" Rolling her eyes, she grabbed her half full coffee mug and refilled it. "Oh, she's Lucy now, not Dr. Davidson?"

"You know, you're the only one up there who doesn't get along with her."

"I'm not going to apologize for that."

"Man, you're stubborn, Jade." Thomas filled his own mug and sat down at the table. "If we were biologically related, I'd say you took after our mom."

Jade ran her finger along the rim of her cup. "I'm not sure if that's a compliment or not."

"Served her well being in the air force."

"Then I'll thank you and as for your Dr. Lucy, she's ridiculous."

After seeing how caring Lucy had handled not only his wounds, but took care of that jerk of a patient, Lucy was anything but ridiculous. "Whatever your beef is with her, you're gonna need to get over it."

"She's taking my job." Jade navigated between the heaters back to her chair. "And she's gonna change my schedule, I know it."

"No, she isn't and she might. Working seven to three Monday through Friday isn't a schedule anyone else gets to have." He drummed his fingers on the table. "She's taking back the duties that you said should never have been yours to begin with."

She waved him off. "Dr. McMasters needed help."

"No, he was lazy and counting the days to retirement." His breath came out in subtle puffs of smoke. The cold air pinched his lungs. "Jade, come on. Pack your bags."

"Dr. McMasters was burned-out and more than ready to retire."

"Doesn't matter why. He didn't want to do his work." He shook his head. "You said yourself that you'd rather be the ER director than work the floor."

"So sue me. I'm tired of clinical medicine all the time and I like having control over the schedule."

"He handed his work to you and you took it. You knew they weren't yours to do in the first place."

Crossing her legs, she clenched her fists in her lap. "Dr. Davidson has to get through her ninety-day probationary period first anyway, so this isn't even—"

"Don't worry. She will." Thomas chuckled as he attempted to navigate around his wounded lip. After a couple of tries, he turned his head to the side and got a few drops of precious coffee into his mouth without spilling it all over his coat. When the bitter taste of the caffeine seeped into his veins he sighed in relief. "Nice."

"Ugh! Whose side are you on?"

"Why are there sides, Jade? Can we all work for the good of the patients?"

"You sound like a greeting card."

"And you sound like you need a time-out." He laughed

when she glared at him. "Seen a lot of kids lately who need time-outs. You're acting like them."

The howl of the winds and the tapping of sleet against the windows made him shudder.

Before he could add anything, she held her hands up in surrender. "I know what you're going to say. Sell the place."

"You can't stay here with no heat."

"The Native Americans lived on the plains and in the mountains here for years."

"They were prepared for it."

"I can get prepared for it. This isn't the first winter I've spent in Montana, you know."

"Great. You planning to skin a buffalo and live in a tee-pee, then? Because that's one way the Native Americans stayed warm."

Her shoulders drooped. "No."

"Jade, you can't even run the fireplace because of the exposed framing."

She sank her chin into the thick collar of her coat. "It's going to be fine. Really. It will."

"It's not *fine*, Jade. This is l-l-looo-nancy." He flinched when the tingling sensation of his nerves waking up radiated to his gums.

Her eyebrow cocked. "Do you know the name of the guy who punched you?"

"You know I can't tell you that."

"Oh, please, there's no such thing as HIPPA in a town like Marietta. As soon as Betty heard it on dispatch, she told Carol Bingley. I promise you, if those two know, everyone knows."

"Then call Carol and ask her." He tried to sip his coffee again, but his lip wouldn't cooperate and he ended up dripping it on his coat. "Dammit."

She grimaced, her eyes focused on his mouth. "You in a lot of pain?"

"Not as much now, but the lidocaine is wearing off. I will be." Thomas grabbed a dishcloth and dried his jacket. "This sucks."

"Sorry."

"Why are you sorry? You didn't punch me."

"But that asshole patient with the jagged ring?" She replied sheepishly, "He's my brother, Junior."

Shock caused the handle of the coffee mug to shift from between Thomas's fingers. A puddle formed on the table. He used the tablecloth to dab up his mess. "Your brother? How do you know—"

"I had to come get him this morning."

"I didn't see you there."

"That's because Tate took Junior into an observation room and waited for me. Gavin asked we clear out the trauma room in case they needed it. Guess Dr. Fancy-Pants was stitching you up." She slouched in the chair and rubbed her temples. "I had to use the rest of the money in my father's account to post bail and for a lawyer's retainer."

Thomas's heart sank. "The money you were going to use to fix up the house?"

"Yes."

"How much of a retainer did you have to fork out?"

"Apparently, my brother has some other matters to deal with. It didn't come cheap."

The urge to scream common sense into her sat on the tip of his tongue. "Jade, let me pay for you to stay in town for a couple of months. Sell the place and be done."

"You promised to help me get the house ready." She shot to her feet.

"And you said you were fixing it *to sell.*"

Without looking at him, she played with the corners of the papers on the table. "Junior called last week and said he didn't want me to. That's why he's here. To talk me out of it."

"But your other brother, James, said to sell, right?" Thomas tried to keep the insistence out of his voice, but if he could get her to see reason...

"Junior said he's too attached to the land to sell."

So much for that.

"Then Junior can buy out you two and be done with it." His rib caught as he took in a deep breath of the increasingly colder air. He needed more consistent workouts than home repair and they needed to be in a warm environment. The few sessions he'd been able to sneak in at Carter's Gym had been more than productive, but Thomas craved getting in the fresh mountain air, hike in the silence, and make his lungs ache from a good day's exercise. Revive his body and get back to who he was before he'd been brutally attacked.

He would have done all that sooner if he didn't have to struggle to stay warm inside and not feel spent as soon as he woke up. A good meal and some much needed sleep without nine thousands layers of clothes would solve most of his aches and pains. At least he'd been able to get a hot shower in the call room early this morning.

The corners of her mouth curled down as she rubbed her temples. The bags under her eyes spoke volumes. "I'm really sorry I dragged you into this."

Disappointment clenched his gut, sending the slow burn of frustration up his throat at his friend's situation. "Is this the brother who always has money problems?"

Silence.

The papers on the table were her father's bills she'd slowly worked through and been paying off for months. Even with the work she'd done before Thomas's arrival and the inside repairs he'd been able to finish, that stack of bills never seemed to thin.

After hearing his friend's plea for help several months ago, Thomas told her he could take an assignment to Marietta and assist her in getting the house ready to be put on the market. Then he'd be on his way.

During his first week here, he froze his ass off every time he walked to his car. The constant, exhausting attempt to visualize the bright sun through the gloomy grey clouds wore on him through those first few weeks of experiencing the harsh winter. As his time progressed, he'd gotten to know the staff, the first responders and more on the house completed, his sprits started to lift and his guilt began to lesson.

After hearing about how beautiful the springs were and never having lived in this part of the country before, he seriously considered the possibility of requesting his contract be extended. It would give him time to explore and they needed additional and permanent ER doctors.

Plus, his pulmonologist in San Diego said it might be the best medicine he could take. He hadn't been totally convinced of such a possibility until this morning.

Getting to know Lucy Davidson a bit more certainly made the idea of staying longer appealing even with the gloomy grey clouds. But if he did, he wouldn't stay in this place. "Jade, I came here to help you put this house back together *to sell*. That's what you said before and when I got here. All you've been able to do is find one problem after another. It's a money pit."

"I know."

"You've already spent more on fixing it than what it's worth."

She sniffed. "You're right, but dad asked me—"

"Your dad left you a disaster. I know he and your brothers stepped up when you came to live here instead of with your mom and her husband."

Her lips went thin as her cheeks reddened. "I was really mad at you for a long time. Sending me away from everything I knew."

"*I* didn't send you away. I only wanted to help."

"And you did." She slouched in the chair, giving him a weak smile. "Don't get me wrong, you helped, but it took a long time for me not to be mad at you for it."

"I'm sorry."

"I look back on it, why did I ever want to stay with her?"

"Love. Commitment. Faith in family. You name it."

"Okay, Freud, calm down." She put her hands up in mock surrender. "I'm guessing the house is the same way, huh? To an impartial eye, it's a wreck. To me, it was where I felt safe for a long time. Hard to walk away from it."

Her confession punched him in the gut. "Your heart is solid, but whether he meant to or not, your dad dumped an unfair situation on you. It's not your job to fix his mess or to hold on to it for your brother. It's your job to handle his estate and *move on* with your life. That's why he put you in charge and not James or Junior. He knew you'd be fair. Sell this place so someone can tear it down and start over."

A gasp escaped her as she wiped away tears. "I can't."

"Why not?"

"Because I told her she couldn't," an oily voice crept in and crawled up Thomas's neck. "That she owed me a favor."

Thomas stood up so fast, the chair crashed to the floor.

Fred popped up from his nap and whimpered.

"What in the hell are you doing here?" Moving away from the table, Thomas wanted plenty of room should this get ugly.

Junior casually moved to the table and picked up the chair. "Better question is, what are you doing here? This is my house."

"It's your sister's house, your dad left it, *all of it*, to her."

Junior's upper lip, twitched as fury flashed in his eyes.

Guess he doesn't like that.

Spinning his ring on his finger, Junior snarled, "Careful, you don't have sugar tits here to defend you."

Rage surged through Thomas's body. His jaw clenched,

making his teeth ache. "Don't you ever call her that again."

"Who's sugar tits?" Jade's forehead furrowed.

"That sweet-assed doctor I saw there this morning." Junior mimicked humping the chair. "One sweet-assed doctor."

Without thinking, Thomas grabbed the chair and moved it well out of Junior's reach. "Enough!"

"Don't like that, Dr. Fat Lip?"

Rolling her eyes, Jade groaned. "As if you couldn't make my life even more complicated, Junior. Now I'm gonna have to apologize to *her*."

Thomas scoffed, "Why should you apologize? He's the one who's an asshole."

Storming up to Thomas, Junior went nose to nose. "You're the asshole. Get the hell out of my house!"

Jade's eyes went as wide as dinner plates as she tried to pull her brother more than an arm's length away. "Junior. He's my guest."

He fought her like a child fighting a mother to get to the candy aisle. "You ain't sleeping with him. He ain't no guest."

"It's not like that. I've known Thomas for a long time. When we were kids and I lived with Mom."

Junior stopped fighting her. "You're the one who called, huh? Got her out of there? That's you?"

"That's me." Thomas held his ground, waiting for Junior's next move. A nod of respect from the man lessened Thomas's anxiety for only a moment. "Why don't you want her to sell the place?"

"I got my reasons."

"You haven't helped her with it."

"Neither have you, freeloader."

And the respect is gone.

Jade finally stood in front of him, her hand square on her brother's chest. "He came here to help me."

"With what?"

Thomas leaned against one of the stripped studs near the window. Even through his coat, he could feel the cold seeping inside. "The house."

Holding his arms out like a circus ringmaster, Junior laughed, "Doin' a fine fucking job. Place looks like shit."

Jade shoved him. "Well, maybe if you'd come and helped Dad while I was working my ass off in California a year and a half ago instead of taking off."

"Why are you taking that out on me?"

"Junior, I'm still trying to make the money to pay the back taxes on this place. Dad didn't pay any for the past three years before he died. A year and a half ago, you rode into town saying you're going to stay and take care of him. Then you take off right after Labor Day. No one knew where you'd gone. You left him here by himself. He died alone."

That raised an eyebrow. As long as he'd known Jade, Thomas had never heard her say an unkind word about her father or brothers. In fact, she'd only spoken favorably of all of them. To see this side of her concerned him.

She shoved him again, making Junior bump into the coffeemaker. Coffee sloshed out, spilling down the cabinet doors.

"Settle down. I had shit to do."

"You always have shit to do, Junior, and it's never to help anyone but yourself and now I've had to use the rest of the money in dad's account to cover your attorney's fees." She ran her hands hard through her hair. "And tell me this. Why the hell is that guy's retainer so high?"

Two reasons, he charges way too much or Junior's got a long list of offenses.

"What is your shit, Junior?" Out of respect for Jade, Thomas asked in the calmest voice he could muster despite his anger being this side of volcanic. "Other than wrapping your car around a tree?"

"I fix cars." With grubby fingers, Junior pulled a pack of cigarettes out of his jeans pocket.

Ironic. "You're a mechanic, then?"

"No, I take them apart. Put them back together." He pointed at the window. The ring that cut Thomas's lip, sat on his finger. "That place out there. It's my shop."

Casually, Thomas leaned against a bare wall stud. "Take them apart, huh. Like a chop shop."

"No, body repair specialist." Junior replied like a kid who didn't want to admit he'd taken the last cookie when he had chocolate on his face.

Jade buried her face in her hands. "Ugh, you make me nuts, brother."

"How many cars you have in your *not chop shop*?" Thomas's heart raced in his ears as he watched every move of Junior's with intense scrutiny.

I'm ready for you this time.

Junior lit a cigarette, took a long drag, and tossed the

pack and lighter on the table. "No one wants those cars. I take them off people's hands."

"Legally?"

"Yeah, legally. Not that it's any of your damned business, Dr. Fat Lip. Unless you want to buy something. Got a sweet ride out there. Just need to fix the grill."

"What did you hit, now?" Jade picked up her coffee and took a long drink.

Thomas wondered if she had spiked it. "Now? Does he hit things often?"

"Enough to cause concern."

Harsh criticism sat on Thomas's tongue, but the frustrated look on his friend's tired face kept him from speaking his true feelings. "No thanks. My car works fine."

Running her fingers through her hair again, Jade looked like she may yank it all out. "Junior, you can't run a business out here. We need permits, have to get zoned for it, pay taxes. There are safety concerns, OSHA—"

"I ain't doin' any of that, shit. No one cares what we do out here. This here's private property." He poured himself a cup of coffee and plopped down at the table. "As long as you own the place, no one's gonna tell me what to do."

This guy's like lice. Gonna take some heavy pesticides and a whole lot of patience to get rid of him.

The look of utter defeat on his friend's face hurt Thomas's heart, but nothing he said would change anything unless she made it so.

As Thomas moved over toward the couch, Fred's nose stuck out from the blankets. Thomas held his hand out, the corners of the pile bobbed up and down and the dog's head popped out and he licked Thomas's hand. "Good pup."

"Thomas?" Jade's voice dripped with sadness. "Can you do me a favor?"

He paused since the last time he promised to do something for her, he ended up in this frozen tundra. "What?"

"I need you to go."

If she'd professed her undying love for him, he would have been less shocked. "You want me to leave?"

Junior threw a few fist pumps in the air. "You heard my sister. She said get the fuck out."

"Shut up, Junior. That's not what I said." She wiped away tears and moved around the table, taking the stack of papers with her. "I've got to take care of something today and I think it would be best if you went ahead and got a place in town."

Keeping his eye on her brother, Thomas asked, "You gonna be okay?"

"I'm gonna be fine. Would you take Fred to Brett's?"

The harshness of reality floated through her tears, but he hoped she'd figured out how to save herself. "I'd be glad to."

When the last load of his bags were in the car, Fred walked out with him, Jade behind them with Fred's blankets. The dog hopped in and sat in the passenger seat.

"Thank you, Thomas, for helping me." The wind slapped her hair in her face. She defiantly brushed it away. "I know it was a lot to ask you to come here, especially in winter."

"A promise is a promise."

"I think you more than fulfilled that when you called CPS that day. Saved me from a fate worse than death."

He hated how matter-of-factly she said it as if she'd become dull to the horrible memories. "Sorry I couldn't help more with the house."

"Oh that?" She motioned toward the house. "I guess the heater going out was a cold shock of reality. Sometimes you can't fix what's too broken."

Thomas noticed a flash of movement in the window. Junior stood with a cigarette hanging from his lip and both middle fingers pointed straight up. "Nice."

Without looking, Jade smirked. "My brother's flipping you off, isn't he?"

"You sure you're going to be okay?"

"He's a harmless idiot." She rested her hands on his arms. "Thank you for helping me so much over the years. It took a lot of bravery to call that day and to step up for me again when... you know."

"I don't think either time was brave, but it was—"

"The right thing to do. Yeah, I know your tagline."

Sadness settled in his gut for her. "I sent you away from everything you knew—"

Jade waved him off. "No, you did the right thing. The adults there weren't good for me. Despite what the place looks like now, Dad and my brothers did take good care of me. Just sad to see the place falling to ruin."

"Wish I could do more."

"You've done plenty. This was a pretty big payback and more than I should have asked of you."

"You saved my life, Jade. I don't think I can owe you enough."

"You've more than kept your promise, Thomas." She looked back toward the house. "It's simply time for the hard choices and to move on."

He gave her a strong, brotherly hug. "Did you want me to get you a room reserved somewhere?"

"Um, no, I'm going to stay with a friend."

The uncertainty of her words worried him. "You sure?"

"I promise."

Fred barked as if to say, "Let's get moving."

"I think you're being paged." Jade laughed and gave him a gentle nudge toward his car. "Go on. Get out of here."

When he got in, the dog tried to crawl in Thomas's lap, but he cracked the passenger window, piquing Fred's interest. He spent the ride into town with his nose crammed up against the one inch of air that poured in as Thomas cranked the heater, hoping he'd thaw by the city limits.

Chapter Seven

A S SHE SLID on her new heavy jacket, Lucy anticipated the crisp Montana chill when she opened her car door. The pure mountain air would invigorate her as the snow would playfully tickle her nose during her short walk to the Main Street Diner.

Thick, wet clumps of ice and snow fell around her as strong winds intermittently pushed her sideways on the icy sidewalk.

This scenario sounded so much better in my head. She laughed at her Hallmark Channel approach to the weather. The very same approach she'd emailed her siblings about this morning after her brother, Peter, texted her that it would be sleeting with a high of thirty-five in Marietta today.

A fat glob of the slushy mix dropped on her shoulder.

As if I didn't already know that, big brother.

Intermittently over the past weeks, the temperatures had bumped to the forties, allowing her to do some much needed walkabouts. Walking everywhere, she'd scanned every shop, every street, every inch of the picturesque town, all while adding those much wanted steps to her daily goal of fifteen thousand.

Today's weather altered her outside walking plans, again. She'd have to make up the steps on the elliptical in the Graff Hotel's gym before she slept for the day.

Lucy zipped her coat all the way to the top as she walked by the pharmacy and linked her purse through the strap. She stuffed her hands in her pockets, holding her keys in one.

Carol Bingley, owner and part of the Marietta grapevine, waved from the window.

Out of the corner of her eye, Lucy saw the father of the croupy child she cared for this morning standing at the pharmacy counter. She popped her head in, asking if he had any questions about the discharge instructions.

In his broken English, he graciously said no as he held a few dollar bills in his hand. His head furrowed as he appeared to be flustered by which bill to use while the child played with his Hot Wheels car at his father's feet.

Entering completely, she inhaled the citrus scented candles Carol kept near the front. They reminded her of spring and warmer days to come.

After a quick review of the discharge instructions in both Spanish and English, Lucy gave her goodbyes and began to head out.

Before she could make it to the door, Carol blurted, "Dr. Lucy, Dr. Lucy we have lip balms on sale, two for four dollars."

"No, thank you, Mrs. Bingley."

"Humpf. Fine, but can you tell this man how much the medication is? I don't know what the words for seven dollars and twenty-three cents are in Spanish."

"They use the same number symbols in Spanish and English. You could write them down."

Carol went wide-eyed like someone tazed her.

Mentally rolling her eyes, Lucy fished a twenty-dollar bill out of her pocket. "You know, it is chilly out there. A couple of lip balms may be nice."

She turned to the father and pointed to the display. "*¿Quieres dos chapsticks para que mantengas humectados tus labios?*"

"*Sí, sí,* thank you, *Doctora.*" The father nodded and pointed. "*¿Que quieres?*"

The son jumped up and down. "*Fresas, Papi. Fresas.*"

"Okay, strawberry. *Un otra?*" Lucy encouraged the child to take the red-topped lip balm.

"*Naranja.*"

"Orange it is. *Excellente.*"

Carol eyed her suspiciously, but when Lucy bought two for herself and handed Carol the money, the woman beamed. "Please use the extra for anyone having trouble paying for the medication today."

"I see." Carol's lips pursed, but she rang up the sale and offered Lucy the change and the pharmacy bag. "I'll cover the medication."

Turning to the father, Lucy handed him the medicine. "*Señor, su medicina hoy es gratis.*"

"*Gratis? No, no, Doctora.*"

"*Por favor, señor.*"

With tears in his eyes, he hugged her. "*Gracias.* Thank you, *Doctora.* My son will get better. Yes?"

"If he doesn't, bring him back to me." Her stomach growled and she said her goodbyes. "I'm off to get some of Gabby's famous orange cinnamon bread. Have a good day, Mrs. Bingley."

More times than Lucy could count, it had been far harder to win over the females in the medical community than the males. If buying a couple of Chapsticks would keep Lucy on the nosy woman's good side, so be it. She couldn't worry about small-town politics now, especially not out in this weather.

As quickly as she could, Lucy walked past Marietta Western Wear then Grey's Saloon as a large wave of sleet pelted her. The icy sidewalk in front of the bank made her slip for a few steps, but she kept her balance. Past the shoe store and finally hitting the front doors of the Main Street Diner.

A wall of warmth along with the smells of bacon and sourdough bread slammed Lucy in the face as she entered.

The cold that had seeped into her bones on the short walk from her car to here loosened its grip. She ran her fingers through her hair to get rid of some of the precipitation. A chilly trickle ran down her neck and underneath the innermost layer of her clothes, making her shudder.

All this, seriously, made her question her impulsive choice to relocate to a place she'd only seen on a map before she'd arrived.

I can't believe I came here sight unseen. Walked right through the wardrobe.

As she made her way to the counter, she realized once

again, she'd run headfirst into a new situation to prove her family wrong and she'd ended up over her head. Being the youngest of four had never been the issue. Lucy loved her siblings; she loved her parents, her stepfather, Charlie.

To this day, Lucy cherished the strong bonds she had with all of them.

No, the problem had never been the birth order.

Her search for her identity began that awful day when she became the child that lived through the horrific crash. When she'd become the poster child for why drunk driving was bad. The day that triggered their mother to smother Lucy with worry and self-doubt. That had been the symbolic carpet that was yanked out from underneath her at the tender age of ten when one selfish mistake had stripped her of her faith in forever.

"Hey Lucy," Gabriella Marcos, owner of the diner, gave her a quick kiss on the cheek as she held a tray of honey-laced biscuits in the other hand. *"¿Cómo estás hoy?"*

"Bien, ¿Y tú?"

"I'm great. Busy as you can see."

"That's good. Needed to get something to eat before I sleep for the rest of the day."

"Late night?" She adjusted the tray on her hand.

A loud sizzle from the kitchen caught Lucy's attention. "Twenty-four hours of it. Griffin making bacon?"

"Twenty-four hours? Don't you need to sleep now?" Gabby blew a wayward lock of her dark hair off her face.

"I grabbed a power nap this morning. If I sleep too long today, I won't sleep tonight. It'll throw my body clock all off."

"Grab a chair. I'll come talk to you in a few and, yes, we've got plenty of bacon for you."

A seat at the end of the counter emptied and Lucy skillfully moved between happy customers and all the waitresses carrying large trays of food.

Before she took her place at the end of the counter next to a burley guy reading the paper, she shivered. "Just how freaking cold does it get here anyway?"

With an all-knowing smile, Flo, one of the local residents and a regular waitress at the diner, slid a large mug of coffee across the counter and filled it to the rim. "The winter getting to you, Doc?"

"Yes." Folding her coat on itself, she laid it perfectly on the seat back before sitting down. She placed her gloves on the counter next to the mug. "I need more sun and more activity. I've read close to thirty books since I've been here and binged watched three TV series on Netflix."

"Which shows you watch so far?"

"I just finished the first season of *Timeless*. Thank goodness, season two has started." Wrapping her fingers around the coffee mug, Lucy sighed at the warmth against her skin. "They have such good stories."

"I never did like time travel ideas much, but I do like this one. Glad they brought it back. Cream?" Flo slid a small bowl of creamers across the counter. "I think I might appreciate the eye candy more than the stories, but either way, I'm gonna watch it."

"They do have some good lookin' people on that show."

Fatigue had set in so deeply that Lucy didn't realize she added three creamers until she started opening the fourth. "Good grief."

Tapping her fingers on the counter as if deep in thought, Flo suddenly snapped her fingers. "Hey! Their leader has the same name as you."

"One of the reasons I love the show." *And if I had a time machine, I'd go back and change what happened to my family so long ago.*

"You just need to get out more."

Flo's upbeat voice pulled Lucy away from falling down the rabbit hole of sadness. "I would love to go hiking except it's too stinkin' cold, Flo."

"Sweet pea, if you're gonna stick around for a bit, you gotta work with what you got. There's a lot of fun to be had in the cold." She gave a mischievous wink. "Because, if you do it right, you go out and do some adventurin' in the cold."

"What's right about that?"

"Comin' inside and *warmin'* back up again."

Diner philosophy. Sadly, it made total sense.

The corner of her mouth curled up. "Well said, Flo."

"I try." The diner's door opened and Flo waved to the newest customers.

"Speaking of warming up, I need some real gloves. I got these in the dollar bin at Target before I moved here." The frayed purple gloves had seen better days.

Flo picked them up with her index and thumb, inspecting them with narrowed eyes. "How have you not gotten frostbite wearing these?"

"Stuff my hands deep in my pockets."

"Lordy, these are pitiful. Try Marietta Western Wear just a few stores down from here. They have some good ones.

"If they don't, I think Big Z's might still have a few pair." The man next her added. "They aren't fancy or nothing, but they'll keep yer hands warm."

"Thank you, both. Still learning my way around here. Seems I didn't prepare for the weather as well as I thought." The idea of ever stepping outside again sent a bone-deep cold through every inch of her body as the steam rose from her mug. She wished she could crawl into it, like a hot tub. "Might as well have a good pair of gloves to keep me warm these days, since nothing else is."

The waitress cocked her eyebrows, making Lucy mentally groan. "Nothing or no one?"

I thought I'd said that a whole lot softer. "Both."

The man went back to reading his paper.

A quick memory of Dr. McAvoy's broad shoulders and swoon-worthy smile warmed her south of her belly button, but she laughed to herself at the absurdity of it.

Keep dreaming.

"No one, huh?" Flo's eyes narrowed and Lucy waited for the typical response like, "What, you need me to set you up with someone?" or "So and so is looking for a date next Friday" or "My friend's son is a nice boy. Lives at home still, but you might like him."

Instead, the waitress gave a knowing nod. "Look, we all have our dry spells, that's for sure."

Dry Spell? More like a dry life. Lucy didn't want to spill her guts about her limited dating history, boring and bad choices, but having so few people to talk to here, the words threatened to fall out.

Resting her forearms on the counter, Flo leaned in and lowered her voice. "But there are other choices to get us through those moments."

Lucy froze, her coffee mug half way to her lips. *Please. I don't need your help with this.* "Flo, I appreciate the advice, but I'm good."

Flo patted Lucy on the arm. "With God making hot coffee, good books, great food and TV shows course you are."

Relief flooded her and Lucy raised her mug as a toast. "He did a fine job with those."

"Bet you thought I was gonna say something else."

The man next to her stifled a laugh as he stayed on the same page of the paper he was on when Lucy sat down.

"Yeah, I did." Lucy opened two creams and added them to her coffee before Flo topped it off.

Sliding a piece of something across the counter, Flo gave Lucy a wink. "But I never rule anything out."

Picking it up, Lucy laughed out loud when seeing the twenty-five cent off coupon for a four pack of double AA batteries. "I'll keep these in mind."

Especially since Dr. McAvoy is off-limits.

Coffee went up her nose at that thought. Lucy grabbed a napkin and pretended she'd sneezed.

Where did that thought come from?

After a month of finding the man annoying, of course he had to be wonderfully gracious, charming, *and* hot.

And so very out of my league.

She mentally corrected herself.

No, not out of my league, but I am his boss. That would be a conflict of interest, especially if he's being groomed for my job or leaving.

A sobering thought crossed her mind. *Of course, if I don't pass my ninety-day probationary period, it really won't matter. I won't be staying.*

She wondered if she could keep her eyes in her head if he walked in the room now. After this morning of getting to know him more and seeing those scars, she dreamed of getting him bare-chested and running her fingers along those old wounds as she helped him forget all about them.

But what would he say about yours?

The thought brought her back to reality for a few seconds, making her pull a lock of hair in front of the irregular spot at the base of her neck before her naughty thoughts regained control. A slow smile crept across her face as another tingle settled low. She sipped her coffee, mentally lost in a sea of erotic possibilities.

"Dr. Davison?" Flo cleared her throat.

"Yes? What?"

"Did you know what you wanted… to order?"

No doubt the warmth radiating off her cheeks right now could be easily seen. She patted her face. "In a few, Flo. Just warming up from my coffee right now."

"Well, I'll leave you alone with your *warm* thoughts. Let me know when you want to order." Flo stood straight and went down the row of counter customers, filling tea and water glasses, and topping off coffee mugs with the skill of an artist. After she'd taken care of everyone, she headed out to check on several tables.

Casey, another waitress and Brett Adams's sister, ran to the back by way of the wooden swinging doors. Her short, pink striped bob a sharp contrast to Flo's high, tight salt and pepper bun to Gabby's loose, dark French twist.

When Casey returned with a stack of napkins and two bottles of syrup, the wooden doors thudded against their stoppers as she passed through. A photo hung next to the doorway, reminding Lucy of the town tragedy that occurred in 2016.

First responder Harry Monroe had been hit by a car when he stopped to help an elderly couple change a tire.

Like every ER doctor, when they heard of such an incident, Lucy wondered if Harry's outcome would have been the same had she been working. It was an arrogant game of "what if", but she had complete faith in the staff that worked that day.

He couldn't have been in better, more caring hands.

She slowly stirred her coffee as her mind replayed the day she'd been in good hands. The day strangers saved her life. The reason she sat here today.

The reason she couldn't fail someone's good outcome.

A joyous laugh pulled her away from her deep thoughts.

With her coffee pot in one hand and a water pitcher in the other, Gabby laughed with a group of customers at a table in the corner with several of the town's first responders.

Lucy had been told of the crisp, clean mountain air having healing properties. The oxygen untainted by mass population, pollution, and people. Maybe that was the reason Marietta seemed to have an unusually high number of handsome men and beautiful women.

Patrick Freeman, one of the paramedics and Jonah Clark, one of the search and rescue guys sat with Amanda Carter as she finished off her coffee. She joked with three other men at the table.

The man next to her at the counter folded up his paper and offered it to her. She graciously took it after he slapped a twenty on the counter, and left as another customer sat at a seat at the other end of the counter. Flo tucked the money in her pocket before clearing the dishes and wiping the empty space down.

Gabby checked Lucy's coffee mug before starting a new pot of coffee. "Why don't you go say hi to the group?"

Good grief. The woman never missed a thing. "I'm good, Gabby. I don't need—"

"My help?"

Lucy couldn't help but chuckle at her own stubbornness. "Sorry, I'm used to—"

"Pushing people away? Being in charge?" Gabby raised a perfectly groomed eyebrow. "*Amiga*, I'm gonna give you some advice that I learned from *mi amor*."

Lucy giggled at the gleam in Gabby's eyes at the mention of Kyle Cavasos. "Yes, ma'am. What did your beloved say?"

"Kyle said, 'Gabby, you're new in town. Make some friends. Go out. Have fun. Quit trying to do everything yourself'."

"Fair enough, but I don't have a Kyle to give me such advice."

"Well, there are other possibilities." Gabby's eyes darted from Lucy to the table of first responders.

Lucy subtly motioned to the group. "Trying to remember three of their names."

"Which ones?" Leaning against the counter, she pointed. "You got Patrick and Jonah on the left. Jonah's a helicopter pilot. Served in the army. Just so you know, Jonah is taken. Then Amanda's got her back to the window and next to her are Daniel, Jack, and Chris."

"Amanda and Kyle came in this morning. I've met each of them when I've been at work."

"Working all the time at the hospital, Doc?"

"Something like that." Lucy tucked the battery coupon in her coat pocket.

"What department again?" Flo joined them as she organized the bills in her pocket.

"Emergency Room."

"Taking over from Dr. McMasters." Gabby played with the loose strands of her hair. "That man needed to retire."

"You can't even believe the paperwork he'd left behind."

Flo agreed. "Yes, I can. It was like trying to get a cat to take a bath making that man use a computer. He flat-out refused to assimilate at the hospital."

Even yesterday, Lucy had found charts from his last week he never closed or dropped charges on multiple files of patient visits had gone untouched. He hadn't signed off on more than half. Lucy'd barely gotten some of them filed before the ninety-day insurance deadlines. "I heard all he does is fish now."

Flo tucked her money back into her pocket. "Got a spot near Miracle Lake you can always find him when the weather's good. Otherwise, he's at home doing a puzzle, reading, or binge watching a TV series. Right now, he's finished up the first season of *Game of Thrones*."

"How do you even know all this, Flo?" Gabby smirked.

"Simple, he comes in here every afternoon right around half past three for a piece of pie and a cup of coffee. Always has that fancy cane with him."

"Guess I'm in the back doing paperwork at that time."

Taking a long sip of her coffee, Lucy relished the low buzz the caffeine sent throughout her body as the realization of her having the social life of a grumpy old man hit. "Dr. McMasters sounds like he's got quite the retirement plans."

"The man needs to find his happy place because, lord knows, he isn't. Got diagnosed with really bad arthritis last year. Hasn't been the same, since." Flo tilted her chin toward the table behind Lucy. "As for you working in the ER, for sure and for certain you'd see our first responders there. They're a good bunch."

"Yes, they are." Lucy ran her finger along the rim of her mug.

"We get plenty in here from the ER. Staff and customers alike." Gabby added. "Never heard any complaints from anyone who's been treated there."

Flo playfully nudged Gabby with her elbow. "I'm pretty sure Griffin and Merlin have made more of Gabby's famous breakfast tacos for the ER employees in the past six months than they ever have in their lives."

"I've had a few of those. They are good, Griffin." Lucy raised her mug to him as he peeked through the window. "My favorites are the bean and cheese and sausage and eggs."

"Thank you. Those are from my *abuela's* recipe book." Gabby squared her shoulders.

He gave the ladies a nod before slapping the bell. "Order up."

"Got it." Gabby gently squeezed Lucy's hand before making another round of coffee and water refills.

Casey maneuvered around a few tables before coming behind the counter and taking the hot food out into the dining room. "Hey, Dr. Lucy. How's your morning?"

She took off before Lucy had a chance to answer. "She's a spitfire."

"Casey's a good kid. You must be one smart woman to be the director of the ER so young." Flo gave Lucy a wink.

Although the comment was meant to be complimentary, Lucy wondered when she would no longer look too young before people simply accepted what she could do. "Thank you, Flo."

Flo's forehead furrowed. "Takes a lot of brains and gumption to think on your feet like that, but something about what I said must have bothered you."

"Why do you say that?"

"Cause you always smile and right then you didn't. Now, what is it?"

The question made Lucy pause. No one had ever asked

her if she thought she was smart. "I'm not as young as you think I am."

With a kind pat on her arm, Flo sighed, "Oh, sweetie. Don't be upset about being young. Just means you've got a lot of adventuring left. Believe me, you'll miss it when you're not and it happens in the blink of an eye."

"Maybe I'm just exhausted." Lucy rubbed the bridge of her nose. "Been up more than twenty-four hours and the sun really hasn't been out for a few days. I'm used to a lot more sun than this."

"Then, let's get you fed so you can go to bed. Lord knows tomorrow's gonna come sooner than you want it to." Flo's banana earrings swayed as she waved to a few more customers. "There's a table in the corner. Be with ya in a minute."

Grabbing a coffee pot, Flo held it up. "Gonna make my rounds. I'll be back to get your order, Doc."

"Thirty-six!" a small voice squealed.

Lucy looked behind her to see a large man holding up a flash card to the child across from him.

"Eleven times two."

The child pursed his lips as his eyes narrowed for a split second before he yelled, "Twenty-two!"

"Nice work, Parker." He held his large hand up and the boy slapped it.

A nugget of sadness lodged in Lucy's throat when she remembered how her mother helped all of them learn their multiplication tables. How she helped them with every page of homework, every project, even when her beaten and broken body could barely stand, she'd help them until they were done.

Without realizing it, she'd kept watching the interaction with the two.

A nod from the man made her realize she'd been staring. Clearing her throat, she mouthed, "Sorry" and turned back around.

"That's Colt and Parker." Flo set the empty coffee pot in front of Lucy after filling her mug again.

"Oh, I just noticed they were practicing multiplication. I wasn't—"

"Honey, Colt is a sight to behold. Don't apologize for appreciating the man. You know, they come in for breakfast each morning, but today, Parker had a dentist appointment, so Colt brought him in for lunch."

"That's nice of him."

"Doesn't matter if it's breakfast or lunch, Parker's gonna order chocolate pancakes." Flo snapped her fingers like a thought had suddenly popped in her head. "Talon, his wife, Parker's mama, goes to vet school. She's close to being done so we'll have another doctor in our little bit of paradise."

"I never knew paradise could be so cold." Lucy shivered and sipped the caffeinated ambrosia.

"It does get cold here, that's for certain. I never have asked you, where you from?"

"Jupiter, Florida."

"Not much snow there."

"Only on TV." Taking a deep inhale as the scents of coffee, sugar, and bacon floated around her, Lucy appreciated the small-town hospitality the diner offered her. "Everything smells good. I'm so hungry; I don't know what to order."

Flo drummed her fingers on the counter. "Well, I think if you get a solid breakfast or lunch or whatever you want to call it, you'll sleep better. How about some eggs, bacon, toast, hash browns?"

"Shelly mentioned some orange cinnamon bread."

"Yes, ma'am. Fresh out of the oven this morning. You want that as your toast?" Flo wrote on her notepad and tucked the pencil back behind her ear.

"That would be great. Eggs over easy please."

"I remember." She ripped the order sheet off the note pad and pinned it to the order wire.

Griffin slammed the bell. "Order up."

"Now Griffin yankin' my chain again. I'll be back." Flo excused herself and headed out to deliver the latest dish.

Lucy nodded to no one and took a deep inhale. The sharp aroma of dark roast seeped into her body and gave that all too familiar buzz that had gotten her through high school, college, and medical school, all before she turned twenty-five.

The group of first responders hopped to their feet suddenly when Patrick held up his phone.

They were out the door before Lucy had a chance to say hello, but they all waved to her as they walked by.

By the time Gabby returned to the counter, Lucy had drained her cup and held it up for a refill.

"Color me impressed." The woman smirked. "That's a lot of coffee for someone your size."

"Trying to clear my head before I go back to the hotel."

"When are they ever going to get your furniture here?"

"They told me last week, seven to—"

"Ten days. Yes, I know. How frustrating."

Not that it might matter.

Should her ninety-day probationary period end early, Lucy cringed at the idea of standing in the front yard, waving to the movers to turn right around and drive her stuff straight back to Florida. "Needed to get out. Walk around for a bit. Clear my head since I'd been inside for too long."

"Cabin fever's gonna get you if you're not careful. It's taken awhile for me and Trinity to get used to the weather. She wasn't a fan at first."

"San Antonio does get a lot of sun."

"*Sí*, but I kind of like the actual seasons. My girl's gotten good at skiing, ice skating without breaking anything, but I'll admit, the gloom can get to me."

Sadness settled in Lucy's gut, thinking of home. "Do you miss it?"

A slow smirk spread across Gabby's face. "On a morning like today, I really do. The grey clouds. The gloom. The bitter cold, but then I think about what I've accomplished here, on my own, and I wouldn't trade that for the world."

"Doc's order," Griffin called.

Grabbing the plate, Gabby placed it in front of Lucy. On it were two thick pieces of toasted and buttered orange cinnamon bread. The crisp aroma of the citrus perfectly mingled with the spice of the cinnamon.

Gabby smiled and took the chair next to Lucy. "This

should recharge you after the scuffle this morning."

"After twenty-four decent hours, it ended with me fighting a drunk who liked calling me names."

"Some people skip manners class in school."

"He more than skipped class. Ended up giving one of my colleagues a fat lip."

"Who did he hit?"

"Dr. McAvoy."

Gabby rolled her eyes. "From what I understand, Junior has never been known for his smart decisions."

"You said his name, not me."

"Don't worry about HIPPA. Kyle was in earlier, but Betty heard the call on the radio from her house so you know everyone in town knows what's going on."

Being new to a small town, Lucy had learned several things.

Sage's chocolate had to be the best on the planet.

Rocco's served an amazing chicken piccata and if anyone told Betty the police dispatcher or Betty's best friend, Carol Bingley at the pharmacy *anything*, the entire county would know it within a matter of an hour.

Grabbing her fork, Lucy cut off a piece of the bread and popped it in her mouth. The soft pastry melted on her tongue as a layer of sweet orange then cinnamon butter followed. Every knotted muscle in her shoulders and neck released and she sighed. "Oh, my gosh, that's so good."

Gabby smiled. "I'm glad. Kyle said for me to save a loaf for Shelly."

"I'm going right by there. I can take it to her." Shoving

down another piece, Lucy laughed. "That is if you trust me to not eat it before I can get it there."

"After we fill you up, I'm pretty sure you can control yourself." Gabriella's eyes darted behind Lucy and she gave her a wink. "Take your time. The rest will be out in a few."

Cutting off another piece, Lucy stuffed the perfectly season bread in her mouth, relishing how it slowly released its flavors.

Regardless of the two cups of coffee she'd finished since arriving, after this meal, she'd be able to go back to the Graff, curl up in those flannel sheets and have sweet dreams about...

"Is this seat taken?"

Chapter Eight

ONCE HE'D DROPPED Fred off at Brett's, Thomas rounded the corner of Front Avenue and the Copper Mountains came into view. He pulled over into the parking lot of the Graff Hotel and stared at their natural beauty.

The jagged peaks jutted into the grey sky. The crisp white snow, a stark contrast to the thick, gloomy clouds that hovered over them.

A loud growl erupted from his stomach and he could think of nowhere else he wanted to eat than Main Street Diner. "Can't think straight right now."

Deciding it was far too cold to walk from the Graff to Main Street Diner, Thomas drove the short distance and found a space no more than thirty feet from the famed Copper Mountain Chocolates and only a block from the diner. When he turned the car off, he noticed a familiar figure in his rearview mirror exiting the pharmacy. "Lucy?"

That sent his heart racing and him scrambling for the door handle. He easily crossed Second Street, but had to wait for the light on Main.

As soon as the crosswalk signaled for him go, he beelined to the corner of Main and Second, but before he could get by the pharmacy, Carol Bingley came barging out of the store. "Dr. McAvoy! Dr. McAvoy! I needed to ask you something."

"Yes, ma'am." He tried to pay attention to where Lucy went, but Carol kept asking questions and pulled his gaze away. By the time he looked up, he didn't see her anywhere. "Dammit."

"And by the way, this man doesn't speak very good English, and I'm concerned he won't take the medicine correctly, even after Dr. Lucy—"

"It's Dr. Davidson." The mention of her name immediately caught Thomas's attention. "Wait. What?"

She pursed her lips. "Yes, she was on her way to the diner when I waved to her to come in. She told the man the directions in Spanish."

"Then why are you asking me about this?" He said a silent thank you that the good doctor's compassion for this family extended beyond the ER doors. "Ms. Bingley—"

"Carol." She beamed.

"Ms. Bingley, I trust Dr. Davidson." The wind whipped by, but Carol seemed unaffected by it. At least they were under the awning and he wasn't getting soaked by wet ice. "We should all be grateful that she's taking the extra step to make sure the family understands how to take the medication in Spanish *and* English."

"I guess. I mean, she did pay for his medication."

"She paid for it?" Thomas shoved his hands farther in his pockets as a slowly growing admiration for his colleague grew and the cold seeped deeper. "I trust Dr. Davidson and so should you."

"Yes, I guess I'm old-fashioned. I prefer a *man* as my doctor."

Nice that sexism is still alive and well in Marietta. "Doesn't mean you can't trust her."

She recoiled slightly, but then went doe-eyed. "Dr. McAvoy, can you explain to me how steroids work again? Maybe you should take some for that lip swelling or I've got some really good lip balm for sale. Two for four dollars."

After a quick lesson on the mechanism of steroids, he went in, shook the patient's father's hand. The man, graciously reciprocated as the child held his hand and played with a Hot Wheels car as he ran it up and down his father's arm into the air, and then ran the car up his own arm and across his face.

By the time Thomas made it to Main Street, his lip was painfully numb, but at least he had two brand new lip balms in his pocket. Orange and cherry.

Every place has got someone like Carol Bingley. The eyes and ears of the town whether you want them or not.

The wall of hot air laced with the smells of butter and sausage caressed his face when he opened the door of the diner.

This is probably what heaven smells like.

A sea of people for the lunchtime crowd, but he immediately noticed a good-looking redhead at the counter.

And what heaven looks like.

Luckily, the chair next to her sat empty. "Is this seat taken?"

She turned and sweetly smiled. "Not at all. How's your lip?"

"Hurts like hell." He sat down without taking off his coat and held up his purchase. "Got some lip balm to help."

"Carol got you too, huh?" She reached over and brushed some of the snow off his shoulder. "What flavors did you get?"

"Orange and cherry."

"I got strawberry and grape."

The idea of tasting the strawberry or grape Chapstick off her full lips had him shifting in his seat.

"Your lisp seems to have resolved."

"I don't sound like Elmer Fudd any m-more."

"I like Elmer Fudd. I think he's adorable. Slightly deranged, but adorable." She winked.

His insides fluttered at her playful flirtation. "I'll kweep that in mind."

"Fabulous."

Without asking, Flo set a cup of coffee and a glass of water in front of him and filled it just an inch short of the rim. "I'll get your milk, Doc."

She paused before leaving. Her eyes narrowed on his lip. "And a straw."

"Thanks, Flo." He coughed, then cleared his throat.

Lucy stirred her coffee in lazy circles. "Guess you've been here a few times."

"A few." Since Jade's kitchen's capability only covered anything you could microwave or peanut butter and jelly sandwiches. "The pot roast is one of my favorites, but the

French toast is good too."

"They really are. Have you tried Gabby's breakfast tacos?"

"I haven't had good breakfast tacos since I worked in San Diego."

"When was that?"

"I was there before I came here." He nervously tapped his thumb on his forearm as the dull pain in his shoulder and his ribs ached, pains that appeared every time he thought of his disastrous assignment there.

"I've been to San Diego. Loved it. Beautiful weather, so much sun." She smiled brightly. "My sister Susan and I had the best time last summer. Spent almost the entire time on the beach."

"They do have good beaches." Picturing her in a swimsuit had his jeans fitting uncomfortably tight.

"We only had one day at the zoo. I didn't get to spend enough time there, but I'd love to go back. Why were you there?"

"Work. Rehab."

Her eyes darted to his shoulder. "Right, you did mention that this morning."

His shoulder pinched him and his rib caught in mid-breath, making him flinch. "And you mentioned you had three siblings, right?"

"Peter, Susan, and Edmund." She grabbed her phone and held up a picture of the four of them. "Sadly, they've all become infatuated with the weather since I've moved here. Winter is far different where they are."

"What do you mean?" The four smiling faces on her phone made the corner of his mouth curl up. "Nice."

She tapped her phone frantically, her eyes wide. "Every time I talk to them now, Peter holds his phone up to the computer screen and says 'Luce, it's twenty-seven degrees there today. Did you know that?' As if I haven't been outside at all."

"They must miss you." A nugget of sadness settled in his chest knowing no such group wondered so much about his day. He and his parents talked, but he had no siblings or even close cousins.

Placing the phone on the counter, she patted it before moving her hand away. "I miss them too, but it was time for a new adventure. Something that was my own."

"I get that. Wanting to carve your way in the world." *More than you know.* Before Thomas would let himself elaborate, he tapped the menu before opening it. "Surprised I haven't seen you here before."

"I'm in here several times a week, so yeah. I figure we would have run into each other before now." She shrugged. "Guess it's all about timing."

"Probably." After scanning the menu he had memorized, he tucked it back next to the napkin dispenser. His still uncooperative lip got in the way when he tried to blow on his coffee. "I'm gonna spill this."

Her hand rested on his arm before he attempted to take a sip. "You need a straw."

As if on cue, Gabby walked by and without breaking her pace, handed Thomas a straw. "Milk?"

"That'd be great, Gabby, but I think Flo—"

Within seconds, Flo had a small pitcher in front of him.

Slowly, he poured in the milk, watching it blend in with his favorite drink to make the perfect mix of dark and light.

Lucy cocked her head. "Only milk? No cream or sugar?"

"Milk is enough."

"*Café au lait*, then."

"*Oui.*"

"*Très bien.*"

Hearing her speak French made his skin tingle. "You spoke French."

"*Oui, c'est vrai.*" She giggled before popping back a slice of what looked like Gabby's famous orange cinnamon bread.

He had to consciously tell himself not to playfully grab her arm and kiss up it like Gomez Adams did to his wife, Morticia. "Nice. How many languages do you speak?"

"Only English and Spanish. I know a few words of French. Enough to get me into trouble at Mardi Gras."

Before talking to Lucy today, Thomas hadn't realized how much he'd missed good one-on-one banter in a non-medical setting. Something casual. Fun. Sexy. "Been to Mardi Gras, huh? The one in New Orleans?"

She sat up proudly. "Sure have. Got the beads to prove it."

The hard burn of cold water up his nose made him choke. He wouldn't ask what color beads she had since the only way the famed black beads were acquired by women, were if they flashed their boobs. The image of her perfect breasts, only made his jeans pinch him in the tenders.

"You okay?" She patted his back.

"*Laissez les bons temps roulez.*" He coughed and dried his face with a napkin.

"*En effet!*"

"You win. I've run out of French words."

"Me too."

He liked seeing this side of Lucy. The casual, relaxed side. One she rarely showed when they were working. Unlike a lot of women he'd met over the years, she didn't hide her intelligence, her strengths.

He'd worked with plenty of nurses and physicians over the years who'd turned into giggling airheads outside of work, only because they were afraid a man might be intimidated by their intelligent minds.

Not Lucy. She seemed to not only be proud of it, but appeared to love her knowledge base and want to share it with anyone who'd listen.

"Where'd you learn Spanish?"

"Went to school in Florida. Took every class I could in high school and college, Did some of my clinicals in the predominately Spanish speaking parts of town."

"She's pretty good." Gabby smiled as she walked by with a tray full of food.

"What about you, Thomas. What language did you take in college?"

"I took computer programming as a second language." *Might as well have shown her my lifetime nerd card right there. Save her the trouble of letting her kick my ass right now.*

Her eyes sparkled and she leaned forward. "Really?

Computers, huh?"

The sultriness of her voice surprised him. *Maybe she has a thing for nerds.*

The idea made Lucy a whole lot more interesting. He tapped his cold fingers on the hot ceramic surface of the coffee mug until he could tolerate holding it without pain. "I couldn't learn an entire language, no matter how hard I tried. But if it was all numbers, I'm good."

"Interesting."

Her appreciative stare caught him off guard, making him wonderfully uncomfortable. "I thought you'd be sleeping off that twenty-four hour shift you finished this morning."

"I took a power nap back in my room. Trying to stay up a bit longer so I can sleep tonight. Too wired to sleep much today, anyway."

"These swing shifts'll screw you up. I'm back at noon tomorrow and have to figure out when to sleep. You?"

"At ten tomorrow for a six week evaluation. Dr. Sinclair and Dr. Watson want me to see where I'm falling short. My guess is one of my employee evaluations will have a few less than complimentary things to say about me." She finished off her coffee. "But it is what it is when you're the boss, right?"

"Right." Mentally, he cringed knowing who might have given her a less than complimentary review. "Lucy, I think you're doing a great job."

Her face lit up. "Really? I especially appreciate that coming from you."

"Why *especially*?"

She stirred her coffee with a spoon. "There are rumors that you're also in the running for the director position."

Her honesty amused him. "You're direct aren't you?"

"No other way to be, really. Time is short. No need wasting it guessing."

The corner of his mouth curled up. He liked this woman. *A lot.* "Those rumors are false. I am not in the running for the ER clinical director."

His pride punched him in the stomach knowing his endurance would fall short for the position.

"I'm glad to hear that, but to be honest, I'd think you'd be all for it."

"I'm under temporary contract. I have no plans to stay in Marietta." Although, sitting here, talking to her, made him wonder what would happen if he extended his contract a month. Three months? Six? A year?

Her shoulders fell slightly and she flipped a lock of hair that had fallen in front of her perfectly freckled face. "Right. Temporary."

His heart skipped a beat at her reaction. *Is she disappointed?*

Flo arrived, a full coffee pot in hand before he could ask Lucy anything more. "She drinks more coffee than I thought someone her size possible."

"It's my ambrosia." Lucy took a healthy swig as soon as Flo cleared the coffee pot out of the way.

Pulling her pencil out from behind her ear, Flo asked, "Breakfast or lunch, Doc?"

Inhaling the luscious aromas of bacon, sugar, and coffee,

his mind ran chaotic with possibilities. "I'm feeling daring. You choose."

"You got it." As soon as she dropped the order, Flo attended to new customers who'd seated themselves at a booth by the window.

Gabby talked to a group in the corner as Casey happily took care of the customers at the counter.

"You know, I've worked a lot of places," Thomas began.

"I understand three a year for the past five years." Lucy turned toward him. "That's a lot of moving around."

"Bad habit. Dad and Mom were both in the air force so I'm used to it."

"Oh, wow. That would make for a lot of moving."

"I think eighteen months was the longest we ever stayed anywhere until they retired on the East Coast. DC." His lip throbbed and he needed sleep, but he didn't want to miss the chance to talk to her more.

"How old were you?"

"Twelve." And the geekist kid on the planet.

She leaned forward. "That had to be exhausting at times, especially in middle school. How did your siblings feel about it?"

Her interest in him made the corner of his mouth twitch. "Only child."

Her forehead furrowed. "Oh, I guess that could have been lonely."

"Not always. We lived in some cool places. Hawaii, Korea, Washington DC, England, Germany." The warmth of the diner permeated his coat. He shed his jacket and hung it on the back of his chair. "But what I wanted to say about the diner was, it feels good to be here. Like a place I'd want to come back to again and again."

"Yes, I know that feeling quite well. It's nice to find a place where you're always wanted, welcomed. Where they smile when you come in the door."

"Sounds like you're describing home."

"I guess I am."

His eyes locked with hers as her words sank in. Even he had a hard time believing he'd professed such a possibility. Staring into her eyes, he questioned his want to move on, to keep changing and never setting down roots.

I wonder.

The bell rang for another order, breaking his introspection.

Cocking her head, Lucy looked at her watch. "I thought you were working until noon."

"Gavin sent me home. Said I was scaring the patients with my split lip."

"Oh, it's eleven. I didn't realize it was so late. Who's covering for you?"

"Tom Reynolds is supposed to come in about now. Gavin said he'd cover until Tom arrived." He took a gentle sip of his coffee through the straw, but moving his lip made it hurt worse. He mentally pushed the pain away. He had to get more coffee in his system or he'd be in full Godzilla crushes Tokyo mode.

She leaned forward, staring at her handy work. "There's some pretty good bruising. You take any Motrin or Tylenol for it, yet?"

"Nope."

"Ice?"

"Other than the wind? No." The sweet caffeine layered on his tongue and he relished the buzz.

Grabbing her purse, she produced a bottle of extra strength Tylenol and handed two pills over to him. "Take these."

"And call you in the morning?" he punned.

"Sure."

When her cheeks flashed a hint of scarlet, his mind raced with endless possibilities. "Lucy, would you—"

"Hey, Dr. McAvoy!" A large man waved to Thomas from across the room.

Thomas waved back. Although he'd treated the man, Thomas couldn't be sure when or for what so he gave the canned response. "Doing okay?"

"Doing great." He began to leave, but his eyes went wide and headed straight for them.

Every muscle in Thomas's body clenched as the man approached, but the patient went right by him and threw his arms out to give Lucy a hug. "Good day, Dr. Lucy. How are you?"

She responded in kind. A radiating, gorgeous smile on her face. "I'm good Mr. Richards. How's your knee doing?"

The older man hopped a couple of times. "Real good, Dr. Lucy."

"Well, look at you. You'll be back to line dancing in no time."

Leaning in, he lowered his voice. "I really appreciate you helping me so much. Dr. McMasters didn't do near as much as you did."

"I'm sorry to hear that."

"Yes, not a shot or pill, nothing for my pain."

Thomas wasn't the least bit surprised to hear the previous director of the ER had done little. Jade mentioned more times than not, the man had been counting the days before he retired and pretty much checked out when it came to doing anything to help his patients.

Lucy gave Mr. Richards an encouraging pat on the arm. "I'm glad we could get you back on your feet."

"I followed up with Mr. EJ just like you said. He gave me some good exercises I can do and I've been doing them three times a day, just like he said. I can get up and down without hurtin' most days."

"I bet your sweet pups, Frankie and Annette, are loving that. You can walk them okay, now?"

"I can. They are so happy to be out with me, not that I can walk far right now. Too cold." He dramatically shivered, then laughed.

How in the hell does she remember his dogs names? I can't remember what I had for breakfast yesterday. Thomas watched her talk to the man as if he were an old friend. While he'd worked with her, he couldn't believe how she always remembered every patient, every diagnosis, and every detail about their visits.

Jade's got it all wrong. Lucy will be a great director.

Mr. Richards gave them each a respectful nod. "I did get

your bill Dr. Lucy and more than glad to pay it. Glad Dr. McMasters didn't send me one from my visit back before Thanksgiving."

Lucy cocked her head. "He didn't?"

"No, guess he figured he didn't do anything, so he didn't bill me. Hospital said there's no charges for my visit and something about the chart not being completed."

"To be fair, there are a lot of charts that need to be reviewed. I'll do some research on that for you, Mr. Richards."

"Don't feel the need to send me a bill, Dr. Lucy. I'm good with nothing since that's all McMasters did. A big, fat nothing." The man extended his hand to shake with both doctors. "Good to see you, Dr. Lucy. I'll leave you to your breakfast."

"Watch out for those icy patches on the sidewalks." She gave him an encouraging pat on the shoulder.

"Will do." Mr. Richards turned back towards Thomas. His bright smile turned into a grimace. "Wow, Doc. Junior really got you good, didn't he?"

The question caught Thomas off guard. "How did you—"

"That kid has a quick punch, but he's a bit of a punk when he's hit first."

I'll keep that in mind. "I didn't say…"

The man waved off Thomas's concern. "When Poppy called it in, it came in over dispatch and Betty heard the whole thing. She told Carol at the pharmacy and now everyone knows."

Thomas smirked at the effectiveness of the small-town

grapevine. "I'll keep that in mind, Mr. Richards."

He whispered, "Be sure you do. That kid's been bad since the day he came out of his mama. I'm sad to say, he'll be that way until the day he dies."

"Hopefully, he didn't give Deputy Logan too much trouble." Flo shook her head. "He's got a knack for that. Sad for his sister, though. I know she's always trying to do the right thing."

"Yep, she does."

"Who's his sister?" Lucy inquired as she finished the last piece of toast.

Crap.

Flo smirked. "Jade Phillips."

A strangled wheeze sounded to his left as Lucy grabbed her coffee mug.

Thomas grabbed a napkin and handed it over to her. "You okay?"

"Jade? As in nurse practitioner, Jade?" She sputtered as she grabbed the napkin and dried her face.

"The very same." Flo pointed to the door. "Henry, your ride is leaving."

"See you later, Docs." Mr. Richards waved and left without waiting for their response.

More orders arrived in the kitchen window and Flo excused herself when another group of customers came in.

Lucy settled back in to her seat and took a few slow deep breaths before placing the wad of napkins on her now empty plate.

"Better?"

She nodded and didn't say a word. Her jaw clenched, her lighthearted mood gone. "Mr. Obnoxious is Jade's brother? Isn't she a friend of yours?"

Shit. "Yes, but I hadn't met the guy until a couple of hours ago."

She dabbed at her mouth. "I'm sure that'll be awkward for her when she finds out he gave you that fat lip."

"She already knows." *And when she found out, she should have kicked his sorry ass to the curb.*

"She does? Oh, right because Betty—"

"No. When I was at her house—"

"That's right. You're staying with her."

Thomas didn't expect to hear snark in Lucy's voice.

Annoyance maybe, but not snark. The idea saucy Dr. Davidson might have a twinge of jealousy made him silently cheer.

"Jade and I have been friends for years. Since we were kids. She's the one who asked me to take an assignment to Marietta."

"That's right. Ethan said she asked you to come help with her dad's place."

"She called about six months ago, after her father died." His stomach growled again and he tried to quell it with his coffee, but spilled some on his clothes when he pressed the mug to his wounded lip to take a drink.

Lucy grabbed a napkin and blotted the front of his shirt at each word. "Right. Fixing. Her. Dad's. House."

Dammit. "Yes, but—"

Frustration dripped from her words. She wadded up the

napkin and tossed it beside her plate. "You're together?"

"No."

"No?" She swallowed hard. "Were together?"

"No. I owed her a favor."

Her eyes narrowed on him. "What kind of favor?"

For a reason he couldn't quite explain, he found great amusement in her wanting to know about his relationship with Jade. It gave him an inch of hope that she might want to get to know him better because Lucy had certainly caught his attention. "Jade and I have never been intimately involved or married if that's what you're wanting to know."

Her eyes went wide as her face pinked. "I didn't ask you that."

"No, ma'am, you didn't."

"What is it, then?"

"Because she saved my life." He tapped his shoulder and ran his hand under his arm, across his left ribs.

"She saved your life?" Her eyes darted to his shoulder as a look of understanding washed across her face. "She was there?"

"Yes."

"I see. Wow."

Gabby snatched a large plate of food out of the pass-through window and placed it in front of Lucy. "Here ya go."

"Gabby, can I get a to-go box. I'm really tired."

Damn. "Lucy—"

"I was wondering. You've been up a long time. Give me a second." Gabby disappeared behind the wooden doors leading to the back.

A sadness settled in Thomas's chest. "You don't have to go."

"It's fine. I just had no idea you and she were, um, so, um, connected."

"It's not like that, Lucy."

Waving him away, she shook her head as she dug through her purse. "It's fine, Thomas. You're an adult. It's nothing you have to explain to me. Really, you don't."

Tentatively, he slid his hand closer to her on the counter. "I think I do."

She placed money next to her plate and put on her coat. "Your life is your life. I have to get going. I'm really, really tired."

"Lucy."

"I need to get some sleep." As soon as Gabby returned with the to-go container, Lucy dumped her food inside and sloppily closed the lid. "I'll see you at work, Dr. McAvoy."

When she hit the door, his food arrived, but his empty stomach sat still and his appetite vanished.

Chapter Nine

WHEN THOMAS WOKE from his nap, the gloomy afternoon he'd fallen asleep to had darkened to pitch. No stars twinkled in the sky and the only light appeared to be from the parking lot down below.

Still overcast and still bitter cold.

But he didn't care about the outside weather, now that he'd found a warm, safe place to sleep. He relished the quiet of his room late at night and getting the best rest he had for the past month.

After he stuffed his face at Main Street and ordered a couple of sandwiches to go, he took his chances that the Graff would have a room he could stay in long-term or at least a few nights until he figured things out.

His agency representative arranged a room for him to stay at the Graff for the duration of his contract and gave him the suite at a discounted rate. There he had a small refrigerator, microwave, and coffeemaker along with a comfortable queen-sized bed, TV, and a perfect view of Copper Mountains.

Once he had his bags inside the door, he stripped, tossing his work clothes in the corner and took the longest, hottest shower he could tolerate.

Right before his body gave in to exhaustion, he took his daily medications then crawled into bed wearing nothing but a smile and immediately drifted off to sleep.

The moonlight shone through the windows, a brief pause in the darkness before the clouds hid the light again.

The soft flannel sheets of the bed slid against his aching muscles and beaten body. He'd been so wiped out, he'd slept in one position the entire time, but it had been worth it. His fatigue had finally loosened its grip on him and he felt revived and rested. Sucking in a deep, easy breath, he relished the fact he didn't have to reach for his inhaler upon waking up or that no shortness of breath woke him.

Grabbing his watch, he pushed the buttons. "Two-thirty. Swing shifts suck."

He'd been out a good ten hours, but plenty of time to get up, work out, then get another nap before going in at noon.

Nothing like some good sleep. Lying in the quiet night, he absorbed the room. The subtle smell of the citrus and sandalwood scented body soap he used before he came to bed. The low hum of the hotel bedside clock.

When working swing shifts and noon to midnight, this had been one of his favorite times of the day when he'd been with his previous girlfriend. He loved it when he'd come home from a shift and she'd decided to stay the night. He'd quickly shower then wake her with gentle kisses. Seduce her with his tongue until she cried out her joy.

He started tenting the sheets thinking about doing the

same to Lucy.

Pushing the sheets away, he took himself in his hand and slid up and down his shaft, as he imagined how she tasted. How she'd react to his touch. Her mahogany red hair cascading around her as he worked down her body, tickling her peaked nipples with his tongue before feasting on her most tender flesh, bringing her to climax. Her hands in his hair as he ate her, hearing her moan his name.

Within minutes he'd taken care of his business and relished the idea doing the same for her. Not that it would happen.

After her joy wiped away with the mention of his friend's name, any shot he had with Dr. Lucy Davidson was out the window.

Rationally, he should be grateful for the loss. *You're leaving in six weeks. Why would you start anything up?*

But Lucy Davidson more than piqued his interest and his emotional brain couldn't think of a better way to spend his days in Marietta than getting to know her better.

Slowly, he got out of bed and made his way to the bathroom. Flipping on the light, he shielded his face until his eyes adjusted. His scars were the first thing that came into focus. The slashes from the knife. The incisions where they tried to repair the damage to his lung. The lateral scar across his deltoid from the surgery to fix his injured shoulder. The circular scars where the chest tubes had been inserted after his punctured lung collapsed.

On the counter, the inhalers he couldn't live without anymore.

He hated this. Hated the inhalers. Hated not having fully recovered from his wounds. He hated that when he ran it took him longer to build his speed and regain his breath than it ever did before the attack. His left shoulder ached most of the time and his general endurance had never fully rebounded.

The obvious scars, he didn't care about since everyone had some. No, what wore down his pride had been the long lasting results that decreased his ability to do the job he'd spent so much time training for. ER physician.

He loved the buzz of a busy level one trauma unit. The unknown chaos that could walk through the doors at any second. The ability to change a person's life for the better. How a sixteen-hour shift would roll by in the blink of an eye.

Not anymore. He had trouble with the pace. The constant bombardment of respiratory illness floated through him. He'd never fully recovered before getting another one. The long, brutal hours.

Now, he had to work the in smaller hospitals so he could keep up appearances and his mental skills without beating himself up every shift.

He pounded his fist on the counter.

I just need the weather to get better, some good exercise and I'll be fine. I can go back to level one after a few months and get away from Marietta.

Lucy's sweet smile flashed in his brain, giving him pause.

Looking at his wounds again, including the bruised lower lip, he painfully smirked at her stolen glances when he changed his shirt.

Good to know my workouts have paid off.

Staring at his reflection, he paused, taking that nugget of Lucy's admiration and holding it close to his soul. "You'll get this done, but it will be harder than you think."

He showered and dressed in his work-out clothes. He'd hoped the recent self-gratification would take care of his building interest in his colleague, but thinking of her again made his cock twitch.

Looking toward the window and the darkness outside, he rubbed his aching shoulder and ribs, a pang of sadness tickled the back of his throat.

Since he moved too much growing up, he never had a serious girlfriend until college. Even during that time, he'd only been with her two years before he graduated and she left for her military commitment. During the next four years of medical school and three for his ER residency, he'd spent more nights alone than he had with a long-term girlfriend and never had a one-night stand.

He didn't regret being particular, but he wondered if the constant uncertainty his parents willingly provided because of their careers and self-made chaos had done far more harm than good when it came to him finding his own stability.

More than he cared to count, their fights, their infidelities, their selfishness when it came to their child, played in his head. When he graduated high school, Thomas couldn't get out of there fast enough.

He spoke to his parents every few weeks, but he hadn't visited in years because they never felt like home. For far too long, he'd been fine with the constant travel, but almost dying gave him a hard dose of reality. He questioned when the running would stop and if he would ever be comfortable setting down roots.

Yet, in the last place he'd look, he'd found a sliver of hope from a woman he never expected.

Lucy gave him a sense of calm he'd attempted to find for far too long. The idea of staying here with her, for her, should have unnerved him but it didn't. And that only aggravated him more.

What are you doing? You can't stay here.

As he tied his shoes, he heard the ding of the elevator followed by a door opening and clicking closed before he opened his. He put his earbuds in, but before he pressed play, the melodious sound of Lucy's laughter tickled his ears as the subtle flowery citrus fragrance drifted around him.

Geez, my imagination is screwing with me. He had no doubt a good run on the treadmill would help alleviate some of his general frustrations and purge his over imaginative libido. An hour and a half later, he'd completed his 5K and lifted free weights, but the ache continued.

I haven't been this worked up since high school. He adjusted as he walked back to his room, the subtle flowery scent still lingered in the hall.

Showered up, Thomas threw on his favorite sweatshirt and jeans. He planned to eat the thick turkey sandwiches he brought back from Main Street while finishing his latest book, when he heard footsteps in the hallway.

Other than the front desk staff, he'd seen no one else

awake and thought nothing of it, but when someone softly sang the lyrics to the Rascal Flatts song, "I Melt," Thomas sprang from his chair.

"Lucy?" He opened his door to look around only to catch a familiar redhead turning the corner at the end of the hall. She wore bright pink long-sleeved pajamas and held an ice bucket in her hand.

"Lucy?"

The loud thumping of ice against plastic echoed into the hallway.

He jogged after her, not wanting to shout her name and wake up other guests, especially if it wasn't her. His heart pounded as he drew closer, hoping he wasn't wrong.

The ice dropping stopped as he reached the room, but the sweet voice continued to sing along to the song. He stepped in the doorway as she turned around.

The bucket crashed to the floor, sending ice everywhere. She pulled her earbud out. "Oh, my gosh… Thomas?"

Without thought, he knelt and began picking up the escaped cubes. "Sorry, I didn't want to scare you."

"What are you doing here?" She crawled around on all fours, reaching under the ice maker for the remaining escapees.

"I'm staying here now."

"What? Why?"

He couldn't help but notice the V-necked collar of the pajamas and how much of her perfectly freckled skin he could see. She'd always worn long sleeved shirts with higher collars under her scrubs, which hid her arms and décolleté.

She stood and flipped hair over her shoulder. "Lover's quarrel?"

"Lucy, come on." With her hair out of the way, he noticed an irregular line at the base of her neck.

"I'm sorry. I didn't... well, yes, I did, but I'm sorry for being quick to judgment." She moved around him, but waited for him to catch up. "What brings you to the Graff?"

"Change of plans since her brother arrived."

"Oh, right." She tapped her lip. "That would be awkward."

He jumped up and walked beside her. "For the best. Jade's selling the place, anyway. Less for her to have to deal with if I'm not there."

"True. I hope that goes easily for her." Lucy let the ice bucket swing casually at her side as neither of them appeared anxious to get back to their rooms. "I'm sorry if I acted weirdly, earlier. At the diner. It simply wasn't news I expected to hear."

"About Junior?"

"Yes."

Relief flooded him. "It's nothing I've kept secretive, me staying with Jade. She told everyone I was coming to help out with the house."

Not that it mattered now. He mentally shook his head at the amount of money she'd already spent to keep her head above water.

None of it she would get back. Not a penny.

"You mentioned she saved your life." Lucy rested her hand on his shoulder. "How? And you don't have to answer if you don't want to."

He stopped and took a deep breath, hoping to get the words out in an intelligible way. "Out of control man. He had a beef to pick with me. Attacked me in the parking lot of the ER after a long shift. Knocked me to the ground. He'd already gotten me a few times with a knife. Jade had a gun. Shot him. Killed him."

The color drained from her face as her eyes widened. "Oh, my gosh, how scary. How awful for both of you."

Both of you. *After all the hell Jade has put you through, you still show her compassion.* Lucy constantly amazed him.

"But I'd think you'd know about me helping Jade from the staff."

"I know a bit, but I'm the boss, remember? I don't hang around the staff other than at work. I have meetings with the hospital directors." She stopped and leaned against the wall, facing him. "Though, I have met several of the first responders, paramedics, firemen, that group at Main Street Diner. They are a great bunch of people, but the staff hasn't been as inviting outside of work, so I'll know the basics, not the details."

He leaned against the opposite wall. His hands tucked flush behind him. "The first responders are good people to know."

"They are great. Gabby, you know, Kyle's girlfriend, she's been really nice and welcoming. She'll be my neighbor when I move in."

"You have a house? Why are you here?"

"I have a house, but none of my stuff. The snowstorms

and some sort of computer glitch have the truck with all my furniture somewhere in Michigan right now so no bed and I'm not sleeping on an inflatable." She rolled her eyes. "By the time it gets here, it may not matter anyway."

"Why's that?" He loved how her hair cascaded about her shoulders like a long winding road, but he wondered about that irregular place on her neck.

That doesn't look like a birthmark.

He also wondered what sound she'd make if he kissed her there.

She moved a lock of hair to cover her neck, apparently noticing his stare. "I have my six week performance evaluation later today. Hopefully, it's better than my last one."

"They weren't good?" Pulling his head out of the gutter, Thomas's heart sank remembering Jade's comments. "I talked to Denver and Evan yesterday morning. The evaluation is painless."

"Glad to hear it. Yes, they are good people. My evaluations have been mostly positive. That I was solid with my professional and organizational skills. The patient surveys that were completed were overwhelmingly positive and, apparently, people have said good things in town. Anything Carol or Betty hear, it gets back to hospital administrators."

"Good to know the grapevine is working well."

She smirked. "Right, but I didn't score as well with some of the employees."

"What's not well?"

"About average for most of them and one you'd think I was the spawn of satan."

Thomas subtly clenched his teeth together. *Jade.* "But that's only one person."

"True." Lucy sighed. "Hopefully, I've improved on my overall employee satisfaction before they offer me the job permanently."

"You're extremely competent. Why is the staff's input so important?"

"The way it's been explained to me is if the staff doesn't like working for me, there's a higher chance of them quitting. Hiring and firing costs money and the professional pool here isn't as high as it is in say, Billings or Livingston."

"Right. They want to keep their staff happy."

"Yes, and I understand it. Denver or Evan could take over as ER director while they looked for someone else, but they can't rehire an entire unit. It's difficult when I can't seem to connect well with many of them." Tilting her head, she sucked her bottom lip. "But apparently my ninja skills did make me cooler this morning, although my actions this morning may have me talking to the hospital's attorney."

"Why would you need to do that?"

"I hit a patient."

"You defended yourself," he answered louder than he intended. Covering his mouth, he lowered his voice. "You defended yourself."

"Yes, but I'm sure someone will argue that I put myself in that situation and should have expected Junior to be combative. That I could have deescalated the situation. Don't you love litigious fortune-telling?" She started walking again. The carpeted floor creaked under their feet.

The sadness in her voice bothered him. He hoped Jade's biting commentary wasn't enough to keep Lucy from the job she appeared to want.

I need to talk to her. "You want me to say something to Jade?"

"Why would you assume—"

"She's said a few things. She's not one of your biggest fans. She thinks she got passed over for the job." *Not that she deserved it by the way she's acting.*

"I can understand why she doesn't like me. No one wants to feel as though they are being replaced. If she'd talk to me, we could at least work together to better the unit, especially since my predecessor really dropped the ball." She ran her fingers through her hair and pulled it back into a makeshift ponytail and let it drop.

"Jade's mentioned that, but has never gone into too much detail." His fingers itched to run through her hair. Feel the softness, the fire of the red against his skin.

"The man never liked the computer and wanted all his charts printed. He hadn't done a QA or had someone on his staff do any QA since the last JHCAO inspection." She rubbed the bridge of her nose. "It's a nightmare in this office. I honestly don't think Evan and Denver understood the extent of the backlog."

"Lucy, I can help you with all that."

"No!" Her head popped up, but she swallowed hard. "I mean, thank you. I can do this. It's what the job is, right? Even Jade would have to admit it's a lot to take on."

Until then, the conversation flowed so easily, Thomas

walked right by his room and they stopped between doors. "That's what she said, but between you and me, I don't think she minded that Dr. McMasters passed her the baton. She's always argued she never needed a physician looking over her shoulder."

"I've had that talk with PNPs many times, but this isn't a personal slam. It's the law and what insurance companies are willing to reimburse for and cover. Besides, you and I have both looked to colleagues for second opinions before. Why should this be any different?"

"When we get or give opinions, we don't have to have someone else sign off on it."

"That's true. I appreciate your gallant offer to speak on my behalf, Thomas." She rested her hand on his arm for a moment. "The last thing I want to do is get between friends. I can fight my own battles."

Her polite decline only made him like her more. "No kidding. Junior never saw it coming."

Leaning toward him, she whispered, "That's the idea."

The quiet nestled between them and Thomas realized they stood closer than he ever expected they would.

Wonderfully close.

Dangerously close.

Taking a lock of hair, he ran his finger down its length and dropped it on her shoulder. "Are you always so stealthy?"

"When I need to be."

I wanna kiss you so bad right now.

Shaking his head, he ran his tongue over the still swollen

area. "Still tender."

"It's gonna be bruised for a bit, but in three to five days, those sutures can come out." Lucy gently cupped his chin with her fingers. The warmth of her touch made his skin tingle.

"Am I hurting you?"

"Not at all." His hand rested on the curve of her hip.

She stepped forward, closing the gap between them. "Make sure to keep taking Tylenol for the first twenty-four hours. Which room is yours?"

She'd rattled her question so quickly, he almost didn't catch it. Swallowing hard, he replied, "Three eighteen. Yours?"

"Three twenty-seven."

"Guess this is good—"

"You want some hot chocolate?" she blurted, her face slightly flushed.

His heart sped up. "Now? Don't you have to go to work in the morning?"

"Yes, but I slept from noon to almost eleven. Worked out and I took another short nap. Woke up about thirty minutes ago. I can't go back to sleep." She tapped her watch. "I don't have to be there until ten. When do you have to be there?"

"Noon. Answer me something."

"Of course."

"If you're the director, why are you working all these weird hours?" *What are you doing? She's asking you where your room is.*

"That's not what I expected you to ask me right now." Her gaze lingered on his mouth as she moved her fingers away. "Not at all."

I hate Junior so much right now.

"What did you expect me to ask you, Dr. Davidson?"

She paused as though she were searching for the perfect words or decided whether she should say anything. "It wasn't about schedules."

"What was it about?"

"Hot chocolate." She sucked on her bottom lip as she rocked sideways. "I do owe you a hot chocolate, right?"

His body hummed with her so near. "You promised Copper Mountain hot chocolate."

"It's too early to go to Sage's." A sexy smirk spread across her face that made his cock stand at attention. "I have instant hot chocolate powder and some marshmallows. It's not Copper Mountain chocolate, but maybe consider this as a bonus for being such a good patient?"

It wouldn't have mattered if she'd offered to serve him hot water in a dirty cup, he would have said yes. He looked down at his old sweatshirt and suddenly became very self-conscious. "Yes, but I need to do something real quick."

"Of course. Do you want me to come over or you come over there?"

"Either works."

"Come over." She pointed. "Three twenty-seven."

"Give me five minutes."

Chapter Ten

*Y*OU SHOULDN'T BE *doing this.*

But Lucy had no interest in what she *should* do. She'd always done what she should do. Now she planned to go with what she *wanted* to do.

What she wanted was to spend some good quality time with Dr. Thomas McAvoy.

She checked her breath and brushed her teeth for the second time since she'd been up, then ran a brush through her hair and checked her reflection in the mirror.

Still wearing her new flannel pajamas, she debated on whether she had time to change her clothes and shave her legs, but figured the best she could do in the short time she had was put on a bra under her pajamas, brush her teeth, and leave it at that.

Otherwise, it looked like she was trying too hard.

Plus, me not having shaved my legs will ensure things won't go too far.

Tossing off her shirt, she wrestled with her underwear and laughed at the crazy of life. The last person she expected to see at Main Street yesterday or at four-thirty in the morning today, was Dr. McHottie.

Thank goodness she'd decided to wear cute matching pajamas Susan sent her last week. Going braless in her favorite dingy *Star Wars* t-shirt and sock monkey PJ pants had never been complementary, but they were broken in and wonderfully comfortable. They did little for her sex appeal.

Of course, if she had her way, Lucy wouldn't need anything to wear when Thomas was around. Especially after the erotic dream she had about him during her power nap this morning. The tingles were so fierce, she had to stand outside the front doors of the Graff for five minutes to simply cool off before she walked on the treadmill at the hotel gym.

That dream would have to stay exactly that, because she was his boss. Getting involved would certainly be a great way to ruin her reputation during her first ninety days.

This is simply one colleague having hot chocolate with a hot... another colleague.

Regardless, she'd have to thank Susan later for the perfect timing of the new sleepwear.

You shouldn't be doing this. What if this ends in disaster and your siblings are right and you're wrong for coming here?

For a moment, the practical side made sense and sent her angst dancing all over her self-assurance. Trying to create this life all her own, away from anyone who knew her history was too good to pass up, even if the job was in one of the coldest places she'd ever lived, she wanted the chance to be Dr. Lucy Davidson, ER Director. Not Peter's or Edmund's or Susan's little sister.

Not Karyn or Neil's daughter.

Not Charlie, the newscaster's, stepdaughter.

Not the girl who survived the crash so long ago, which changed laws.

Just Lucy Davidson, a damned good doctor and valiant woman.

She braced her hands against the sink as her practical side spoke again.

What a brilliant way to be taken seriously—date a coworker.

There had been no discussion about fraternization. Denver nor Evan hadn't said a thing about it and there was nothing in her contract banning it, yet it could make or break her credibility.

Seemed unfair how women were judged more harshly in the court of public opinion about situations like this. So far, Marietta had proven to be a good fit with good people. Certainly, seeing Thomas McAvoy wouldn't be career suicide. Right?

Even before she came here, her fifty-plus hour weeks left little socialization time outside the ER. The guys she had met only seemed to be interested in commenting how short she was, asked her how much money she made, or tried to mansplain her job to her.

One guy wanted to fiercely argue about politics and when Lucy factually and calmly offered her rebuttal, he went to the bathroom and never came back.

Of course, he'd left her with the check.

In the last few years, she had a couple of boyfriends, nothing that lasted more than a year and no one who made her heart race like Thomas did.

It's just hot chocolate. It's just hot chocolate.

Filling the small coffee maker to the top line with water, she turned it on, set up the powdered hot chocolate in the mugs she'd purchased since she'd been here. A light dusting of chocolate powder floated out on the counter next to the bag of mini marshmallows.

The last of the minty toothpaste tingled on the corner of her mouth and she quickly wiped it away before buttoning her shirt.

She checked herself in the mirror again and self-doubt crept in. "Maybe I shouldn't, but I'm tired of having no social life. Susan always has dates, but that's Susan."

For years, Lucy had compared herself to her older sister, who'd always been called a classic beauty. Her long chestnut hair, green eyes, and freckle-free skin had boys lined up as soon as their mother and stepfather said Susan could date.

Lucy's dark red hair, brown eyes, and too many freckles hadn't brought about much interest.

She certainly wasn't ugly, but simply not as classically pretty as Susan, who had far more suitors and three marriage proposals over the years. More than Lucy could have ever hoped for.

Giving herself another quick look, Lucy checked her smile. "Good enough, I guess."

For whatever reason, the scar on her neck seemed to stick out like a sore thumb. It hadn't gone unnoticed that Thomas stared at it. She hoped she'd been subtle enough when she covered it with her hair.

Lucy had never been ashamed of her wounds, but she

wanted the option to discuss why she'd gotten them on her terms. Otherwise, conversations with new friends became too emotional and uncomfortable. The last guy she'd dated never looked at her the same way once he'd seen her scar, heard her story. She'd be damned if she'd let anyone else look at her with such pity again.

She grabbed her makeup brush, just as there was a soft knock on her door that sent her heart racing.

"Crap. Okay, okay." Smoothing down her jammies, she moved a large lock of her hair in front of her right shoulder, covering her neck, then gave her reflection a thumbs-up before opening the door.

"Good evening. Good evening." Thomas had changed from his grey Boston Bruins sweatshirt to a button down blue plaid that brought out the colors in his eyes and emphasized the broadness of his shoulders.

Oh, goodness. This may not be a good idea.

She subtly grabbed the sides of her pants to keep her hands from running up his chest and ripping the shirt open.

It might be a great idea! "I'm getting the water ready. It's not fancy, but it's powdered hot chocolate. Or would you prefer tea?"

"Hot chocolate is great. How long have you been here?"

She glanced around the room. Three suitcases laid open against the far wall. Some clothes were folded, others were haphazardly tossed in.

It was either clean up the room or check my teeth and put on a bra.

Attempting to appear casual despite her rising anxiety of

him seeing her room so unkept, Lucy tapped the coffeemaker to get it started. "March. The day before orientation."

"Six weeks? That's right. You said you don't have any furniture." He picked up the book on the top of the to-be-read stack and flipped it over. "When do you think your stuff will get here?"

"I've heard seven to ten days at least twice. The next potential move in day is Monday." The gurgling of the coffeemaker filled the room and immediately, hot water dripped out into the mug.

"*Astrophysics for People in a Hurry.*" Thomas held up the book with the galaxy on the cover.

Great. Now he knows what a nerd I am. This is already a disaster. But Lucy wasn't going to apologize for wanting to learn more about the world and beyond.

She tilted her chin up. "I think Dr. Tyson is very interesting. He presents a subject I don't know a whole lot about in a fun, interesting way. At one talk, he said to embrace curiosity."

Lucy watched Thomas study the book.

He's either reading the back cover or pretending to read the book but he's actually deciding the most polite way to get the hell out of here.

"Have you read *The Pluto Files*?"

What? "What?"

Placing the book back on the stack, Thomas shoved his hands in his pockets as though he'd admitted something he hadn't planned to. His cheeks dusted with a light shade of crimson. "I thought it made a lot of sense, demoting Pluto.

It does change what I learned in elementary school about the planets though."

Holy crap. He's a nerd too. Lucy's ovaries jumped for joy. "I haven't read that book. I'll put it on my list."

As if Dr. McAvoy couldn't get any sexier, he'd gone and all but admitted his super geek status.

If I'm not pregnant by the end of my ninety days just by standing in a room with him, it'll be a miracle.

He closed the distance between them, his hands still in his pockets like a nervous teen. "He's got a bunch of books. Seen his lectures a time or two. Funny guy."

"I like that show *Cosmos* he did," Lucy whispered, her breath quickening as Thomas approached. "It's very... um... intense."

Having him within arm's reach, Lucy couldn't help but rake her eyes over him and her blatant observance didn't go unnoticed.

Thomas raised an eyebrow before placing his hand on the curve of her waist. "You're an amazing woman, Dr. Lucy Davidson."

Her body hummed from his touch. The click of the coffee maker reminded her of the hot water. "Want any hot chocolate?"

"Not right now." His gaze rested on her mouth.

"Good." Taking a small step toward him, she licked her lips in anticipation of knowing what his felt like against hers. She hoped they were as good as she'd dreamed about. "Thank you. And you're—"

Gently, he kissed her before letting her finish her

thought.

The soft brushes of his lips against hers set her body on fire. Turning his head slightly to the left, he tenderly sucked on her bottom lip then his tongue traced along the seam of her mouth before slowly sliding it halfway into her mouth and out again. He flicked her top lip with his tongue followed by featherlight kisses.

His agonizingly slow and erotic techniques ignited the passion inside her. With each touch, nibble and suck, every nerve he ignited, shot straight south. Tingles danced over sensitive flesh as he moved his hands up her waist, the outside of her breasts and to her back. She could imagine him intimately kissing her, making her body sing while taking his time before bringing her to an earth-shattering climax.

The overwhelming craving for him washed over her. Lucy grabbed his shirt, pulling him and deepened the kiss.

Immediately, he moaned in pain and pulled away, holding his hand to his face.

Realization hit her hard when he pulled his hand away and his swollen lip caught her attention.

"Oh, gosh, Thomas, I am so sorry. I wasn't thinking. Are you bleeding?"

A chuckle escaped him as he dabbed at his bruised lip. "Glad to know I can get that brain of yours to take a break."

"It's not taking any sort of break, Dr. McAvoy. Believe me, it's running overtime where you're concerned."

"Really?" Despite his wounded mouth, he managed a dangerous smile that just about caused her panties to spontaneously combust.

"Crap, I thought I said that to myself." Lucy threw her hands up in frustration, but wouldn't deny the obvious. "Okay, yes. I'm attracted to you and would like to see more of you… I mean you more."

"Either one works."

Even with her cheeks flaming red from embarrassment, Lucy couldn't help but laugh. "I'll keep that in mind."

"Sorry to ruin the moment."

"It's not your fault." *But I'm gonna punch Junior in the face next time I see him.*

Because if that was how Thomas kissed with a wounded lip, Lucy could only imagine what he could do when every luscious bit of him were healthy.

Oh, goodness. The possibilities.

Chapter Eleven

"KUNG FU, HUH?" His lower lip moved, shooting pain into his gums. Finally getting a nibble of what Lucy Davidson tasted like had been better than he hoped it would be, but then his damned lip. "You started when, in middle school?"

"Yes." Lucy handed him a mug covered in small marsh-mallows floating on top before she curled up in the chair opposite him. "A friend told me about it, said it had helped her and she was about my size. It's a smarter martial art since it uses my opponent's momentum against them instead of brute force."

"You let them do most of the work. Dammit." He touched the mug to his mouth. The heat of the ceramic burned his tender skin. "Hot."

"Oh, gosh. I've got some ice we can add." She began to stand, but he motioned for her to stay seated.

"It just needs time to cool, Lucy. What were you saying about Kung Fu?"

"At least let me get you a straw." Within seconds she'd returned with a cup of a few cubes of ice and a couple of coffee straws. "Sorry, it's the best I've got for now."

He dropped the thick cubes into the thick chocolate and stirred with the straws. "Then I'm having warm chocolate instead of hot?"

"Yes, Dr. Smartypants."

"Okay, Dr. Badass." *And perfect ass.* All those years of martial arts had kept Lucy more than in shape.

Thinking about having his hands on her body only made it more difficult for him to reposition gracefully without embarrassing himself. Good thing he wore jeans and not sweatpants because in sweatpants, there would be nowhere to hide his enthusiasm for his beautiful colleague and her company.

She took her seat again and took a long sip of her hot chocolate. "You asked about martial arts. It would have been foolish for me to try and come straight at Junior like I would have been trained to do, let's say in American Karate or Aki-do. Scrawny or no, he certainly would have knocked me on my ass if I'd thought I could overpower him through brute force."

"I don't know. You're pretty fierce. I can't see you backing off from much of anything or anybody."

Her eyes lit up with delight. "That's the sweetest thing. Thank you."

"What made you start in Kung Fu again? Bullies?"

"Something like that." She moved her dark red hair over her shoulder as she appeared to get lost in thought. "My mom thought it would build my confidence and coordination."

Something like that? He wondered if she'd suffered the

injury because of someone's malicious act. Fury uncomfortably twisted his insides at the idea of anyone hurting her.

Calm down, man. It was only one kiss.

One amazing, intense kiss.

If it weren't for his busted lip, it was possible they would
be on the fast track to Nakedtown.

"Did the Kung Fu help?" He repositioned in his chair,
hoping to alleviate some of the pressure on his fly. "Were
you able to use it?"

"Yes." She stared at him for a few seconds before she appeared to blink her way out of her thoughts. "You mean did
I use it to defend myself?"

"Yes. I'll give you an example. Junior. When he grabbed
you. How did you get out of it?"

Placing her hand on her head, she mimicked her previous
movements. "I held his hand against my head when he tried
controlling me by pulling my hair."

"I wondered why you did that."

"I'm surprised you noticed. It all happened pretty fast."

"I notice a lot of things about you, Lucy Davidson." He
toasted her with his mug, but set it back down again.

Her eyes twinkled with excitement. "That's either the
sweetest or creepiest thing you could have said right now."

He let out a throaty laugh. "Which one am I? Creepy or
sweet?"

"I haven't decided yet, Dr. McAvoy." Placing her mug
on the table, she rested her elbows on the armrests of her
chair as her sultry voice danced over his ears.

God, how he wanted to kiss her. Kiss every inch of her,

every day for a long, long time. "I really hate him right now."

"So do I."

Good to know she's thinking the same thing I am.

"In three to five days, those sutures will come out."

"I'm a quick healer." And he'd drink three gallons of orange juice and eat a bucket of apples if he thought it would heal him faster.

"I'm glad to hear that. Maybe we could try again sometime."

The pajamas hugged her body beautifully. In the past hour, he'd come to appreciate pink in an entirely different way. "What about tomorrow?"

"Tuesday? Your sutures won't be out by tomorrow."

He rested his elbows on his knees, soaking her in. "I can spend time with you with my beat-up lip."

"I doubt you'd want to. I'm working in the office all day doing QA. Exciting stuff."

"Who doesn't love reviewing chart after chart? Catching mistakes and checking the minute details. Good times." He chuckled. "*Laissez les bons temps roulez.*"

She raised an eyebrow. "*Oui.*"

"You spoke French." Playfully sinking to his knees in front of her, he stretched out her arm as though he planned to kiss all the way up. "Do it again."

"*C'est vrai*... Gomez."

Thank God she got the reference. Thomas had tried this before only for the affectionate gesture to fall flat. Instead of kissing her arm, he brushed his cheek against her wrist, avoiding his wounded lip.

A healthy dusting of crimson colored her cheeks. "Be careful. I'd hate for you to… um… hurt yourself."

"I won't." He subtly inhaled the ginger and citrus scent on her skin.

"What were we talking about?"

"Work. I'm in noon to midnight today, then come in at seven Wednesday evening and work until seven, but I would be glad to come in and help you with charts."

"Not necessary. Thank you," she replied breathlessly as she leaned forward. "What about Thursday?"

"Another seven P to seven A on Thursday and Friday and Saturday then off two days." He hated swing shifts. He needed to find something far more stable, but that required working daylight hours. He could quit moving every few months., establish roots somewhere.

Here?

Until yesterday, the idea alone would raise his blood pressure, but after talking to Lucy and sitting with her today, staying in one place rapidly gained appeal.

Especially watching her react to his touch.

As he ran his thumb along the sensitive skin of her palm, her eyes remained laser-focused on him. "I-I-um…Thursday and Friday, I have to work in the office, but in the unit Saturday morning seven to seven at night."

"Then, I'll see you at check out." Before sitting back in his chair, he kissed the back of her hand and flinched as pain shot into the roots of his teeth. *Dammit.*

But they were dull compared to the stretch in his jeans. He had to carefully sit back while his body ached for her touch.

She twisted a long red lock around her finger. "I'm off Sunday morning and until Monday midday."

"Sunday evening?"

She ran her fingers through her hair, gathered it in a makeshift ponytail and flipped it behind her. "This Sunday? I don't know. *Timeless* is on at nine."

"The time travel show?" It took a few seconds for him to realize her playful tone. "Can I convince you to watch it on demand the next day?"

"Possibly." The corner of her mouth curled up.

"It's Tuesday morning now. The stitches can come out Friday morning. Swelling for sure will be gone."

She picked up her mug. "Sunday it is."

"Here's to Sunday." They clinked their glasses together and she took a long drink.

"Now, what were we talking about?"

For a moment, Thomas couldn't remember, but seeing her long copper lock fall about her face, he blurted out, "Hair pulling."

"Right. Right. Instinctively, people would have pulled to get away, but I wouldn't have gotten anywhere doing that and it would only hurt like hell." She lifted her hair off her neck and fanned it with her hand. "Again, I have to assume anybody larger than I am is going to be stronger, so I'm always thinking of another way to come out of the situation in a positive way. Sorry, I guess the hot chocolate is warmer than I thought."

Guess I haven't lost my touch. "Does it work for everything?"

She pressed her lips together before answering, her hair cascading about her shoulders. "It can work for a lot of things, but not everything is one hundred percent. The thing is, you have to be willing to get hurt if you need to use your techniques. You just make sure the other person is hurt worse."

Hurting Jade's brother ranked high on Thomas's to-do list right now. "I think I'm liking Kung Fu more and more."

"It's also amazing as physical therapy." Hopping to her feet, she extended her arm. "Grab my wrist."

"What?"

"Grab my arm like you want me to come with you."

I do want you to come with me, not that I have any perma-nent place to take you. Cautiously, he wrapped his hand around her tiny wrist. "Now what do I do?"

"Make sure you have a solid hold. Don't let go." She yanked her arm straight back and got nowhere. "See, if I pull straight back, not only is it what you'd expect I'd do and what I instinctively do, but it won't get me anywhere. I'm not strong enough to force your hand off, but if I do this…"

She twisted her arm toward his thumb and he could feel his hold weakening. Within a second, she'd freed herself.

"What did you do?"

"Your thumb is your weakest point. If I apply enough pressure and twist just right, it gives away. You can't hold on to me, but I can't stand there like they do in horror movies. My feet need to be running as soon as I get free."

"Interesting." Her pure excitement about the martial art

only made him want to head to the studio owned by the Scott brothers. "I've tried some martial arts and boxing classes. Don't remember them teaching me any of this."

If I had known some of this before San Diego, I might not be missing a piece of my lung right now.

"Or I can… stand up."

He did as she asked, standing beside the table. "What do I do?"

Holding her arm out. "Grab my arm again."

"Okay."

When he laid his hand on her arm, she leapt forward and her elbow flew toward his gut. She stopped short of knocking the wind out of him. "Again, the obvious thing for me to do and what you'll anticipate is I pull away, but if I slam my elbow into your solar plexus or gut, I catch you off guard."

She moved in closer, grabbing a handful of his shirt. The sweet scent of chocolate swirled between them as his body tingled with her so near.

"What are you doing?"

"Giving myself a better shot at getting away." Her eyes zoomed in on his lips.

He swallowed hard. "You want to get away?"

Gently she tugged at his clothes. "See, if you were distracted from that punch to the gut, I could yank your face down into my knee, ram you in the nose or hit something delicate to help me put distance between us."

"Like his nuts."

"And toes. I don't care who you are, a crushed toe hurts."

"True."

Her hands still rested on his chest several beats after she'd completed her instructions.

Leaning down, he brushed her cheek with his. With his finger, he traced along her jaw, then her elegant neck. "You're a badass, you know that?"

She shivered. "I don't think I'm a badass. Just well prepared."

"Is that what badasses do?" He breathed her in. She smelled of chocolate and ginger. "Prepare."

Her breathing quickened when he gently licked the pulse point above her collarbone. "No, um… badasses prepare to be prepared. Oh my, that feels good."

The jagged scar had been sutured long ago and he wondered again, if it had anything to do with the bullies she'd mentioned before. He smiled against her skin. "Tell me more about how badasses prepare."

"O-kay. Bruce Lee worked out for hours a day. Trained, um, constantly and when he was in the movies, he made it look, um, effortless. Oh my." She grabbed handfuls of his shirt when he brushed his lips against her ear. "Thomas."

His opposite hand rested on the small of her back, holding her close to him. She cupped his face and pain shot through his lip, his jaw, making his teeth hurt. "Crap."

She jerked her hand away. "You okay?"

"Not really." Pulling back, he shook his head as his tongue pushed on the sutures to calm the wicked pulsations in his lip. "I think I might need to take some more Tylenol."

"I'm so sorry." Glancing at her watch, she touched her

forehead to his. "It's almost six."

"Sorry to keep you awake."

"It was worth it." She nuzzled his nose. "So Sunday?"

"Sunday."

"Thank you for the hot chocolate, Dr. Davidson."

"You're most welcome, Dr. McAvoy."

As he walked back to his room, Thomas knew two things for certain.

Something traumatic happened in Lucy Davidson's life long ago and Marietta had started to look a whole lot more interesting.

Chapter Twelve

"COME ON, THOMAS. Two more." Paramedic Kyle Cavasos yelled as Thomas struggled to lift the heavy barbell.

The shift had been rough. Thomas never sat down the entire twelve hours. Along with the normal chest pains, lacerations, and late night ear infections he'd treated, he'd been spit in the face by some crappy kid with the flu. Another woman came in crowning and they barely got her to a labor and delivery room before out popped a brand new baby girl as two guys fought in the hallway over paternity.

Deputy Shaw had to be called in to referee.

As soon as Dr. Sean Gallagher came in, Thomas took a shower in the call room and headed to the gym.

What Thomas hoped for was a great workout, a big breakfast, and a good, long nap.

So far, he was zero for three.

"Thomas, come on. Two more, man." Kyle encouraged as he spotted Thomas.

The muscles in his arms burned. His left shoulder gave way slightly, but he recovered with Kyle's help. "Shit. That's it. I can't do anymore."

"Good set."

"It sucked." Sitting up on the bench, Thomas rubbed the sweat from his face, the salt burned his lip. "I'm still not back where I was."

"Why the setback?"

Thomas lifted the side of his shirt, revealing his scars. "Stabbed by a crazy-assed patient."

"Holy shit." Kyle's eyes went as wide as dinner plates. "What happened?"

"Jumped me in the parking lot after a shift." He glanced out the window, seeing the fire department building across the street, snow still on the ground in small piles.

The front doors of the police station flew open and out strutted Junior with some guy in a suit. Rage slammed Thomas in the gut, sending a foul taste coating the back of his tongue.

"Hey, Doc. Did he get your shoulder, too?" Kyle asked, pulling Thomas out of his anger.

Searching his brain, Thomas tried to recall the evening, but everything happened so quickly, he couldn't be entirely sure what occurred when. "In the fight, he tore my rotator cuff. They repaired it with everything else."

His eyes never strayed from Junior as though he were afraid to let his guard down for a second. Not until Junior got in his car and drove away did Thomas breathe comfortably.

That guy is trouble. I can feel it.

"After all that, guess your face seems like a walk in the park." Kyle grabbed some free weights and began a set of bicep curls. "How many stitches did you get?"

"Lucy put in about six."

"She's got suturing down. What did Junior hit you with?"

"Some sort of weird-looking ring." Sitting back down, Thomas dabbed his face again and flinched when the bruised skin bit back. "I can't believe he got the one up on me."

"Junior's a sneaky bastard," Brett Adams called from across the gym as he ran on the treadmill. "He's weaseled his way out of so many things. Pleaded down sentences because the jails are full."

"His attorney is a slimeball." Kyle completed his set of curls and dropped the weights with a thud.

"An expensive slimeball. I'd guess Jade's spent everything she's got for that guy's retainer," Brett added. "And her brother won't lose a wink of sleep when he skips town and leaves her holding the bag."

"I wouldn't shed one tear for that guy to be behind bars." Fury fueled Thomas's body to move. He motioned to Kyle to spot him again. "Let's do this."

"You sure?"

Rolling his shoulders, Thomas lay on the bench again and willed himself through a set of twelve. By the time he finished the last lift, his muscles uncontrollably burned, but a piece of his pride had been restored.

"When do you work again, Dr. McAvoy?" Brett shook his hand after he finished his run.

"What day is it?"

"Tuesday."

"I'm going in at seven, work a twelve." He replayed his schedule in his mind. "Off Wednesday, then back for three twelves. Seven P to seven A."

Then I'll get my date with Lucy.

That thought alone gave him enough energy to complete another set.

"Knock. Knock." Thomas held up coffee as he entered Lucy's office. On every available surface there were files, papers, and expandable folders.

Her eyes sparkled and she almost lunged for the coffee. "My hero. Your sutures look good."

"Two more days and they'll be out." The idea of kissing Lucy with two functioning lips made him pace off his rising libido. "I came by your room this morning after working out, but housekeeping said you'd already left."

She held her hands out wide. "As you can see, I've got a ton of work to do. This office is a nightmare."

The stacks of work made Thomas's eye uncomfortably twitch. "What is all this?"

"Best I can tell, it's every patient he ever saw. Apparently, Dr. McMasters liked everything printed."

"Good God." Wandering around the office, Thomas picked up a file and opened it. "This is from four years ago."

"There's no rhyme or reason to anything in here. Nothing. It's as though he walked in and threw everything up in the air."

"No doubt." The place would have sent anyone with OCD into a catatonic state. "Anything in this closet?"

"I'm afraid to look." Lucy took a sip of her coffee. "Oh, this is perfect. Just the way I like it. Thank you."

He reached for the door handle, but Lucy jumped up and took his hand away. "It's fine, Thomas. I don't need the help."

Her redirection annoyed him. "Lucy, relax."

"I know, I know, but I'm good. Didn't you just get off this morning?" Without letting go of his hand, she guided him back toward her desk and dropped his hand as someone walked by.

"Yes, I met Kyle at Carter's Gym before going by Main Street and getting some breakfast. Thought you might need some coffee." Glancing around the room, he asked again. "Lucy, why won't you let me help you?"

The smile that lit up his morning became tense. "Because I like doing things a certain way and it's *my* job."

"And dropping my hand. Is that doing your job?" He'd never been a big fan of PDA, but her trying to hide their interest in each other hit him wrong. Frustration simmered under his skin.

Her fists clenched in her lap a couple of times before she answered. "Look, I like you. I really do, but this is my job and I'm going to do it, no matter what."

"No matter what. What does that mean?"

"It means I can't get distracted, not by anybody or anything. I have to be successful. This job is everything to me."

"I never said it wasn't, Lucy, I'm offering to help, not

take over."

She gave him a quick hug. "I appreciate the coffee and the offer, but I've got to work and I need you to go."

Chapter Thirteen

*W*HAT WERE YOU *thinking?*

Two days later and Lucy still couldn't believe she'd brushed off Thomas so quickly.

A wonderfully nice, hot guy brings you coffee, offers to help and you ask him to leave? No wonder you're still single.

Rubbing her temples as she sat at her work covered desk, she asked herself again, "What the hell is wrong with you?"

Lucy brushed it off on anxiety and frustration of what she'd uncovered in this pile of crazy called her office.

And one of the people she did need to talk to had to be the last person Lucy wanted to see.

"Jade, can you come in here, please?" Lucy stood in the doorway of her office right as Jade walked by.

"I have to go."

"It's noon. Your shift is until three."

Zipping up her jacket, Jade sighed. "Allen came in for my last three hours. I have to take care of something."

"Nice to end a Friday shift at noon. I need to talk to you before you go."

"Right now?"

"Right. Now." Walking back into her office, she hoped

her assumptions of what she'd found was incorrect, but when Jade's eyes went wide as she walked in, Lucy's heart sank.

"Where did you get that?"

Lucy hoped the frustration that bubbled in her stomach didn't echo in her voice. She needed to get Jade to work well with the bombshell that was about to drop if things were going to work out for the better. "It busy out there?"

"Not bad for a Friday afternoon, but it's early." Jade's tired eyes stared at the expanding file holder on Lucy's desk. "How do you have those files?"

"What? These? Or that? Or those?" Lucy tapped the holder, then the pile of papers next to her and finally the long table behind her, full of paperwork, before pulling out a tin of mints. "Mint?"

"N-n-n-o, no thank you." With nervous fingers, Jade tapped the holder on the desk.

"Any idea why this was in the closet back there?"

Waiting for Jade to say something, Lucy hoped her assumptions were way off the mark. Sadly, Jade's reaction only encouraged Lucy's worry. "Look familiar?"

"How did you find those?" Jade snapped, then cleared her throat and calmly asked again. "What made you look for files in the closet?"

"Dr. McMasters."

"Oh?" The nervousness in her voice verified what Lucy already knew.

"When Mr. Richards saw me at the diner a few days ago, he mentioned he never got a bill from his November 2017 visit and that Dr. McMasters didn't do anything for him."

"And, Mr. Richards seems to look good these days. Out walking his dogs around three or four every afternoon."

"He is better, but I thought that was weird. Him never having gotten a bill. I looked through the system and found it, but no charges had been dropped. In fact, the chart had never been closed."

A look of relief washed across Jade's face. "Okay, and?"

"No one red-flagged it. Nothing. Just his admission face sheet and an initial record of vital signs. Very limited notes from the triage assessment and who saw him that day, but no documentation of his visit from the MD otherwise. No charges."

"A lot of things get lost in medical records and billing. Denver and Evan have talked about giving that section a bit of an overhaul." She tapped her watch. "Are we good? I've got stuff to do."

Standing, Lucy walked around the desk and handed Jade a file. "He has Blue Cross Blue Shield and thankfully we have a year to file, which is lucky."

"Lucky, indeed. The hospital may still get reimbursed." The papers shook between her fingers.

"In fact, all these in this holder are Blue Cross and Blue Shield."

"How… weird." She swallowed hard, her eyes scanned the room. "Why do you have all this in here?"

"Well, since JCAHO is going to be here next year, I found out that Dr. McMasters didn't do any quality assurance since the last time joint commission came."

Jade's eyes scanned the piles of papers. "What a disaster.

Sucks for you, doesn't it?"

"On so many levels." Walking away, Lucy stood by the window. The cloudless, sunny day had been a much needed reprieve from the winter grey skies. Sunshine had helped her fight her doubts about her ability to do this job, but how she handled this critical moment would certainly make or break her chances of keeping it.

But she could easily lose any chance with Thomas if Lucy turned Jade's mistake into the hospital directors.

"Why are you showing me this?" Jade dropped the papers on the desk like they'd scared her.

Please let me be wrong. "You really don't know?"

"Should I?"

Just come clean, Jade. "Fine, I'll spell it out for you. I did a search and found multiple charts around the same time that were never closed."

"Didn't you have an employee evaluation this morning with Denver and Evan? When did you even have time to research any of this?"

Lucy had to admit, Jade had a flair for deflection. "That was yesterday morning."

"How did it go?"

"Better than I expected." In fact, both hospital administrators were beyond impressed with what Lucy had accomplished so far. Even mentioned her ninja skills.

"As I was saying, these charts are similar. They have initial vital signs, patient intake, but no documentation from Dr. McMasters."

"Maybe they lost the piece of paper that he wrote on."

Please don't fight me on this. "One or two maybe, but not a dozen."

"A dozen?" Swallowing hard, Jade took a step back. "That many?"

"Dr. McMasters never documented anything about these patients, but someone saw them. *Someone* wrote prescriptions for them. Ordered narcotics on them."

"Narcotics? Where?"

She may not know how deeply this goes. Pointing to the chart, Lucy tapped the paper. "Here."

Picking up the paper, Jade appeared to study it. Within a few moments, her hands began to shake. "I don't… didn't."

Lucy expected defiance, even denial, but not distress. "Are you okay?"

"No." Jade tossed the paper on the desk. "Patients get pain medication in the ER. So what?"

Mr. Richards said he didn't get anything for pain. "You did see all these patients, right?"

"Yes, well, I didn't see Mr. Richards. Dr. McMasters saw him." Pulling her jacket tightly around her, Jade looked away. "But I did my job as you can see. Congratulations, you solved the mystery. Here's a Scooby snack."

"But his signature on here is different from his regular one." When Jade didn't answer, disappointment settled in Lucy's gut. "I verified all this by paying Dr. McMasters a visit yesterday afternoon since the writing looked strange to me."

All the color drained from Jade's face. "You went to see him? What did he say?"

"Speaks highly of you." Lucy lied. The old curmudgeon couldn't say a nice thing about anyone, especially not any women who he felt had no business in medicine higher than a "ward" nurse. When Lucy left, she couldn't have been happier that the man had retired since he had to be the last person anyone needed to see in the ER or in any other medical setting.

"What did he say?" Jade asked urgently through clenched teeth.

Moving back behind the desk, Lucy sat down. "He said you promised him you'd take care of making sure all his patients' charges dropped. You'd file from the last few months before he retired. That I shouldn't worry because you always kept everything really organized for him in this file folder. Told me what it looked like and that he left it in the closet on his last day for you to finish."

Jade swallowed hard when Lucy tapped the desktop file holder in front of her. "Dr. McMasters always liked things printed. It helped me keep him organized when he wanted everything on paper."

"I see that." Lucy hated this. Hated that Jade wouldn't just come out and confess what she'd done so they could fix it. Firing a strong nurse like Jade would only hurt morale and make Lucy the monster Jade had painted her to be.

But she wouldn't let the woman roll over her or set up the hospital to be fined tens of thousands of dollars.

Tilting her chin up, Jade replied, "He didn't like the computer. I tried several times to get him to use it. Even had him sit right next to me, walked him through every step several times, but he had no interest. Wanted everything on paper."

"Which is one of the many reasons it was time for him to retire."

"I swear. He still bragged about using mail-order and paying with a check everywhere. He hated computers and refused to even have one at home," she scoffed. "I'm surprised the man has a cellphone."

Opening the lid, she ran her fingers along the color-coded tabs. "Truly, Jade. This is wonderfully simple, great tools, but I have to ask you one thing."

"What's that?"

Removing two of the folders, she placed the sign off sheets from those two and Mr. Richards's chart side by side on the desk. "Can you tell me what's wrong with this?"

Without looking down, Jade backed away from the desk. "Not really."

Watching all those hours of *Lie to Me* on Netflix, Lucy knew Jade was hiding something big. Hopping to her feet, Lucy tapped on the papers. "But e-signature for the doctor, in the doctor's signature on an official document. My guess is he never saw some of these people."

"He saw them when they came in. Glanced at their face sheets."

"Them walking by him and him actually treating them are different things."

"He stood at the desk and saw every single patient that walked in."

Exhaling a long breath, Lucy said a silent prayer. "Fine.

We can work with that, but you're going to have to get him to review these. Sign these."

"I don't need a doctor looking over my shoulder, telling me I'm doing a good job. I'm a more than qualified health care provider!"

"That's not the way liability and insurance works and you know it. I have no doubt that you're more than qualified, especially when it came to Dr. McMasters, but the rules were specific. You have to operate under a doctor's supervision, especially in the ER."

"I did."

"No, according to these and him, he didn't sign off."

"He didn't close the charts. Big deal. I'd bet there are many doctors here who don't or think they did." Jade dropped her purse at her feet. "Do you know how many times I tried to get the man to learn that? By the time we got to that part of the lesson, he'd all but zoned out."

Lucy agreed. "After talking to him yesterday, he didn't seem like the want to learn anything new type. In fact, he said he rarely had to even get up from the central ER desk that last week if you were working. Which means if he never laid eyes on the patient, these aren't valid, Jade. If you file them, they're fraudulent."

"Who would know? It's not like Blue Cross and Blue Shield is going to send their minions out to make sure the doctor saw every patient."

Lucy laughed from shock. "You're justifying this?"

The buzz went off. Jade frantically went through her purse before pulling out her phone. "I have to go."

Moving around, Lucy stood in the doorway. "Wait. Yes, you're right. No one would probably ever know. There are so many claims that go through insurance offices every day that no one would probably even notice the different signatures. The charges are normal, not inflated, everything looks fair for the most part. They look like every other charge and chart that's gone through here."

Jade's lower lip trembled. "And?"

"In fact, if Mr. Richards hadn't mentioned he never got a bill, we wouldn't be talking right now."

Stomping her foot, Jade snapped, "If everything you say is true, why are you making an issue out of this? Why does it matter?"

"Because if it *is* caught and they do bounce them back, it is fraud. We need to do everything in our power to make sure we cross all the Ts and dot the Is just the way insurance wants it." She motioned for Jade to sit down, but she refused. "I don't like the system either, but insurance companies don't want to give up a penny unless they have to and they are ruthless when it comes to fraud."

"I know that. I dealt with them many times."

"Yes, you have, which makes me wonder." A sudden epiphany hit Lucy. She walked to the desk and picked up the file holder. "If you're so adamant that these wouldn't bounce back, why didn't you file them?"

"I… um…" Jade grabbed her phone and tapped the screen. "I really have to go."

"You need to stay here and help me figure this out."

"I don't need to help you with anything. You wanted my

job—"

"It was Dr. McMasters job. Not yours." Lucy pleaded. "Jade, I know your heart was in the right place. McMasters dumped this situation on you. He needed to retire but you should have gone to the supervisors for help and not taken over everything."

Locking her arms across her chest, Jade snapped, "I'm guessing you've told Denver and Evan about this?"

"Not as of yet. I wanted to see if we could work together first before letting them know what had happened."

That bit of information caused Jade's eyebrows to hit her hairline. "Why? Why wouldn't you? It would be a great way to get rid of me."

"I don't want to get rid of you. I want to work with you."

Jade looked as though she'd been slapped. "I don't understand you at all."

"I'm not the evil person you've decided me to be. I want to do what's best for this unit. This community." Lucy sat on the edge of the desk. "If you'll help me, we can get these corrected and sent in."

"How? You going to call all the patients back and have them reenact their symptoms for the day?"

"You and he will sit down, you go over the patient's chart with him, he signs it."

"McMasters? He won't come back here. He said he's done and that guy only does what's best for him and only him."

"I can get him to come back." *Especially after seeing these charts.*

"I doubt that."

"How much you want to bet I can?" After spending the afternoon with the man, Lucy had no idea how to make things right, but she needed Jade on board before anything would work. Otherwise, she would have to go to the hospital directors, Denver and Evan, and Jade would lose her job. Firing one of the most solid employees would not be a great way to instill confidence in the staff.

Lucy worried she'd opened a can of worms that had been better left alone.

Shifting her feet, Jade retorted, "You're saying we'll need to sit down and go over these however many charts and charges, make sure things were filled out, documented, and filed right?"

"Quality assurance does it all the time. It'll take one day, tops." Lucy mentally crossed her fingers. *Come on, Jade. You can make this right.*

A momentary flash of relief blinked across Jade's face before her forehead furrowed. "The day that happens would be the day my prince charming walks through that door, so next to never."

"Does Prince Charming have to walk through my office door? Can he walk in the front doors of the ER? Just this building?"

"Get over yourself."

Ugh! Stop it. Lucy threw her hands up in frustration. "You'd rather the hospital be out tens of thousands of dollars and fined instead? Come on, Jade. You're better than this."

For a few moments, Jade appeared to be contemplating Lucy's words, but turned a one-eighty and began to walk out the door. "I get what you're saying, but I don't have time to deal with this right now. I've got a brother who's making me crazy. A house that has no heat. Property I need to sell. I haven't seen my dog for the last few days."

"Thomas mentioned you were having some troubles."

That stopped her in her tracks. She came stomping back into the office. "You've talked about me? Why? Where?"

The size of Jade's eyes told Lucy she'd hit a nerve. "The other morning. We talked about a lot of things. How you two knew each other as kids. What happened in San Diego."

"What else?"

We kissed. Ugh, how we kissed. Lucy's knees trembled at the idea of what his one hundred percent working order lips could really do. "Not much else."

"You know, huh? That I had to kill someone?" Jade adjusted and readjusted her purse on her shoulder.

"I'm sorry you had to—"

"I don't need your pity."

Lucy massaged her temples, hoping to cut off the migraine that would certainly erupt the moment this conversation ended. This woman was simply impossible to reach. "Please, quit being defensive. I wanted to say I can't imagine having to kill—"

"My husband." Tears ran down her face. "Yes. It's awful to have to kill someone you love."

If Jade had slapped Lucy with the file holder, Lucy would have been less surprised. "Your, your husband?

Thomas never said he was your husband."

The anger that had colored Jade's face for the past several minutes morphed into a devilish grin. "Yes, my husband. My more than *jealous* husband."

"Jealous? Why would he… I see."

"And he had every right to be. Thomas and I worked together a lot. Have known each other since we were in middle school. Are good *friends.*"

Thomas said they were never involved. "Great. Everyone needs friends."

With a look of the cat that ate the canary, Jade moved toward the door. "We done here?"

It took a few seconds for Lucy to regain her snap. *You can't think about that now. Fix this first.* "No, Jade. You've got an obligation to get this done. Do what's right."

"Is that what you do? What's right?"

"I try to, but I'm not perfect." *Apparently, picking guys who screw around with married women is one of my many imperfections.*

"You perfectly punched my brother in the junk the other morning. I'd say you have perfection down."

"What does that—" Lucy shook her head in frustration, her head pounded from this foolishness. "I get to defend myself. That doesn't have anything to do—"

"Junior is harmless."

"And I guess Thomas got that cut on his face from shaving."

Jade's lips thinned. "My brother… my brother is complicated."

"Family sure can be, but that doesn't give them free reign to do whatever they want when they want to." As much as Lucy wanted to sympathize, something uncomfortable twisted Lucy's gut about Jade. Something she couldn't quite put her finger on.

She's hiding something more.

"What would you know about family chaos?" she scoffed, her eyes welled with tears. "You can't possibly know anything about it."

Instinctively running her fingers down the lines on her arms, Lucy exhaled a long breath. "We all have our scars of life, Jade. You can't let them decide who you are or you'll never be who you really are."

Which is why I have to make this job work. I can't go back.

"You're not my shrink or my boss or my friend, so don't start throwing all sorts of trite advice my way." Jade stormed out of the office.

The whoosh of the ambulance doors echoed through the hallway.

Watching from the window, Lucy saw Jade run to her car.

Behind her, Copper Mountains' peaks jutted into the thick clouds that had formed in the past hour.

The wind caused the hedges outside Lucy's window to dance, but she couldn't see it through her angry tears.

He lied to me. And I fell for it.

When will I learn?

Chapter Fourteen

THE AFTERNOON SUN shone through the windows, bringing in a much needed brightness to the gloom that had hovered over Marietta for the past couple of days.

After her confrontation with Jade, Lucy felt spent, but the idea of Thomas lying to her, had her brain on overdrive.

She sat in the office for a couple of hours, trying to sort her thoughts as she reviewed the rest of Dr. McMasters' unclosed files, finding the same questions over and over again. "What a total mess."

The paperwork only distracted her for so long. After finding yet another open chart from her predecessor, she threw her pen down on the desk. Berating herself at being so out of sorts about a man she'd only known for six weeks and had hardly talked to, Lucy got up and stretched.

Like ships in the night, she and Thomas passed each other at check out.

"Maybe I misunderstood or Jade had simply thrown the idea of Thomas's lying in there to deflect from the true matter at hand." Even if Thomas and Jade had been involved past or recent present, she assumed they weren't now. Yet, all of these instances gave Lucy pause when deciding how involved she wanted to get with Thomas.

How well do I really know him?

He's locum tenens, a traveler. A temporary assignment and hasn't said a word about staying.

Yet, the idea of taking a backseat to the potential of what, like? Love? Lust? Simply getting to know him better? Bothered her more than taking a chance.

That scared her most of all. All she wanted to do was jump into the dating pool with both feet when she'd been so used to dipping a toe and overanalyzing the water, the depth, the temperature.

For so long, she'd been too cautious about her choices in men, which had led her to heartache due to overthinking and then not thinking enough.

Could this be a happy medium? Was there such a thing when this kind of attraction existed?

Would this be a distraction to keep her from doing what she needed to accomplish here in Marietta?

She scanned the piles of work again.

Everything she needed to accomplish.

I can't do this alone, but I have to. I can't bail on this now.

Throwing her hands up in frustration, Lucy growled. "I'm done. I need air. A workout."

A short walk to the Graff got her brain out of the computer. The afternoon sun danced around her like a warm hug and the crisp air seeped into her body. The brisk chill cleared her thoughts and she could begin to think without her mind being clouded with worry.

The snow had begun to melt and she almost felt hot in

her heavy coat.

When she reached the Graff parking lot, she faced the Copper Mountains and sighed, wondering what mysteries and adventures lay in wait up on the trails. She hoped with the warmer weather, she'd get a chance to explore sooner rather than later, but the amount of work that had been left by her predecessor dimmed her hopes of having any sort of fun anytime soon.

The mountains glistened, the sun sparkled off the white-capped peaks.

Who would have thought a former beach bunny would embrace the arctic winters of Montana? A laugh tugged her mouth up at how quickly life could change.

She ran her finger along her arm.

Both good and bad, I guess.

When she couldn't get her brain to stop banging into itself or problems appeared to have no true solution, she did what she always did. Worked out, then talked to her family for some much needed grounding and common sense.

"How is the weather there, Lu?" Peter's handsome face filled the screen.

"You tell me. You're the one always sending me messages about it." She combed her hair still wet from her post-exercise shower.

He held up his phone and tapped the screen, his eyes comically wide. "It's a high of fifty-five today. Fifty-five! That's almost freezing."

She laughed. "It's twenty-three degrees above freezing, Peter."

"What are you two talking about?" Edmund asked, joining the conversation.

"Hello, Edmund!" Lucy waved to her brother just three years older than she. "How are you?"

"Warmer than you are, I'd suppose."

"You'd suppose right." A slight breeze blew in the open window next to her. She shivered and curled up in the chair.

"When are you going to come home?"

"Why don't you think I can do this?"

Peter smiled. "I know you can do this, Luce. We just want you back here."

Edmund added, "Montana is too far away. Quit this obsession over snow and this assignment and come home."

Her pride took a hit with his words, but she smiled through it. "It's not an assignment. It's a job. A directorship."

"It's too far away." He grabbed Peter's phone and held it up to the laptop camera. "Fifty-five? That's insane!"

A hearty chuckle escaped her. "Call me a glutton for punishment."

"Seriously, Lu." Peter leaned forward. "Why would you leave?"

"You know why. I need to make my own space, Peter. I need to be me."

"I need to be meeeeeeee!" Edmund sang off key. "You can have your space here, Lucy. It has to suck out there. No family."

As much as she loved her brother, he'd been nothing but a pessimist for the past few months. Of course, with everything he'd been dragged through, she could understand why.

"Come on, Edmund. It's not that bad and I think you'd love it here. You've always loved skiing."

"On water."

"Well, this is frozen water. You ski on a thing called snow," she joked.

His face scrunched up as if he were trying to understand what she said. "Frozen water? That's just crazy talk. Fake news, I tell you."

Peter joined in. "Never seen the stuff. Only heard about it. I don't think it exists. Don't believe in it one bit."

She picked up her phone and typed in the home zip code on the weather app. Holding it up, she joked, "Seventy-eight and sunny, there? That's positively scorching."

Behind them, the ocean view from Peter's home made the pangs of homesickness settle in Lucy's chest. *Dealing with my heart would be so much easier if my family were here.*

Edmund continued as he pointed behind him. "Hear that? Those waves are saying, Luuuuucy. Luuuucy, come home."

"I do hear them." She could almost feel the summer sun on her body. The way it would dance across her skin with featherlight touches—like Thomas's lips on her ear.

That thought alone encouraged her to stay in Marietta a bit longer and confront him on what Jade had implied.

She glanced at her watch. *Only three.*

"Need to be somewhere?" Peter cocked his eyebrow. "Meeting someone?"

"Me? Who would I be meeting here in the frozen wastelands of Montana?" But Thomas had to go into work at seven. She'd listened for the familiar ping from the elevator or the slam of the hotel door, hoping to catch him coming or going.

"Lucy. Come on. Quit avoiding the question. Let me be the big brother on this one."

"I promise you, there's no one. Now, what time is it there again? You two or three hours ahead of me?"

He looked at his brother. "I find that I don't believe her. Do you, Ed?"

"Nope, not one bit." Edmund added.

"Boys, I love you always and forever, but I'm fine. I promise." A sharp bark from outside made her stand up. "Wait a minute."

Glancing across the street, she saw Mr. Richards rounding the corner from Second Street with his three miniature pinchers on leashes. The dogs' feet moved as quickly as their tails wagged. With a smile as bright as sunshine as he waved to all the kids at the movie theater as they walked by, apparently having no problems keeping up with his pooches.

"You okay?" Peter asked.

Edmund joined him. "Lucy, everything alright?"

"Yes, yes. I can see one of my patients is walking his dogs. Very nice man came in my first week. Took a slip on the ice, partially ripped his ACL." When she finally looked at her computer screen, both of her brothers had gotten as close to the camera as they could where she could still see their faces. She let out a laugh.

Peter pointed to the beach. "Ouch. No one would slip

on ice here."

"Unless they spilled their drink." Susan tilted her face into view.

"Susan! How are you? How's the wedding planning?"

A flash of sadness moved across Susan's eyes. "It's not. I broke it off yesterday."

"I'm so sorry to hear that. You okay?" As much as Lucy pined for a life as exciting as Susan's, she didn't wish for her relationship drama.

"Yeah, yeah, I'm fine." She ran her fingers through her hair before gathering it into a messy ponytail and pinning it on the back of her head. "Guess third time wasn't a charm."

"I guess not."

"How are you? Anyone interesting there you want to tell me about?"

"Yeah, Lu? Anyone you want to tell us about?" Edmund stood behind Susan and he was quickly joined by Peter.

"We're listening."

How much she'd missed the playful banter between her and her siblings. Their caring for her well-being, their worry about her being so far away. "There's nothing to tell. There's no one—"

A knock on her door, made her pause. She held her finger up. "Hold on, someone's here."

"Oh, oh, someone's there. Someone's there!" Susan excitedly clapped her hands. "Let's see who it is. Take us with you, Lucy!"

"I'm not expecting anyone." Since she'd not heard the elevator ding or a door slam, she assumed it might be one of the other guests on the floor. She scooped up her computer and walked with it on one arm to the door.

As soon as she opened it, she wished she'd left the computer on the table.

There, freshly shaven Thomas stood in a black button down, dark jeans. In his hands a bouquet of flowers and a picnic basket. "Good afternoon, neighbor."

Heat warmed her cheeks then headed straight south. "Hello. What's all this?"

"It's a balmy fifty-five right now. I wondered if you'd be interested in going hiking with me for a quick afternoon date."

If her ovaries hadn't noticed him before, they certainly noticed him now. In fact, they were doing their own happy dance right now.

He might have lied to you. Those words whispered in her ear sending her libido from full fire to simmer. "I'm so glad you came by, I have something I wanted to ask you, but aren't you supposed to be working today at seven?"

"I gave the first few hours of my shift to Gavin. I have to go in at ten, but I'll work for him another time." He gave her a curious look. "Is that a yes or no on the picnic?"

"It's a possible maybe." She motioned for him to enter then laid the computer on the bed. "I wanted to apologize for being abrupt the other day. I had a lot on my mind, but I do appreciate your offer to help me. Thank you."

"I wondered."

"Now, I have to ask you something."

"Right. First, this." He handed her the flowers and put

the basket next to his feet. "Shoot."

As soon as the door clicked closed, she took a deep breath. The sweet smell of the bouquet floated around her, bringing her angst down. She relaxed enough until the question that had bounced around in her head drifted out of her mouth, "Were you and Jade ever lovers?"

When his eyes went wide, Lucy realized she'd already asked the question she'd been thinking about for the past few hours. "I'd meant to work up to asking you that."

"What?" He stepped back. "Jade? No."

The tight grip of betrayal evaporated, but Lucy didn't want to throw caution to the wind. She'd been lied to before by a man she cared about and she wouldn't go there again. "You're sure?"

"I'd know if I'd slept with anyone. Why'd you ask?"

"I talked to her today."

"You talked to her today. About what?"

Should I tell him his friend might have committed insurance fraud? "I had a few questions about some charts she had with Dr. McMasters. That's it."

His eyebrow cocked. "You sure that's it?"

"Yes. I mentioned what we'd discussed about your time in San Diego."

The muscle in his jaw clenched. "And she said what?"

"That she shot her husband."

"She did."

Taking a step back, Lucy clasped her hands in front of her. "Her *jealous* husband."

A look of understanding washed across his face. "She said

that. Her *jealous* husband?"

"Yes." Crossing her arms across her chest, Lucy waited for the excuse that was sure to come.

"She's right."

Lucy sucked in a breath. "She is?"

"He was jealous. Hated anyone else she talked to. Men. Women. Dogs. Air."

"If that was the case, why didn't you tell me?"

Cautiously, Thomas took the flowers from her hands and placed them next to the computer. "I didn't say anything about the man being her husband because I felt that part was Jade's story to tell. She's never talked much to me about it and I'd guess not a lot of people in town know much either."

"Trauma can be difficult to discuss." She soaked in his body language, changes in breathing... the mouth-watering smell of his spicy cologne.

Ugh, focus!

Thomas reached out and gently took her hand. "Believe me, Jade and I have never been intimate. Nothing more than childhood friends. Nothing."

For a long moment, Lucy studied him. She looked for all the signs of lying she'd learned from binge watching *Lie to Me.*

Good eye contact. No sweating. No nervous twitches. He's solid in his stance, no shifting of his feet.

She glanced down at his hands in hers. *He's tenderly holding my hand. No stress there.* "Nothing between you two."

"Nothing."

"And why should I believe you?" But she already did.

Dammit.

"I believe him." Susan piped in. "I think he's telling the truth, Lu."

Thomas's forehead furrowed. "Please tell me you heard that."

Biting her lip, Lucy tried not to laugh as her eyes went innocently wide. "Heard what?"

"I think he just might be," Peter added. "But I need to look him in the face, first."

"I don't like this guy. Who is he?" Edmund's grumpy commentary rounded out the trio. "Guys lie. They always lie."

"Lucy, what's going on?" Thomas looked around. "Is someone else here?"

Subtly, she pointed to the computer. "When you arrived, I was talking to my siblings."

He turned and waved. His face shaded with a dusting of scarlet.

They all waved back.

"Let me see the flowers again and I'll tell you if he's lying," Susan requested. "The bouquet has to be the right size. Too small he doesn't value you enough, too big, he's hiding something."

"Is that true?" Edmund scoffed.

"No idea." Peter shrugged. "But good to know."

How Lucy loved her siblings. Even from thousands of miles away, they knew how to make her day better.

Thomas scooped up the flowers and held them near the screen. "Hope these meet your approval."

Susan clasped her hands together and sighed like some fairytale princess. "Awwwww. That's so sweet. He's telling the truth, Lucy."

Peter gave a thumbs-up. "The flowers are a nice touch. Her favorites are peonies, but good luck getting fresh ones in Montana. It's fifty-five there today."

"You don't say?" Thomas pulled out his phone, his fingers sailed across the screen. "It is fifty-five!"

"Smartass." Peter nodded. "I might like this guy."

Susan let out a lusty laugh. "I know I do."

No one had been able to hold his own against her siblings and certainly, not so quickly. The banter made Lucy's heart happy.

"I'm not so sure." Edmund put his eye near the camera as though he were looking through a keyhole. "Who are you? What's your name?"

"Thomas McAvoy." Thomas gave them a grandiose bow.

Her siblings mockingly oohed and aahed for a few moments.

Leaning down, Thomas waved. "Hi, you must be Peter, Edmund, and Susan."

"Hiiiiii, Thomas." The trio smiled.

"*Dr.* Thomas McAvoy." Lucy laughed.

"Oooooooh! A doctor!"

"Never seen one of those before." Edmund playfully rolled his eyes.

As Thomas tried to get a word in edgewise, her siblings decide to simultaneously bombard him with questions.

Who are you?

Where are you from?

How much do you bench?

What books do you read?

Do you have a criminal record?

Can you read?

How tall are you?

Are you really a doctor or do you just play one on TV?

Did you know it's fifty-five degrees there today?

Are there any warrants out for your arrest?

You hurt my sister, I'll kill you.

Lucy picked up the computer at Susan's last comment. "Okay, time to go. Love you. We'll talk with you soon."

"Wait." Thomas counted his answers off on his fingers. "Thomas McAvoy. Washington DC. Two-hundred-fifty. Anything I can get my hands on."

Lucy cocked her head. "What?"

"Someone asked me what I read."

Peter raised his hand. "That was me."

"No. Yes. Six-two. I really am a doctor. Yes. No. I won't hurt your sister."

When he finished, her siblings applauded with Edmund's claps far less enthusiastic than Peter's or Susan's.

Thomas bowed again. "Thank you."

"How did you do that?" Susan asked.

"Got a decent memory. Majored in math. Like the details. That's why I like ER." Thomas placed his arm around Lucy's shoulders. "Any other questions you want to ask."

"Not for you. Hey, Lu." Peter leaned his face close to the screen. "You gonna let him help you?"

Turning his gaze at Thomas, Peter added, "She never lets anyone help her. With anything. Nothing."

"Changed her own diapers because she didn't like the way anyone else did it." Susan nodded. "And there was the time she taught herself to read because she didn't want anyone else to teach it to her."

"And she grew her own vegetables because the grocery store didn't lay them out in a particular order." Edmund piped in.

"Ha, ha, ha." Lucy stuck her lip out. "I'm not that obstinate."

For a moment, her siblings looked wide-eyed then all broke into laughter. Thomas chuckled as well.

As much as she loved her siblings, she had enough of their good humor for today.

"Okay, well, we've got to go." Lucy stepped forward and picked up her computer. When she moved back, Thomas slid his hand down to rest on the top of her butt. Her body tingled with anticipation.

"Wait, wait, Luce. Which one of us did you want to come out and give this guy the third degree?"

"None of you. Bye."

"Wait! Wait!" Peter called out. "On three."

The siblings bounced their fists in the air and counted to three.

Edmund threw his hands up in victory. "Rock wins every time."

Lucy smirked, her heart missing them even more. "I love you all."

"We love you, Lucy! We miss you!"

"See you next month, Lucy, when I come out and give this guy the third degree." Edmund held up his fists.

"Ha. Ha." She closed the computer, placed it back on the table and plugged it in, then set the flowers in the sink. "Oh, my gosh. I'd forgotten I had that on."

"That thing is off, right?" Thomas raised an eyebrow.

"Yes, it's off."

"And we're good? You believe me when I say nothing intimate has ever happened between me and Jade."

No stuttering of words. No breathing changes. He's not trying to shield his mouth or any other part of his body. Easy, causal speech. "Yes, I believe you."

"Good." He pulled her into his arms.

"Your lip."

"Is fine." He kissed her without apologizes, probing her mouth with his tongue, then nibbling her lips. "The sutures came out a few hours ago."

Lucy grabbed handfuls of his shirt to keep herself standing. His kisses knocked the wind out of her. She pulled back, breathless. "Is this your way to convince me to go hiking with you?"

"I don't know. Is it working?"

"Maybe, I haven't decided yet."

"Must be off my game." Thomas brushed her lips with his, then kissed her cheek and made his way to her ear. "Lucy."

Lucy's heart raced in anticipation of what he would do. "Yes, Thomas?"

"Would you go hiking," he whispered before gently sucking the sensitive skin under her lobe, "with me."

Having him to herself with no computers or work. She wouldn't have to think about Dr. McMasters's charts or quality assurance or the number of other things that had filled her mind up over the last several weeks. "Yes, I would be happy to go, um, hiking with you."

"How much time..." His words tingled across her skin as he kissed across her neck to the other side. "Do you need to get ready?"

She calculated the minimal amount of time she could get ready. "Give me fifteen minutes."

Nuzzling her neck, he pulled away, then kissed her hand as he headed to the door. "I'll wait for your downstairs."

When the door clicked closed, Lucy fell back on the bed and sighed, her body on fire from Thomas's attention. "So glad I just shaved my legs."

Chapter Fifteen

"OH, MY GOODNESS. It's beautiful." Lucy gasped when they walked around a large boulder and had a perfect view of Miracle Lake. "It's almost too pretty to be real. The different blues, the water, the sky. This is amazing."

Thomas thought the same thing of her as he panted, winded from the steep trail they'd walked up to get here.

Describing Lucy Davidson as a force would be an understatement. She'd proven herself to have staying power at work, but for the past two hours she'd smoked him hiking all over the trails park ranger Todd Harris had suggested.

After that bit of knowledge, he wondered how her endurance would be for other things. She might kill him.

But it would be worth it.

The cold air simultaneously burned his lungs and revived him. Two years ago, before he'd been stabbed by Jade's late husband, he could run a mile in seven minutes and scale a sand dune without breaking a sweat.

Now, his body had to work twice as hard to get the same amount done. He blamed it on the smog and toxins and constant illness exposures in the big city ER where he'd been assigned. When Jade asked him to come here, he thought the clean mountain air and a smaller unit would give him new life. Get him back to his once great shape. He could exercise in pure oxygen and get off his inhalers for good.

Every time he took them, he felt like that twelve-year-old adolescent boy who was going to get his ass kicked at school. Patting his pocket, he felt the outline of the rescue medication should he need it, but he would need to be damn near lung collapse before he'd take that in front of Lucy.

Thankfully, today's walk had been the best workout he had in a long time.

As much as the fresh air slowly repaired him, he couldn't help but wonder if the company had been the best medicine of all. He hadn't felt this good in weeks. Months.

Years.

Looking at Lucy's excited face as she watched the lake breathed hope into him, making him desire... what? Stability.

A home.

With her.

Don't jump the gun. It's a hike. A picnic. Nothing more.

A chattering caught his attention. She pulled her ski cap farther down her head, covering her ears. "It's beautiful, but the sun's going down and it's starting to get colder."

Wrapping his arms around her, he pulled her close. The ginger and lemon scent of her hair floated in the clean air and he greedily inhaled. "Better?"

"Yes." She snuggled into him.

Standing here with her in the quiet of the afternoon only enhanced a calm he'd been searching for since he'd arrived in

Marietta.

For years, he'd wandered, worked, and did nothing else. The unchallenged restlessness he'd felt in his gut for so long calmed when she stood near. Whether they were crazy at work or simply having hot chocolate, Thomas couldn't shake the idea that Lucy held the key to his peace of mind, body, and soul.

Could it be that easy?

The deep blue of the lake contrasted with the fading blue sky in perfect balance. The light winds moved across the water, sending endless ripples.

"Wouldn't it be cool if there was a lake monster?" Lucy giggled as she tucked her chin into the jacket collar. She reminded him of a turtle, poking her head out of her shell.

Her joke broke his introspection. "You mean like Nessie?"

"Sure. Why not? Doesn't this place look like it could use a lake monster? It's isolated and cold. I'd guess the locals would protect it."

"It's possible." The cold whipped by them. He glanced at his watch. The sun would start to set in the next hour. "Maybe we should make some shirts. Start a rumor."

"What do you think they'd call it?" She shivered. "It's Miracle Lake so would we call her Messie?"

"Messie?

"You know like Ogopogo in Okanagan Lake or Chessie in Lake Champlain."

"Or Nessie in Loch Ness."

"Yes. Yes, exactly."

He liked her sense of humor. "What about Miracle Lake Monster?"

She turned in his arms, facing him, a look of amused frustration on her face. "You're no fun. Where's your imagination?"

"Fine. I see that mountain over there. I'm glad there's not an evil eye over a boiling lake of lava."

"You really are wonderfully nerdish."

Let me pull out my inhaler and you can see how nerdish I really am. He said a silent thank-you that she understood his Tolkien reference. "I'm glad you got that. I'd hate to think my imagination fell flat."

"I'd bet your imagination would fall anything but flat."

"I'm not good about coming up with good names for lake monsters." Having her in his arms, his brain went straight to the gutter. "But I could come up with other suggestions of things. That could happen. In the mountains."

"Really." Her voice went low, sultry as she played with the drawstrings on his coat. "Anything you care to share?"

Good. Her mind is in the gutter, too. "I can think of a couple of things."

"Really? Just a couple?" She stood on tiptoe and kissed him.

Her touch made his cock sit straight up. "Wait. Wait, a few more just came to mind."

Brushing her lips against his, she smiled. "Glad to help stir your imagination about the outdoors."

What was it about her that had him thinking like a

horny teenager, which basically meant he wasn't doing any *thinking*. "Not thinking of the outdoors. Thinking of cherry pie."

Her eyebrows furrowed. "Why cherry pie?"

His hands rested on the small of her back. "I'm thinking about those few things."

"Yes?"

"Then adding cherry pie to them."

For a second, she stared at him with confusion.

"With whipped cream." He licked his lips.

Her eyes went wide with understanding. "Oh, I see."

"Because you can't have dessert without whipped cream."

"Yes, whipped cream does make *dessert* quite delicious." Her eyes darted quickly from his face to his crotch and back. "Although, there is something to be said about tasting things without condiments. Bring out its natural goodness."

Dirty girl. "Glad you think so."

"How's your lip?"

"Better."

She ran her thumb across his chin. "It looks good."

"Wanna test it?" he whispered, hoping she'd say yes.

"You sure? You're not in any more pain?"

I want you so bad, I wouldn't care if I were. "Nope."

A hard gust of wind slammed into them, sending them stumbling sideways.

Her teeth chattered again. "Can we test it in the car?"

"Good idea. I think I left the picnic basket in the car."

"Ready to go?" Reluctantly, he stepped away, but his rib pinched him, sending him into a coughing fit. Sharp pains shot through his chest, temporarily knocking the wind out of him. He struggled to catch his breath in the thinner air.

"You okay?" She called from the bottom of the hill and began back up again, but he held his hand up.

"I'm okay." He wheezed as he made his way toward her. "Air's dry. Something caught in my throat."

Lucy met him halfway. "You sure you're okay."

"What are you, part mountain goat?" He meant to say it jokingly, but when she looked at him curiously, he realized his words came out harder than he intended.

Dammit. Trying to impress her and I end up with chest pain. Great job, idiot.

"Come on, Frodo." Interlacing her fingers in his, she took his hand in hers and walked with him back to the truck.

By the time they were in the car, both of them appreciated being out of the chill of the falling temperatures.

"Picnic basket." He panted as he tried to take long, deep breaths. "Hand warmers."

"You okay?" She removed enough for both of them.

"Fine." The tightness in his chest didn't give. He coughed again and cursed when his muscles wouldn't cooperate. *I'm not taking that damned inhaler in front of her.*

"Thomas, you look like you're having trouble breathing. Anything I can do?"

"No. No." He wheezed as his heart rate increased. The panic sat on his chest like a boulder.

She grabbed his hand and held it to her heart. "Breathe, Thomas. It's okay. Focus on my voice."

"Lucy." He coughed. "I'm. Sorry."

"Nothing to be sorry about. Breathe."

As the seconds passed, the tight muscles around his chest began to loosen, but not enough to keep his concern at bay. Dread of taking that inhaler constricted his airways, making it difficult to fully exhale.

"Thomas, please take your medication." She gripped his hand, her kind words caressed his ears. "It's fine."

"Dammit." Turning his back to her, he pulled out the inhaler. After the second puff, his chest muscles relaxed and he could completely exhale. With his breathing intact, he could now better deal with the matter at hand.

His complete embarrassment. When he turned, she held up two hand warmers and popped them, laying them in his hands.

"Goodness, it got cold, fast." She shivered as he turned on the truck, blasting the heater. "Fifty-five in the mountains is certainly different than fifty-five on the beach."

He appreciated her not asking any questions. "You need to get back right now?"

She glanced at her watch. "No, but I start at seven in the morning."

"I have to be there at ten. I won't keep you out much longer. Just wanted to show you something."

The corner of her mouth curled up as she opened her purse. "What exactly were you planning on showing me?"

That got his cock to stand at attention. "It's a surprise."

"A surprise? I'm all ears." She opened a small tin and popped back a mint.

They drove a short distance and came to a secluded spot

and parked. Reluctantly, Thomas turned off the truck after finally warming up from the heater blasting full force.

"Todd said this is a good place to come see the moon come over the water."

"Who's Todd?" She unbuckled her seatbelt.

"He's one of the park rangers. Works out at Carter's."

"I don't think I've met him yet."

The only sounds around them were from the car winding down.

She shuddered and held the hand warmers close. "Oh, wow. That heat is amazing."

"I've got a blanket in the backseat." He reached for it, but she rested her hand on his arm. "What?"

"Or we could curl up in the backseat with the blanket."

She didn't have to ask twice. Without opening his door, he crawled into the bench seat.

"Well, that's one way to stay out of the cold." She waited for him to spread out the blanket over his lap and folded it back for her.

She joined him, bringing the picnic basket with her before snuggling up next to him. "This is nice."

"There's a couple of sandwiches in there. Some water."

Lucy opened the basket and they each helped themselves to food from Java Cafe.

For the next few moments, they watched the moon slowly rise over the water of Miracle Lake as they ate their dinners. The gentle ripples reflected off the image of the night sky.

With it still being chilly, Thomas didn't worry about encountering any large game, especially since they were in the truck, but sitting next to Lucy had his libido simmering like a caged animal.

The ginger and lemon scent of her hair tickled his nose when she removed her ski cap.

"That was delicious." She handed him a mint.

"You trying to tell me something?"

She turned towards him. "Just getting ready."

"For?"

"Didn't you want me to test something?"

It took him a second to remember what he'd asked, but as soon as he did, his body was like a match thrown into parched forest.

"What? Yes. Yes, I did." He popped back the mint and chewed frantically.

She nuzzled his nose and leaned in to kiss him. "Please tell me if I hurt you."

"I don't care if you do. Just get those lips on me."

"Yes, sir." Pressing her mouth to his immediately made his jeans a size too small and he ached to pop the snap to give himself some relief.

Her tentative kiss only drove him increasingly mad with desire as she touched him, but still felt like she weren't close enough. As if he'd never have his fill of her.

He ran his hand up her leg and rested it on her hip.

Her cheeks flushed she straddled his lap. "Hope this isn't too bold."

"I like a woman who knows what she wants."

"You know, I'm vertically challenged. This is easier for

me to get to you."

"I'm all yours."

She unzipped his coat, but as he tried to wrangle out from it, he couldn't get good leverage and ended up awkwardly shifting her off his lap.

She giggled.

"Sorry. Sorry." With the coat finally off, he tossed it in the front seat.

As the moon continued its slow climb into the night sky, Thomas became increasingly more fascinated by Marietta or, more specifically, the woman on his lap.

Shedding her coat, she let it fall to the floor, then ran her hands up his arms and rested them on his shoulders. The smell of peppermint on her breath. When she slid her tongue between his lips and swept it across the roof of his mouth, the burn of mint lingered, making his lips tingle.

"You okay?" Her lusty voice tickled his ears.

He managed a moan as she traced along his jaw and kissed the pulse point at the base of his neck. "You've got a talented tongue, Lucy Davidson."

"First time I've heard that one." She giggled and ran her thumb along his lower lip. "Looks pretty good."

"You do good work."

She raised an eyebrow. "I bet you do too, Dr. McAvoy."

"Kiss me again, Lucy Davidson, and I'll show you how good my work can be."

Chapter Sixteen

I'M DYING. EVEN though his body protested from the hike and his lungs still hurt from the thin air, he'd been riding high from his date with Lucy not six hours ago. He hoped the momentum of their affections would be enough to get him through the next four hours and he wouldn't be beat-up exhausted from pushing himself so hard.

Her affection and the rescue inhaler he had to sneak back to take in the doctor call room would get him to seven in the morning.

How much longer can I do this?

Taking his thumb, he retraced where she'd kissed him until his lips were swollen and sore.

Damn, the woman was going to kill him with her passion for life. If they took that step, she might kill him in the most beautiful way possible.

Nothing like la petite mort.

He smirked. *Guess I do know a few more French words.*

Regardless, he dreaded how beat-up he'd feel after going to bed, but if working out in the mountains meant he got to *hike* more with Lucy, he was all for more physical therapy.

Cheerfully, he whistled as he exited the doctor's call

room, feeling the best he'd felt in months.

Lucy made the weight of his world lift and float away.

She'd given him something to care about again, something to hope for. Something to believe in.

"I cannot believe you."

What?

Jade came around the corner, her hair pulled back in a loose, messy ponytail. Her makeup faded and splotchy. "I need to talk to you right now."

Seeing his friend frazzled and frustrated worked as the perfect buzzkill. "It's three in the morning, Jade. What are you doing here?"

"Were you whistling?" She glared at him then raised an eyebrow. "Like-I-just-got-laid whistling?"

He stifled a laugh. "What do you want, Jade?"

"I need to talk to you."

"Okay." *This should be fun.*

She walked next to him, her pace quick to keep up with his long strides. "You talked to Dr. Snootypants about me."

"I did. Thanks for throwing me under the bus, Jade. Telling her your husband had a good reason to be jealous."

Her rapid footsteps stopped. "She talked to you about that?"

Thomas turned a one-eighty and glared. "Yes, Jade. She did. I had to explain the entire situation to her. Thank God she believed me."

Thank God her siblings believed him or that hike might not have happened.

That wonderful, sexy, exhilarating hike.

Jade scoffed, "Why do you care what she thinks? It's not like… whistling?"

"Yeah, whistling."

"If she's so important to impress, why didn't you just tell her everything?"

"Because I had this crazy idea that I wanted to respect your privacy. Not everyone knows your entire situation, but they know I'm your friend. I came here to help after you helped me." He opened and closed his fists as he shifted his weight. "I wanted to let you tell her on your own terms what happened, but you're too damned busy being pissed at her because she's doing her job."

"I don't care what you tell her about my history. I couldn't give a crap what she thinks of me." She bit her lip as if she couldn't quite believe he'd bitten back or that she'd snapped at him. "I'm sorry, Thomas. She flustered me with something. I guess it just fell out."

"Hell of a way to be a friend, Jade." Turning his back to her, he continued until he reached the central ER desk and scanned the patient board and charts. "Three patients. Nice."

Luckily, the evening ER traffic stopped pouring in about two hours ago. Most had been treated and discharged with minor ailments like ear infections, allergic reactions, and easily repairable lacerations. Now, they were down to a chest pain, a sex injury, and the same croupy kid from a couple of days ago.

For an early Saturday morning, the unit had been unusually slow. Thomas didn't dare say that out loud, though. One thing he never did while working in the ER was utter the words "it's slow, dead, or we're not busy". If done, for certain, all hell would break loose within an hour.

"But I still need to talk to you," Jade mumbled. "Privately."

Sitting behind the desk, Nurse Dave Fletcher yawned as he read a...

"Dave, are you reading, what? A romance?" Thomas chuckled.

Without taking his eyes off the page, Dave nodded. "Sort of. It's *The Body Movers*."

"You sure that's a good book to read in the ER? May not instill confidence in our clientele."

"It's a romantic comedy."

Walking around the desk, Thomas held his hand out and Dave put the book in his palm. "I didn't know you like rom-coms, Dave. Seems you'd be more of a thriller or blood and gore kind of guy."

"I get enough blood and gore here. I want something that makes me laugh. Something that's not constantly serious."

"That's one pink cover," Jade commented. "*The Body Movers* by Stephanie Bond. Any good?"

"Pretty good. The romance part's decent. Closest thing to reading a woman's mind as there is, Dr. McAvoy. A romance novel."

Giving Jade a sideways glance, Thomas asked, "Does it work?"

"I haven't had any complaints."

Medical assistant Sue Westbrook, Nurse Shelly Westbrook's aunt, chuckled. "Sure, Dave. Sure."

"Just doing my homework so I'm always ready for a test." Dave shrugged. "Anything wrong with being prepared?"

"Not a thing, Mr. Boy Scout."

"Where's everyone else?" Thomas handed the book back.

"Lillian's outside getting a smoke. Teresa's in room one checking on the croupy kid. Allen is in the break room getting lunch."

"I hope we can get this kid well. Sucks to be sick." *A four-year-old shouldn't keep having stridor after epi treatments.* He hoped this last one Respiratory Therapist Teresa Mason gave him would help him clear.

"Basically in a holding pattern right now, Dr. McAvoy." Sue took a long drink from her Black Widow mug. "We'll text you if we need you."

One of the things Thomas loved about working in the ER had to be the people. Not the patients as much as the staff. It took a special personality to be ready for anything that walked through the door. The unpredictability of a shift and what patients would be seen presented its own chaos.

Strong and capable doctors, nurses, medical assistants, paramedics, respiratory therapists and anyone else on the team could be as chaotically unpredictable.

A rapid foot tapping only emphasized his point.

"I. Need. To talk. To you," Jade mumbled through clenched teeth.

"Fine." He pointed to an observation room. When they went in, closed the door, he leaned against the window where he could see any new patients being roomed. "You okay?"

"No, I'm absolutely not okay." She paced. "I'm losing my mind."

You just now figuring that out? "Why?"

"Junior isn't talking to me."

"Sorry to hear that." *Not that I should be worried about that. The sooner he gets out of your life, the better.*

"No, you're not."

"You're right. I'm not." He ran his tongue across his well-repaired lip, thinking of how his lips and tongue made Lucy cry out his name but a few hours ago.

"He's mad at me because I told him I planned to sell the place."

That pulled Thomas's attention away from his erotic memories. "You're going to sell? When?"

"Isn't that what I said?" Burying her face in her hands, she leaned against the wall. "I've lost so much money. I can't believe how much I've lost."

This would be a perfect time to tell her 'I told you so', but what would that accomplish? "Why the change of heart?"

"I have you to thank for that."

"Me?" Movement caught his attention, but it was Teresa coming out of the croupy kid's room. "Why me?"

"After him punching you and joking about it, I tried to excuse him. Then he made the comment about him getting to run his business without any permits or zoning changes as long as I owned the land, I knew this would never get better." Fat tears ran down her ruddy cheeks. "And I know you don't like him. You have every right to hate him, really, but he's always talked to me. Even when I didn't see him for long periods of time, we always spoke. Always helped each other. We have some great memories of sitting outside, laughing. Joking. Getting one another through tough times."

Her voice dripped in sadness. Thomas hated he couldn't fix this for her, help her more than simply listening. "I'm sorry, Jade."

She tapped her front teeth, tears ran down her face. "And I think he's into something bad. Really bad."

"Like what?"

"I don't know. It's only a feeling."

Her confession made his jaw clench so tight, it hurt. "Jade, you can't keep the place because of your brother. The memories there. Get out of there."

"I am and I will." Her shoulders slumped as she sat on the end of the bed. "I feel like I'm letting him down. My dad down. Generations of my family down."

His heart hurt for her, but Jade's insistence for doing right by her irresponsible family had been one of her short-comings. More than once, he'd tried to talk some sense into her, but she'd refused to listen. It had almost cost her and him their lives. "If your dad cared about that land and the house, he would have made sure it stayed in the family. He would have done something other than sit and let things rot around him, but from what you said, he gave up a long time ago."

"I know. He did when he could, but after he lost his job

and the cancer came into play… life went downhill for him." She stomped her foot. "What's wrong with me? I can't quit upsetting people. My brother. Dr. Snootypants."

"Me."

"You." She grabbed a box of Kleenex and used several to dry her face and blow her nose.

When she settled back in, Thomas asked, "Why were you even talking to her in the first place?"

Jade's forehead puckered. "She didn't say anything to you?"

"Other than your comment about your ex being jealous. No. Why?"

"She… didn't… say anything?"

Worry slammed into Thomas's brain, making his eye twitch. "Don't do this to me, Jade. I've kept my promise and come here to help, but you can't screw me over on this."

"You like her, don't you?"

"Yeah, I do."

"Does that mean you might stay in Marietta?"

Hearing someone else ask him what he wondered about himself hit him hard. "No, I don't plan to stay."

When the words were out of his mouth, he immediately regretted them.

What the hell?

Jade shook her head as though she were confused. "Does that mean she's leaving? With you?"

"We've had one date." *One incredible date.*

"Must have been a good date because you're whistling." She sniffled.

He didn't want to talk about this now, especially not with her. Instead, he took a rule out of Jade's *How to be Avoidant Playbook.* "Why did you ask if Lucy had talked to me?"

"No, no. It's fine. Honestly. It's going to be okay." She waved him off and grabbed another Kleenex. "Sorry to bother you. I just couldn't sleep."

The angst in her voice didn't offer him any comfort. "Why? What's wrong?"

"That house is an icebox. Can I sleep in the doctor's lounge?"

"You know I can't let you do that." He propped the head of the bed up and locked a bedrail in place. He motioned for her to lie down. "We'll block this room off for you. There. Sleep in here for awhile."

Her eyes welled with tears. "You're a nice guy, you know that?"

"Don't tell anyone. It'll ruin my street cred."

"You don't have any street cred." Jade quickly snuggled in as he found a pillow and pulled two blankets out of the warmer. As he threw it over her, she sighed. "Thomas, I'm exhausted."

"Sleeping in a freezer would be draining."

With fat tears rolling down her face, she sniffled. "I'm flat-out tired of fighting the men in my life. My dad. My brother. My husband." Her breath hitched. "My dead husband."

Damn. Her words made him flinch. "You didn't have a choice, Jade. He was going to kill you. Both of us."

She played with the hem of her shirt. "I could have chosen not to marry him. I could have left him the first time he hit me. I could have gotten him to believe there had never been anything between us."

"He wasn't going to believe anything you said."

"But if I had tried harder."

"Don't do that to yourself." Leaning against the doorframe, Thomas noticed how the sadness had drained all the hope from her eyes. "Jade, you can't change what happened, but it was a damned brave thing you did."

"I killed someone, Thomas. There's nothing brave about that."

"There is when you have everything to lose." He pulled up a chair next to the bed.

"Look, I don't think I can offer any true words of encouragement. I know you're a strong woman and you deserve a hell of a lot more than what you've had so far in life, but unless you believe it, nothing's going to change."

For a long moment, she said nothing. Tears stained her clothes.

"What you need right now is sleep. Things will make more sense afterwards." Standing, he patted her on the shoulder and turned out the light. "Take a nap in here. I'll come wake you at seven."

Before he shut the door, she asked, "Have I ruined everything?"

"What do you mean?"

"I mean, have I ruined everything in my life?"

"Jade, I haven't seen anything you've done you can't recover from." At least what he knew about.

"I hope so."

"Get some sleep, Jade." He stepped back, but she called out to him again.

"Thomas?"

"Yes?"

"I'm glad she makes you whistle. You've needed to whistle for a long time."

Without a word, he nodded and left the room because as much as Thomas *loved* to whistle, the fact he *loved* it scared him more than he cared to admit.

Chapter Seventeen

THE STEAM HAD barely drifted off his body when he heard a knock at the door. His muscles unknotted from the hot shower, his lungs relaxed, his breathing easy, especially after taking his medications this morning.

Hunger pains growled, but the thought of walking ten feet to get anything for breakfast seemed like a mile.

No, Thomas needed to collapse in bed and sleep a solid eight hours, except it would be delayed because of whoever interrupted those plans.

"No housekeeping," he grumbled as he grabbed his sweatpants. In his exhaustion to get to his room, he'd probably forgotten to put the do not disturb tag on the door.

Another soft knock as he slid his pants over his hips. "Okay, okay. No house—"

"Good morning." Lucy smiled and held up a bag and two to-go coffees in a drink holder. "Main Street Diner delivery."

His fatigued receded, seeing her smile. "Good morning. What's this?"

"You've worked a lot of shifts this week. Thought I'd bring you some breakfast."

She shifted her weight, her eyes wide as she continued to stand in the hall. She wore a workout tank top and running pants with a sweatshirt tied around her waist. "May I come in?"

It took a second for him to realize he'd yet to move out of the way. "Right. Yes, please come in."

When she walked by him, the subtle ginger and lemon scent she used floated by him. He inhaled, soaking in every bit of her. Despite his exhaustion, he suddenly revived enough to want to pull her into his arms and kiss her until she sighed his name.

She lowered the bag and drink carrier to the table and set up their meals, the action only emphasizing the beautiful lines of muscle in her shoulders and arms.

"I guessed at what kind of tacos you'd like, but figured you'd be more than hungry after working all night."

His heart skipped. It had been a long time since someone had done something this nice for him. "This is great. Thank you."

When she turned to face him, her head cocked. "I can go if you want."

"Why would I want you to leave?"

"You're still holding the door open. Didn't know if that was one of those nonverbal requests."

Glancing behind him, he realized he hadn't moved from the doorway. He quickly moved aside, allowing the door to close. "Sorry. Tired."

Two breakfast tacos for each of them along with a loaf of the orange cinnamon bread and large coffees sat on the table.

As soon as Lucy's hands were empty, Thomas pulled her in his arms and kissed her. He'd only meant for it to be a quick, thank-you-for-thinking-of-me kiss but, tasting her lips, Thomas wished he'd worn jeans.

She sighed against him and threaded her fingers through his hair, pulling him flush to her. "Glad your lip is better."

"Thanks for that, Doc." He nuzzled her neck, kissing that special spot at her pulse point. "Good to have two working lips."

"They work... um... really well. Feels so good."

Holding her in his arms felt like the most natural thing in the world. Even when her hands ran across his scars, he didn't flinch at their memories. In fact, there was nothing on his mind except getting to know Lucy Davidson a whole lot more and for a very long time.

She tilted her head back. "Aren't you tired?"

"Exhausted."

"Hungry?"

Pushing a lock of hair out of her face, he whispered, "Not for food."

"Oh my, Dr. McAvoy. What should we do about that?"

"I can think of a few things." His hands gently tugged at the sweatshirt she'd tied around her waist. It fell to the floor.

"I'd do something similar for you, but all you're wearing is pants." A nervous giggle escaped her as her fingers gently brushed his back.

"I can put on more clothes if you want."

"Please don't." A sly smirk spread across her face. "But I could meet you halfway."

"Sounds interesting. Tell me more."

Lucy pulled off her shirt, revealing a colorful running bra that perfectly highlighted the curve of her breasts. "Something like this?"

"I like it." His fingers brushed over the swell of her breasts before he noticed something peculiar. "A zipper?"

She nodded. "Someone was thinking because sports bras are ridiculous to get on without clasps and if they're in the back, it's a nightmare. This is so easy to get on...and off."

"Thank you, bra designer person."

"Agreed." Inch by inch, she moved the zipper lower, until she unlocked the base of it and the bra fell loosely on her body.

His mouth watered with anticipation of tasting her sweet flesh.

"Take it off me," her whisper insisted.

Without a word, his hands ran up the curve of her waist and under the bra, pushing it away and off her arms. He cupped her perfect breasts, his thumb teasing her nipples as he kissed the pulse point of her neck and along her collarbone.

She moaned, her hands on his waist, her fingers under the waistband of his pants.

He smiled against her skin. "You like that?"

"Yes."

Sinking to his knees, he kissed her belly button, up her chest, before brushing his lips over her peaked nipples.

"Thomas." She panted, urging him on.

"You like that? What about this?" He brushed across the

sides of her breasts before cupping them and running his thumb over her mounds again, kissing between them.

Her head fell backwards. "Please, don't stop."

"Yes, Dr. Badass." He cupped her butt and pulled her flush to him, taking her breast in his mouth.

He should be bone tired, barely able to stand, but something about Lucy had him wide awake as though he'd chugged a gallon of coffee.

She moved away from him, backing up to the bed and sitting down. "Thought we'd be a little more comfortable here."

On his knees, he followed her, but only pulled her into his arms. He relished feeling her naked skin next to his. "How far do you want this to go, Lucy?"

He worried he's screwed up the momentum when she didn't answer right away.

"I didn't bring anything. I thought you'd be tired and I didn't want to be assumptive."

That wasn't the word he expected her to say. "Why assumptive?"

"I know you don't plan to stay in Marietta. I didn't want you to think you had to if things went too far between us."

Her honest answer surprised him, but then again, it was Lucy. She'd been nothing but honest.

Thomas took her hand and kissed it. "Maybe I should rethink my plans, then."

"I'd like that, but you don't have to say that because I'm topless."

He sat back. "So am I."

She cupped his face. "I'm serious, Thomas. Please don't tell me what you think I want to hear. I'm a big girl. I can take it if we're only out to feel good."

The flicker of hope in Lucy's eyes only matched his. He should be asking her to leave, run away from what she wanted, but for the first time, he realized he wanted it too.

He couldn't resist it anymore.

He wanted a home. A life. With her.

"Lucy, I'm not gonna lie. I like you topless. I am out to feel good, but I am thinking of staying longer." *Although I don't think I can work in the ER after this assignment.*

Her smile lit up the room and warmed his soul. "Really. How much longer?"

"How long are *you* going to be here?"

Tears welled in her eyes. "A while."

"A while it is."

"You promise?"

"I promise."

"I still don't have condoms. You?" Her fingers ran up and down his spine, making him shudder. His craving of her exponentially increasing.

"Nope, but I promise to have some next time."

She sniffed. "You always keep your promises?"

"Always. I can still make you feel good."

"How's that?"

"I still haven't eaten breakfast." He lowered her down on the bed then worked his way down her body, feasting on her breasts again.

She writhed under him, her hands in his hair as his

tongue and fingers mimicked each other over her nipples.

His other hand slid down, cupping her over her pants. His finger tracing the seam between her legs.

"You're killing me, Thomas." Lucy gasped, her hips began to rock. "Please. More."

Thomas smiled against her skin. "Like I said, I like a woman who knows what she wants."

His tongue traced down her stomach to her belly button, his hands on her hips.

She lifted and slid her pants down, but he kept her panties in place.

A slow smirk spread across her face. "You don't want to—"

"I want to. I plan to. You have no idea how many times I've wanted to eat you, but I want to take it off you."

"I like a man who knows what he wants."

"I want you, Lucy Davidson." The honest words cut him to the core. Never had he wanted anyone more and it unnerved him more than he wanted to admit, even to himself. "I want you."

"Show me." She panted. "Show me how much you want me."

"With pleasure." Inch by torturous inch, he pulled her panties south.

"Yes," she whispered. "Yes."

As soon as he had them off her hips and pushed her pants and panties down past her knees, she toed them off, kicking them across the room.

He kissed her inner thigh as he worked his way back up.

His hand moved over the slope of her belly then brushed over her nipples, making her back arch into it as he licked her silky folds.

Sliding his fingers along the seam, he tenderly opened her engorged lips and ran his thumb over her clit.

Lucy gasped as he slid his finger inside her and kissed her intimately. His tongue swirled and taunted her as it glided over her sensitive nub.

"Thomas. Oh, yes." Her knees fell wide as her hips rocked. She rested her arms over her head. "Please, don't stop."

He added another finger and slowly moved them in and out, without lessening his worship of her. She smelled of sunshine and lemons. Her skin soft and delicious.

Her cries of delight only urged him on as he could feel her tighten around his fingers. This was what he'd dreamed of, wanted when he thought of her. To make her call his name, writhe under his touch.

As she urged him on, his hips rocked. The soft fabric of his sweatpants moved against his cock. Thomas said a silent thank you he hadn't put on jeans because his tenders would be strangled about now.

His tongue darted out to tickle her lips, to taste her more before moving up her body to kiss her breasts again.

"Thomas." She gasped as he took a nipple in his mouth.

His thumb circled her clit. The rhythmic movement of his fingers never lost tempo as he licked her nipple and he wiggled his thumb. She tightened around his fingers. "That's it, Lucy. Let me make you feel good."

"Yes, yes." Within seconds, Lucy arched her back, the pulsation of her climax around him as he pushed deep inside her.

She rode his hand as his tongue danced on her nipple, her hands in his hair.

Her exuberant reaction to his touch almost pushed him over the edge, but he relished seeing her satisfied smile.

"Feel good?" Thomas asked, already knowing the answer.

"Very." She sighed and looked up at him as he stood.

Seeing her naked in his bed had to be a dream come true, especially with the healthy blush of red in her cheeks. "You're beautiful."

"Am I?" Her brow immediately furrowed. "You know what else I am?"

"What?"

"Hungry." Without pause, she sat up and moved to the edge of the bed. Grabbing his pants, Lucy yanked them down.

Chapter Eighteen

LUCY HADN'T PLANNED for the morning delight. Honestly, she only wanted to share some breakfast with Thomas and be on her way. She assumed he had to be exhausted from not only their hike, but working all night. This morning, she'd woken up to second day post-workout sore muscles, which she expected after yesterday's walk in the mountains, but she had two perfectly working lungs.

Thomas had the endurance of the Energizer Bunny for certain, but even that bunny eventually ran out of steam.

Give him his food and go.

Give him his food and go.

That had been her plan, but when he answered the door wearing nothing, but sweatpants, her lust took over her brain.

Now, here they were an hour later before they sat down to eat actual food.

Both had stuffed their faces with Gabby's tacos and orange bread before they came up for air. As Lucy watched Thomas finish another piece of bread, she couldn't help but notice the scars on his body.

"Can I ask you something?" She pulled her legs up to her

chest as she curled up in the chair across from him.

"Yep." Thomas finished off the second breakfast taco and sat back. A look of bliss on his face.

"How much damage did the knife do to your lungs?"

He froze. "What?"

"I know you have lung damage. You'd have to. I see where those entry wounds were. You ended up with chest tubes from those injuries and now probably have some scar tissue." Leaning forward, she held out her hand. "How bad was it?"

He took a deep inhale before exhaling a long breath. "You know, when I was a kid, I had asthma. Pretty bad case of it. Got teased a lot for needing inhalers. Dad didn't help much with that either. Said if I would exercise more, think harder, better, it was all a state of mind and that if I wanted it bad enough, I could be off those inhalers."

"What an awful thing to say to a child. That's like insisting that megadoses of Vitamin C will keep you from getting vaccine preventable illnesses." Wadding up the napkin in her hand, Lucy threw it out of frustration. "How archaic."

Thomas agreed. "Taking my father's advice, I decided I didn't need them anymore. I exercised hard. Believed I could beat asthma. I quit taking them right before my twelfth birthday."

"You quit. Just like that?"

"Yep." Leaning back in his chair, he draped his arms over the armrests.

Disappointment settled in her chest at him not taking her offered hand. "You went cold turkey? How'd that turn out?"

"Horrible. Ended up in the ER then in the ICU for a couple of days before being admitted to the floor."

"Your parents must have been worried sick."

He shrugged. "My mother punched my dad in the ER when she found out what I'd done."

"Nice. Good coping skills there."

"That was pretty much their relationship. Fight. Make up. Fight. Make up."

A nugget of sadness pinged her heart. Sadly, his story wasn't unusual, but it hurt more because he'd experienced it. "Sounds chaotic."

"It was, but there were two people who made the biggest impact on me that day. The ER doctor and the asthma nurse."

"Glad you had someone watching out for you. Asthma can be really scary."

"That doctor saved my life. That nurse gave my life back to me." Thomas yawned and stretched.

"How so?" His response made her look at her watch. "Maybe you should go to bed. It's past nine. You've been up since yesterday."

"Maybe, but this nurse. She showed me and my parents how to manage my asthma really well. Gave me a plan."

As he spoke, Lucy pulled the covers back. "I guess that worked out well."

He paused. "Got off inhalers by the time I got to high school and through puberty. I've never had to take them again, until a couple of years ago."

"How much damage did the attack cause?"

"He stabbed me a few times. Lost part of my upper left lobe, but some of the lung is still there."

Lucy couldn't help but grimace. "How long did they say recovery would be?"

Thomas played with the seam on the armrest. "It's been long enough for me to know if I'll get one-hundred percent back if that's what you're asking. I haven't."

"How much have you gotten back?"

"More than most. Less than some."

"That's a nice evasive answer. Obviously, not enough to make you happy."

"No. Marietta has been good for me, though. I do feel better, not one-hundred percent better. It sucks."

Lucy held her hands out and pulled him to his feet. "Why does it suck?"

"Hate being dependent on anything."

Holding his arms out, he motioned for her to come to him. She snuggled into his bare chest. "Inhalers are no different than insulin or heart medication. They help us live better quality lives with what we have."

"They make me look weak." He yawned again and Lucy pulled away, guiding him to the bed. "After how intensely you hiked yesterday, worked last night, and faired this morning, I'd say you're anything but weak, Thomas McAvoy."

"I still hate needing them."

"Right now, you need sleep." She snapped her fingers. "Come on, off you go."

"You're so bossy."

"That I am."

Thomas gave her a slow blink and crawled beneath the covers.

"Sweet dreams, Thomas."

"After this morning, I've got enough to keep me busy."

When she tossed the trash away, a wad of something hit her and fell to the floor. She turned and saw his pants at her feet. Looking up at him, he had a mischievous, sleepy grin on his face. "Can't sleep with clothes."

"I'll keep that in mind." Her body tingled, remembering how he felt against her, in her. How he kissed. Tasted. If he weren't so exhausted and if she'd brought condoms, she might consider crawling into that bed with him and giving him another thing to dream about.

A soft snore filled the room, making her smile.

When she threw the trash away in the bathroom, she noticed his medications on the counter. The dreaded inhalers he hated and she could understand why. She had heard frustrations from patients over the years for needing any chronic medication, but this time, Lucy couldn't help but say a silent thank-you. Because without them, Thomas wouldn't be here.

Without them, she wouldn't have found someone to fall in love with.

Love?

The word hit her as she began to leave. She glanced back at him sleeping and the word whispered to her again.

Love.

Dammit.

Chapter Nineteen

THE MOMENT HER head hit the pillow last night, her dreams were sweet and plentiful. She woke this morning rested and more than revved up to see Thomas again.

Good grief the man knew how to kiss... everywhere.

Glad she got the chance to return the favor. How she loved how he felt in her mouth. The way she made him writhe with pleasure, how he begged for release.

She let out a long sigh at that mental replay and shuddered from delight.

Now, she'd have to stand outside for an extra few minutes to cool off, but how it would be worth it. Spending time with Thomas made the hours until their Sunday date this evening seem farther away than it had before they'd gone hiking.

Before they had breakfast together.

To be fair, Thomas was far more than his talented tongue. He made her laugh, kept up with her during the hike, and cherished her body like a worshipper at the altar. Plus, he intellectually challenged her without being intimidated by her knowledge base. Too many times, she'd dated guys, only to discover they couldn't handle a smart woman, but not Thomas. If anything, he seemed more turned on by her brain as much as her body.

That made her want to spend more time with him.

A lot more time with him.

I love that about him.

Even though she'd said it to only herself, the word love caught in her throat, making her cough.

Love him? No way. No, this is like and a whole lot of lust.

She tossed back a mint and cleared her throat.

Besides, you can't love someone who's leaving.

But his words of promise gave her hope he'd stay.

A while.

That image settled her angst and allowed her libido to kick into high gear. She'd hoped to see him this morning at the hotel gym, but no such luck. With him working from seven last night until seven this morning, she figured he might be sleeping in.

"Mineral oil. Fiber One. Suppositories." Carol's voice floated around the pharmacy on this quiet Sunday. Only Lucy and another couple of women were in the store. The two others spoke quietly on the cosmetics row.

"Ms. Bingley, can you say that quieter please?"

"Oh, Dr. McMasters. Don't worry about it. Constipation is a common side effect of pain medication."

Peeking around the corner of the aisle, Lucy saw the local curmudgeon, his cane in hand. She debated on talking to him, hoping to convince him to come in, correct and close the charts in question, but when Ms. Bingley said enemas out loud, Lucy had to stifle a laugh and hid in the vitamin section.

"Ms. Bingley, please."

See, this is why people know everything about everyone in town. Carol Bingley worked more efficiently than any gossip rag.

She dramatically sighed and put her hand to her chest. "I'm so glad you got your prescription situation figured out from a couple of months ago. I hated to think of you being miserable in pain."

"Yes, thank you, Ms. Bingley." He motioned for her to bag his things faster.

A little boy ran out away from the two women and right up to Dr. McMasters. He pointed to the man's colorful cane and shouted, "*Culebra! Culebra!*"

Carol's forehead puckered. "What did he say?"

"He said snake." Lucy walked over and tilted her chin towards the head of the cane. A silver serpent sat on the head of it; an easy grip for Dr. McMasters's gnarled fingers.

At first the doctor didn't smile, but when the boy jumped up and down, making hissing noises, a smile cracked across his face. "Hiss, hiss, buddy. Yes."

"A snake? That's terrible, Dr. McMasters." Carol's eyes went wide and shuddered. "Wherever would you get such a thing?"

"Amazon. I get everything on Amazon." Leaning against the counter, he handed the cane to the boy who stared at the snake with wide-eyed fascination. He pulled out his phone from his pocket, holding it up. "I can even order it on my phone."

"Computers are amazing things." Carol shrugged and

scanned the remaining bowel products the man appeared to need. "I know they've made it easier for me to keep inventory."

"I love them. Get to write to my son. He's deployed right now. Get to see my grandkids every week." He beamed. "Get to watch all my TV shows no matter where I am."

"Computers are fantastic," Lucy added, but Jade's words replayed in her head.

He doesn't like the computer.

And Flo's.

He wouldn't acclimate.

Seeing a bit of movement to her right, Lucy noticed two women smiling at her. They motioned the boy to join them.

Reluctantly, he gave the cane back and pointed to Lucy, taking her hand. He escorted her to the two women. *"Es doctora, mami."*

"Mucho gusto." Lucy extended her hand and each woman responded in kind.

The bell rang as Dr. McMasters slowly left. He walked with his cane and his careful gait and the large bag of supplies he'd purchased.

"Vroom. Vroom. Mama!" The child's sweet voice called out. The same child she'd cared for a few days before. "Vroom! Vroom!"

The little boy drove it along any surface he could place it and next to him, two women talked back and forth about which over the counter medicine to get.

Lucy knelt to return the hug. "How are you?"

"I good. Better." He wheezed before a hard, stridorous

cough.

"You sure?" *That doesn't sound completely better.* "I'm Dr. Davidson. *Doctora Davidson. Trabajo en el hospital.*"

"*Ja, ja, la doctora.*" The shorter of the two nodded and responded in kind. "He *mejor*. Better, but he have… have… *como se llama ese silbido?*"

"*Silbido.* Wheeze."

"*Sí, sí.*"

"That should get better. He's taking the medicine?" Lucy repeated the question in Spanish when the mother apologized for not completely understanding her.

"Yes. *Sí. Hoy.* Last day."

"Okay, if he's not better. *No mejor el lunes.* Come back to the ER. *Urgencias.*"

"*Otra ves?*"

"He's been back already?"

The mother's forehead furrowed. "*Sí*, but doctor see him. Say my son. *Mejor.*"

"Okay. Please come back if you need."

The child held up his toy car for her to take. "*Es amarillo.*"

"It sure is yellow." When Lucy held it, she realized it wasn't an authentic Hot Wheel, but a plastic knock off. Most likely he'd gotten it out of a fast food kid's meal and it certainly hadn't held up like a metal toy. A long, rectangular piece was missing out of the side panel. "*Donde?* Where is this?"

"*No sé.*" The boy shrugged and took the car back. He ran toward the front of the store and the women quickly followed, waving over their shoulders as they stopped at the counter to pay for their items.

Pride swelled in her chest. It felt good that she could do what so few others here could. Granted, there wasn't as much of a need for Spanish speakers in Marietta, but she couldn't imagine how terrifying it had to be to go to another country for honest work and not be sure if anyone would understand what they said. That held especially true if someone ended up in the ER.

For the next few minutes, Lucy made her way around the store searching for nothing in particular. With Thomas sleeping in today, she simply wanted to be somewhere other than the ER, the director's office behind a pile of files, or the Graff.

The front bell attached to the door rang as the child's rapidfire questions went silent. Her phone beeped.

Checking it, she discovered a missed voicemail from the moving company informing her she'd have her furniture in seven to ten days. Again. *Of course I will.* "Great. Guess I need to stock up again."

In the basket, she threw another bottle of her favorite shampoo, a pack of razors, deodorant, mouthwash, toothpaste. As she passed the family planning section, she eyed a colorful box of condoms.

The bell rang again, signaling another customer had arrived.

After yesterday, it was more than clear that Thomas and she were more than attracted to each other, but were they ready for that next step?

Intense foreplay was one thing, but sex?

Was that where she wanted to go with him?

She tried to mentally count the reasons why she shouldn't.

He could still leave.

Then she reviewed the reasons why she should buy the box. There were too many to count, which put a wicked smile on her face. Still, him heading out in a few months bothered her.

But enough to walk away from him?

Could she risk her heart if he left when his contract expired?

Was he worth it?

She remembered the way his tongue danced over her body. When he said he'd read *The Pluto Files.*

Yep, it's worth the risk.

But before she could place it in her bag, a snarky voice interrupted her thought.

"Big night planned?"

The box fell to the floor and landed behind her.

Taking a soothing breath in, Lucy exhaled as she turned. "Yes. Sunday. I'm going to dinner. With a friend."

"With Thomas?" Jade picked up the box and appeared to inspect it. "Trojan Pleasure Pack. Forty count. Isn't that a little ambitious, even for Thomas?"

Snatching the box away, Lucy tossed it back on the shelf. The heat of embarrassment radiated off her face. "Why do you care about this?"

"You're brave. Most townies buy their condoms in Bozeman since Carol's gonna tell everyone."

Lucy nonchalantly scanned the store, hoping no one was within earshot, especially no one she'd treated in the past month and a half.

Oh, who am I kidding? Carol Bingley probably has microphones planted all around the store. The entire town will know about this by the time I get to work. "What? Now you going to tell me large isn't the right size for Thomas?"

Jade cringed like she'd smelled something foul. "How would I know? It would be like knowing what size condoms my brothers need. Gross."

"Well, that gives me all sorts of relief." Lucy sarcastically replied, but honestly felt better hearing it.

"I thought about our conversation from the other day."

"Great." When Jade said nothing else, Lucy realized she'd leaned forward in great antici… pation. "And?"

"I screwed up. It's mine to fix. I don't need your help." Dark circles of eye makeup sprinkled over the bags under Jade's eyes as if she cried herself to sleep and hadn't bothered to look in the mirror before going out.

Lucy couldn't help but wonder what demons the woman appeared to be fighting to drive the batshit crazy look in her eyes.

Reaching out to touch Jade's arm, Lucy insisted, "You do need my help if you want to keep this from blowing up in your face."

Jade took a step back, out of Lucy's reach. "See, that's just it. I don't want your help. I want to prove to Denver and Evan that I can do this job. That maybe they'll consider adding a position I inquired about months ago."

"Which is?"

"Nurse educator."

Now we're getting somewhere. "And you plan to fix this with the charts, how?"

"I'll get Dr. McMasters to correct the charts like you said. Take them to his house if I have to, but I will get him to do it. Scream at the man if I have to."

"Screaming at him. Jade, please. You're going to get more flies with honey."

"Or booze."

Or apparently laxatives. "Great. Number seven thousand why it was time for him to retire." Lucy put her basket down.

Jade counted off on her fingers. "Looks good on my re-sume, I can make my own schedule, I get to go to conferences, and arrange staff education."

"What about the charting and the billing and the night shifts?"

"You can keep all that."

"This isn't apple picking. The good with the bad." Lucy ran her fingers through her hair in frustration. "I'm only going to say this once. You have to work with me on fixing these charges and charts."

"And what if I don't? You'll downgrade me to QA to go through those mountains of files in your office?"

"That's no downgrade. They need a full-time person to get the hospital ready for inspection next year. Those charts are a full-time job."

Jade flipped her hair over her shoulder. "I think I'd rather drill nails into my hands. People who do that job are tired or can't work the floor anymore."

"Or are really good with the fine details of it all." Clenching her fists by her sides, Lucy mentally counted to ten to keep from screaming. "Jade, I'm trying here."

"Why?"

"Why what?" Lucy threw her hands up in frustration.

"I don't know why you'd want to. It's no secret I'm a major pain in your ass and you're trying to help me. Why?"

"Because I've read your file. You're a damned good nurse with a lot to teach. The staff looks up to you and looks to you for guidance so I think proposing a nurse educator position is brilliant." Clasping her hands in front of her, Lucy prayed for the strength to stay professional, but Jade had the perfect ability to strip away any patience Lucy had left. "I want you on Team Marietta. To help the hospital grow and flourish and whatever other plans the directors have, but I won't, can't, have you compromise the integrity of this facility with filing those charts without me helping you."

For a moment, Jade stood there wide-eyed and still, but soon gave Lucy a slow clap. "Did you practice that speech in the mirror?"

"I give up." Scooping up the basket, Lucy turned to walk away. "Do what you want with your life, Jade. Don't say I didn't try to help"

"Well, I'll say it again. I don't want your help."

A sudden realization hit her in the gut. *Ugh, she sounds*

like me when I talked to Thomas. For the first time, Lucy understood what Jade was all about.

I don't want your help. How many times had Lucy said that to anyone who offered? She couldn't even begin to count them all.

"Jade, I get it. You want to prove to everyone you can do this all on your own." Lucy stuffed her hands in her pockets. "I get it."

"Then let me do it."

Carol leaned over the counter, her ear pointed towards the two of them.

"If she stretches her neck any farther to hear us, her head is going to fall off."

Jade laughed. "She looks like she's attempting to morph into a giraffe."

"You ladies okay back there?" Carol called out.

"We're good, Ms. Bingley." Lucy waved. "Just getting a few things. Still got any of those lip balms?"

"Oh, yes, I do!"

"Be right there." As Lucy began to leave, she stopped before passing Jade. "I know you don't like me."

"That is true."

"But I will give you until Friday to get this cleared up. If you can't do it, I'm going to go to Denver and Evan about it because if you won't take my help, maybe you'll take theirs." Making her way to the front, Lucy placed her items on the counter as Carol said each item out loud.

"Shampoo. Is this any good?"

"I love that kind. Smells like lemons."

"Not much for lemons." Carol unscrewed the top and sniffed and put the cap back on. "Still not much for lemons."

"To each his own." Drumming her fingers on the counter, her nerves buzzed and her heart raced. Out of the corner of her eye, Lucy could still see Jade milling about the store picking things up and putting them back.

"Razors. Toothpaste. Deodorant. Mints. We still have lip balm, two for four dollars."

Jade slowly made her way to the counter, keeping Lucy on edge. Just the woman's presence caused Lucy to go on high alert.

Good grief. After talking to her, I feel like I just poked a bear with a stick.

The tapping of nails on the counter caught Lucy's attention. "What?"

Pursed lipped Carol waited for an answer when Lucy doesn't remember hearing the question. "Dr. Davidson. Lip balm? How many?"

"Sure, sure, throw them in."

"What flavors?"

"I don't care." Lucy snapped. "One of each."

Carol's lips pruned. "You don't have to be rude."

"Sorry, just have to go to the bathroom."

"I get that. It's all that coffee you drink." She wagged a finger at Lucy. "If that's everything, that'll be—"

"Wait. Wait. Dr. Davidson." Jade called out.

Lucy groaned. "What now?"

"You forgot something." The large box of condoms appeared on the counter.

Carol raised an over plucked eyebrow. "Condoms?"

There couldn't be a word in the dictionary that properly described the depth of Lucy's embarrassment at that moment. What else could she do, but play along. "That's very kind of you, Ms. Phillips."

"I saw you looking at it in the back and realized you hadn't picked it up." Jade replied sweetly. "I'd hate for a *single* woman like you to be unprepared."

Thomas's words of badasses were replayed in her brain, but it didn't do much to quell Lucy's complete mortification.

"Did you need the *forty* count, variety pack, pro-phy-lac-tics, Dr. Davidson?" Carol enunciated each syllable with perfect church lady judgment.

When Lucy looked up, she half expected Carol to have on a white wig with tight curls and wear horned rimmed glasses like the Dana Carvey character on *Saturday Night Live*.

When no such costume appeared, Lucy said a silent prayer. "Yes, Ms. Bingley, please add them to my purchase."

At least I might have a good laugh about this.

Some day.

Jade playfully patted Lucy on the back. "Okay then. Glad to help. See you at work, *Dr. Davidson*."

If she doesn't drive me out of town, she's going to drive me mad.

"Evan." Thomas took the seat across from his boss as the noises of the diner echoed around them.

"Thomas. What can I do for you?"

"Sorry to bother you on a Sunday morning, but I needed to talk." Thomas coughed and tried to take a deep breath. His lungs constricted from the cold air and the oncoming virus he'd most likely caught a few night ago. He couldn't exhale enough to let his lungs fully deflate. "I'll be right back."

After a quick trip to the bathroom and a dose of rescue medication, Thomas returned. "Is there anything in my contract about fraternization?"

"Not that I know of. Why, you and Dr. Davidson going to make it official?"

Thomas wished he could be surprised, but he should have known. "There really is no privacy in this town, is there?"

"No, sir. There isn't."

Flo arrived and placed an empty mug and a small pitcher of milk in front of Thomas before filling the mug just short of the rim. She narrowed his gaze at him. "Guess you don't need a straw."

Thomas chuckled. "No, ma'am. I don't."

She refilled Evan's coffee with a promise to be back and get their order. As usual, the diner was filled to capacity with happy locals.

"You were saying about you and Lucy?"

Drumming his fingers on the table, the thoughts that he'd juggled the entire twelve-hour shift needed a sounding board. "Yes. We're going out tonight. First date."

"Need suggestions? Rocco's is a good place for a first date. Romantic. Nice wine list. Serves a great chicken piccata." Evan tilted his head. "Unless she likes a good steak or something fancier. Then I'd say the Graff."

"I'll be sure to remember those, but I'm not asking just about that." His knee bounced in nervous tempo, his pride hanging on by a thread. "I'm having trouble in the ER."

"What part?"

"The pace. The long hours. The swing shifts. I think I need to consider another job."

"You're leaving?" Evan said it louder than Thomas expected, lowering the sound in the room for a moment.

"No, no, not at all."

The volume in the room went back up.

Thomas leaned forward. "I can finish my assignment, but I think you might want to consider another person for the job. Someone younger. Not as beat up as I am."

"I'm sorry to hear that, Thomas. I think you're a great doctor."

"I'm beating myself up on all these odd shifts. I can't get my body clock right. I need a job where I work during the day, sleep at night." Lifting his coffee mug sent a sharp pain down his arm. The thudding of his heart echoed in his ears. "I think there's something we can do that will keep me here and benefit the hospital."

Evan smirked. "You got it bad."

"What?"

"Yep, you got it bad." He motioned for Thomas to continue. "Tell me your plan and let's see if we can all find a happy medium."

By the time their date had arrived, Thomas couldn't believe how fast Evan and Denver agreed to his suggestion. The preliminary contract sat on his bedside table and he'd made the decision to stay put.

To stay in Marietta, with Lucy.

Now all he had to do was tell her and hope it was exactly what she wanted as well.

Chapter Twenty

"I SHOULD BE stuffed from dinner, but I promised you a hot chocolate." Lucy grabbed Thomas's hand as they quickly headed toward the Copper Mountain Chocolate Shop.

The short, chilly walk from Rocco's had her revived and excited. The evening had been romantic, the conversations casual, but Jade's situation had Lucy's stomach in knots.

The wine had helped loosen the angst and she'd been able to enjoy Thomas's company. With that box of condoms back at the hotel, she hoped she'd get to enjoy him a whole lot more later because if Jade didn't get things cleared up by Friday, she and Thomas might not be on speaking terms.

Stealing a glance of his gorgeous profile made her heart skip a beat.

She'd recovered from broken bones. She could easily recover from a broken heart if this didn't work. Right?

The moment the door opened to Copper Mountain Chocolates, the world smelled of endless possibilities. The layers of cocoa, vanilla, and cinnamon floated in the air, almost coaxing people forward toward the display case to choose a treat to take home.

In it, rows of perfectly designed goodies for even the pickiest chocolate connoisseur. Dark chocolates. White chocolates. Truffles. Clusters. Chocolate with sprinkles. Chocolate cubes with pink salt.

Behind the counter, sat a polished copper pot full of Sage's famous hot chocolate.

Lucy had only had it once before, but likened that copper pot to a cauldron and wondered if Sage had sprinkled her food with magic to make customers crave more.

Of course, with Thomas by her side, Lucy craved more, but it wasn't hot chocolate she wanted from the after-hours menu.

"What do you think?" He softly talked close to her ear. "See anything you like?"

Her brain tried to decide if the extra time on the treadmill would be worth the calories. Her mouth watered with anticipation to see how many champagne caramels she could greedily stuff in her cheeks.

But Lucy knew exactly what she wanted and if she did something about it now, they would certainly be arrested for public lewdness and she could kiss the director's job goodbye.

Still, it couldn't hurt to flirt a little. "I see plenty I like. You are talking about the chocolate, right?"

"Of course." He gave her a lopsided smile, his luscious lips looked far better than they had days ago.

Happy butterflies bounced around in her stomach as he held her hand and kissed her wrist. The tender brush strokes of his lips on her skin lit her body on fire. "For now."

Sage greeted them with an award-winning smile.

They ordered their hot chocolates and watched her scoop out a large ladle of the thick drink from the copper pot. She poured it into a ceramic mug nestled in a saucer, then repeated. On top, a thick layer of whipped cream and a sprinkle of cinnamon.

"My mouth is watering just looking at that." Thomas smiled and grabbed a couple of spoons. A thin line of whipped cream drizzled down the size of his mug as they made their way to a table near the window.

For a few moments, they watched people walk by outside and the sun's brilliant colors fade into the evening blues.

A comforting warmth settled in her soul. She never thought she'd be brave enough to live anywhere that no one would know who she was or what she'd been through, but she'd walked through the wardrobe and made her own corner of the world.

"This is really an amazing little town, but I have to be honest. Until I saw the job posting, I'd never heard of it."

"You do have to know it's here to find it. Not too many stumble into town by accident."

Lucy pointed. "Guess Brett's letting Duke get out more."

Across the street, K-9 Officer Brett Adams strolled along, his German shepherd, Duke, happily leading the way. The dog stopped to sniff every ten feet or so and wagged his tail when anyone approached.

"I can tell you, I didn't know anything about this place until Jade moved here as a kid." He pointed. "They've got Fred out, too."

"Who?"

Tilting his chin toward the window, Lucy noticed Casey, Brett's sister, walking with a floppy eared dog that stopped every few feet to sniff something too.

"That's Jade's dog, Fred."

"She's from here, then?" After realizing that Jade's defiance to ask for any help only matched her own, Lucy promised herself she would attempt to be more patient when dealing with the woman. But Jade would be difficult no matter how patient Lucy promised herself she'd be.

"Her father's side has been here for a couple of generations. Before then, she lived with her mother and stepfather, next door to us, when we were in middle school."

"What brought her here?" Maybe if I understood her better, I would know how to talk to her.

He aimlessly moved the spoon in his hot chocolate. "Because I called CPS on her mom and stepfather."

That stopped Lucy's mug half way to her mouth. She set it back down as her heart leapt to her throat. "Oh, gosh. CPS? I had no idea."

He sat back and ran his fingers through his hair before slouching in his chair. "Bad stuff was going on. I couldn't sit by and watch her be destroyed by them. I called CPS and she came here to live with her dad and brothers."

How heartbreaking. "How old were you?"

"Fourteen."

Reaching out, Lucy placed her hand palm up on the table. "I can't imagine how hard that must have been for you."

"My parents weren't all that supportive of me calling.

Said I should mind my own business, but I couldn't sit by and watch that happen."

"Mind your own business? Why would they refuse to get involved?" *My family would have never done such a thing. If anything, my family would have been too proactive.*

"My parents were too wrapped up in their own selfishness to care about much else." He paused, then gave a knowing smile. "Even me."

"You've been friends a long time, then?" A ping of jealously burned up her chest at their longtime friendship, but hearing of Jade's less than happy childhood, her anger toward the woman began to lose its grip and sympathy replaced it.

"She's the closest thing to a sister I've got."

"Sounds like you did the right thing helping her."

He sat up and he placed his hand on hers. "I hope so."

The sadness in his eyes hurt Lucy's heart. What a burden to be placed on a child, but it spoke volumes about his moral compass, despite his parents' negative influences.

This hadn't been the conversation she wanted to have with him tonight, but it had shed a strong light on a sore subject.

His finger gently stroked the sensitive flesh of her palm, sending shivers all along her skin. *Oh, my goodness.*

Thomas shrugged, a look of frustration in his eyes. "At least she's planning on selling the place."

"Who's planning to sell?" Sage came by and cleared some dishes from another table.

"Jade Phillips." Thomas turned to face Sage. "Her dad's

property."

Giving a knowing nod, she agreed. "That's some of the prettiest land in the county. Has a beautiful view of the mountains. She won't have any trouble finding a buyer."

"Hope she does. She needs to. I think she'd be a lot happier if she did."

"You know, Junior's giving Jade a hard time about selling the place. You should get Maddie Cash over there to talk to her. She's really kind about people who are having a hard time letting go of property or figuring out what they want to do. She's really honest and you can trust her to do just about anything, except when it comes to chocolate."

"It's her kryptonite, huh?" Lucy stirred the whipped cream, watching it swirl into the rich dark liquid. A wave of cocoa and cinnamon drifted up.

"There was a short while she promised to give up chocolate cold turkey, but it didn't stick."

"Why on earth would anyone want to give up chocolate?"

"New Year's promises and alcohol can make people do crazy things." Sage gave them a wink. "But all's good. She always brings some of my Himalayan pink salt caramels as an introduction to new clients."

"Sounds like a win-win to me." Thomas licked the whipped cream off his spoon and placed it next his mug.

Lucky spoon.

Sage excused herself when another family of customers entered.

The youngest exclaimed and pointed, running toward

their table. "It's the doctor, Mom. It's the doctor."

"Good evening, Dr. Davidson." The mother smiled as she stomped her feet at the door before joining her child.

"Dr. Welford gave me this great pink cast. Wanna sign it?" The child tugged on Lucy's arm.

"I don't have a pen."

"I do." Sage held one up at the register.

"Come on, Dr. Davidson." The child encouraged.

"Your pubic awaits." Thomas kissed the back of her hand. "Go on."

"I'll be right back." She quickly said her hellos to the family and Sage let her borrow a marker.

Within a minute, Lucy returned to the table and away from the cold air that hovered around the door.

"You're a popular woman." He chuckled. "I've never asked you, Dr. Davidson. Why medicine? Why ER?"

The excitement of seeing the happy child faded for a moment, but Lucy remembered being about that age when her life changed forever. Pulling her hair away from her neck she tapped the skin. "See this?"

"Yes."

"I was in a car accident."

Thomas pushed his hot chocolate to the side and rested his elbows on the table. "What happened?"

"Long story short, we were going to the grocery store and a guy decided to hit us head on. It was one of those older cars where if you sat six, three were in the front, three in the back."

"Where were you?" He extended his hand out and she

rested hers on top.

"In the middle in the front."

"And you lived?"

"Amazing, huh? Broke my legs, which is really why I started Kung Fu. For rehab."

"Makes sense. Anyone else hurt?"

"My mom broke her hip, my siblings were bruised up, but my dad was the driver so… instant." Tears threatened to fall. Even after more than twenty years, the pain of the day would unmercifully surface. "They really can't explain why my face didn't get all cut up. They think my dad's arm blocked a lot of the glass."

"The scar on your neck?"

"A big chunk from the windshield lodged there."

His eyes went wide. "It didn't hit anything?"

"Someone had to be watching over me, because it nicked the brachiocephalic trunk. The chunk positioned where it not only cut, but applied pressure. If it had been removed in the field, I would have bled out." She pulled away, regaining herself instead of turning into a blubbering mess. "The only reasons I'm here are every member of that paramedic and ER staff that day. They were the most compassionate group of people I'd ever met."

"That's what made you go into medicine?"

She nodded as she grabbed a napkin, dabbing the corners of her eyes. "Unbelievably good group. I'm forever grateful and wanted to be as good as they were."

"And your mom? Did she make it?" He almost looked regretful that he'd asked the question. "You mentioned she died."

"She survived the accident, but had long-term physical difficulties from it. Airbags would have made all the difference in our situation."

A slow smile spread across his face. "That's how you knew so much about them."

"And that's why I got so mad at you about it when you told me I was wrong."

Thomas ran his fingers through his hair. "I should have known. You're always so calm and disciplined. For you to get that upset, I should have known it was personal."

He knows me all too well. "What about you? Why medicine? Why ER?"

"Because I watched the show and thought it looked cool." He gave her a playful wink. "God's honest truth. I wanted to be George Clooney then John Stamos."

"Are you joking with me?"

"Nope and it was the fastest way I could get away from my parents."

"That's an awfully long bit of schooling to get away from your parents."

He paused, his fingers drummed on the table. "Probably, but then if I'd done something else, I wouldn't have met you."

"That's true and that's a very short, trite answer about why you'd spend four years of college, four years of medical school, and a sleepless three years of residency to be George or John." She moved her hot chocolate to the side and leaned in. "Seems you could have moved to Hollywood and become those guys for a whole lot less money and time, Dr. McAvoy. So what's the real story?"

"It's really because of that doctor and nurse that helped me when I got so sick."

"I wondered."

"But you have to admit, being Clooney or Stamos is a good goal."

"I like the real story better."

A slow smirk spread across his face. "You really don't put up with anyone's crap, do you?"

"Nope. And that's why you *love* me." Lucy could feel her eyebrows hit her hairline when she saw his eyes go wide. "Oh, my gosh. I'm so sorry. It's an expression. It's just an expression."

"It's okay, Lucy. I know what you meant." Thomas let out a hearty laugh.

"Good. Good. Glad you... okay." With nervous hands she tried to hold her hot chocolate but couldn't get an inch off the saucer without spilling it. Instead, she sat on her hands like a child with too much energy.

Breathe, Lucy. Breathe.

He slid the mug back in front of him and took a drink. A line of chocolate stayed on his upper lip when he finished. "Why did you move to Marietta, Lucy? Seems there would be plenty of ER director jobs closer to Florida."

She homed in on his chocolate lip, wondering what it would be like to lick it off his perfect mouth. "For someone like me, it's a bit harder to get a job like that."

"Someone like you? What do you mean?"

"Even though I trained at a really busy hospital and have worked there as an attending for a few years, most hospitals want to see more years on the resume."

"Got it. They want you to have more experience."

"Yep. And age."

"You're what thirty?" He playfully cringed when he said the number.

"Close, thirty-two."

"That's right. You're three years younger than I am."

"I get underestimated all the time. My age. My size. My gender. So that's why I like to do everything on my own."

She heard the snark in her voice come through. *Don't ruin this nice evening by getting worked up about something you can't change right now.*

"That must get frustrating." He took another long sip of his drink. "Doing it all on your own. Not having anyone there to help."

"It can be. But it is what it is, right? Work with what you have. Use what you can. Learn as much as possible and change the minds of those who are willing to listen."

"And maybe accept help when it's offered." He raised his mug and she followed suit.

"Sounds like good words to live by." They clinked their mugs and each took a sip. "A smaller hospital, level three is a bit more feasible for me to start out in. Maybe I'll move to a bigger town or the hospital will grow. Hard to say."

"You don't think you'll stay here?" He cocked his head.

"I'm still deciding if it's a good fit for me."

Thomas reached across the table, his palm up. "I think

you're a good fit for me."

With nervous fingers, she took his hand. "You do?"

"I do. Why else did you want to move to Marietta?"

She smiled. "You're going to think I'm crazy, but I wanted to see snow."

"Snow."

"Snow. It's hard to come by in Jupiter, Florida."

"I'd guess so."

"You have any trouble asking for an assignment here?" The rich flavors of chocolate, cinnamon, and milk layered perfectly on her tongue. She had to consciously tell herself not to blissfully sigh with each sip.

A flicker of sadness in his eyes. "At first, I did."

"Why locum?"

"You asking why I travel?"

"Yes."

"I told you my parents were in the military. Moving's in my blood, I guess." The sadness in his voice was a stark contrast to the smirk on his face.

"But they settled in DC, eventually?"

"Yes. Retired within a year of each other. Both are computer geeks."

"Is that where you get your love of math?"

"Guilty, but I guess once a computer geek. Always a computer geek. They got private contractor jobs and stayed put in DC. Still there." His thumb brushed her palm, sending tingles through her body. "I never thought they'd stay in one place, but I guess when you find where you belong, you don't keep running."

Her mouth went dry at his touch. "Running?"

He pulled his hand away. "Moving."

She leaned forward, already missing his touch. "Got any issues I should know about?"

"Issues? I don't talk to my parents much. We've come to an understanding over the years."

What a curious comment. "An understanding?"

He looked down and stirred his hot chocolate. "My parents were the couple that everyone wanted to be like, but honestly, they are a disaster."

"How so?"

"They cheat on each other all the time. Fight. Make up. Cheat. It's a weird relationship." A hint of pink colored his cheeks, his jaw clenched.

"Are they still married?"

"They are. Forty-three years. I don't know why. They're weirdos."

A nervous giggle escaped her. "I'm sorry. I don't mean to laugh at that. You."

He rolled the spoon in his mug. His eyes were intense and focused on her. "They said it keeps a relationship interesting. Exciting."

"Cheating?" She nervously tucked a lock of hair behind her ear, but realized she'd exposed that scar at the base of her neck and let the hair fall back. "You don't agree?"

"I think it's a copout for not wanting to totally commit to someone, for not wanting to find new ways to discover each other. Surprise each other." Thomas narrowed his gaze. "I think it's an excuse to say they lack imagination for sex."

A thrill ran up her spine. "I see. That's important to you?"

"What?"

"Commitment? Surprises. Imagination for, um, sex." Despite her embarrassment, Lucy said a silent thank-you to herself for getting the Trojan variety pack.

"I think it's the more selfless, creative thing you can do. Go all-in, love someone without limits. Find ways to get them excited. Turned on. Climax." His voice, low and sultry, danced across her skin.

Lucy scooted her chair forward as another couple sat at the table next to them. "Well, just so you know. I think our hiking adventure was wonderfully creative."

For a moment, he stared at her, the corner of his mouth at a slant.

"What are you thinking?" *Because I sure know what I'm thinking.*

"That it's time to get creative." He finished the last drops of his hot chocolate before standing and offering his hand. "Ready?"

"I thought you'd never ask."

Chapter Twenty-One

T HOMAS COULDN'T BE a gentleman any longer.

As soon as the door closed to his room, he pushed her hair aside, kissed the back of her neck, unzipping her dress. "I've wanted to touch you all night."

It fell to the floor, revealing Lucy wore a tiny pair of black panties and a matching peekaboo bra. "Maybe next time we could order pizza and stay in."

"Damn, you're gorgeous." He ran his hands up her hips and cupped her breasts, sweeping his thumbs across her nipples.

She pressed her bottom against his crotch and extended her hands up, clasping her fingers behind his neck.

His hands moved down over her body, the slope of her belly, the curve of her hips and up to cup her again. When he looked up, the window drapes were wide open. Being on the upper floor, no one could see them, but he could see the moon as its light spilled over the mountain peaks.

After what they'd done to each other up there, he'd never look at those rocks the same. The idea of it had him so hard he could have hammered nails with his cock. "Lucy, I want to be inside you."

She turned in his arms and tucked two fingers in the front of his pants pockets and tugged. "Then let me do something about that."

Her hands slid inside, her fingers ran along the length of him, but her brow furrowed.

"What?"

She pulled out a condom package from his pocket. "We might need this."

Taking it out of her hand, he tossed it on the bed. He kissed the tip of her nose. "In a minute. I wanna taste dessert first."

"Oh? Got any whipped cream?"

"Nope, I want you all natural."

"Then let's get you served." She grabbed his tie and led him to the bed. "What can I get you?"

"Turn around." He sank to his knees and pressed his face against her belly. Quick fingers moved her panties down her legs and she stepped out of them leaving her in her bra and heels.

"Now what?" She giggled and wiggled her hips.

Resting his hands on her hips he guided her down on the bed and kissed up her inner thigh, starting at her knee.

Her sweet scent lit his body on fire. He wanted to taste her again and again. Thomas wanted her more than a man should be allowed, especially a woman he cared for.

Loved.

Lucy moaned his name as he nibbled the crease between the meeting of her thigh and pelvis.

Loved.

The word should have scared him, made him run for the door, but, for the first time, it brought him peace. Comfort.

The restlessness of his soul calmed and he wanted nothing more than to stay here, with her, in Marietta.

Her silky, wet folds engorged with his touch. Her ginger and lemon body wash mixed with her natural scent had him this side of crazy.

She smelled so good and he bet she tasted even better.

"Do you know how long I've wanted to do this to you?" He slipped a finger inside her. "Since Friday."

She let out a small gasp. "It's Sunday."

"That's too damned long." His tongue slid between her lips and brushed her clit.

She moaned and relaxed her legs. "Thomas."

"That's it." He coaxed as his hands ran over her thighs and cupped her bottom. Thomas flicked her sensitive nub with his tongue before sucking it. His fingers kneaded her ass as he pulled her closer, feasting on her tender flesh.

Sitting up, she pushed him away and grabbed his tie. "Take your clothes off. I want you skin to skin." Lucy panted, her face flushed with desire.

"Whatever the lady wants." Thomas couldn't tell when the last time he'd undressed so quickly, but in less than a minute, he'd stripped naked and knelt back down to pleasure her and kissed her inner thigh. "Now, where were we?"

"Right about here." Lucy reached around and unhooked her bra and was about to toe off her heels when he stopped her.

"Leave them on."

"Reeeeally?"

"Why not?"

"Goodness, Dr. McAvoy, you are full of surprises."

He climbed on the bed, hovering over her as she laid back. "I want to show you every single one of them."

"How long you think that will take?"

Even though Thomas knew she meant it as playful banter, the truth slipped out. "I dunno. Forty, maybe fifty years."

She froze. "Are, are you serious?"

"Yes." His heart slammed into his chest at the honesty.

"But I thought…"

The ink wasn't dry on the contract. He couldn't tell her the details. Not until they spoke to his medical travel agency tomorrow. "I decided I like Marietta more than I thought I would."

"You really are staying, then."

"I told you I would. That okay?"

"That depends. How many surprises do you have tucked up in that brain of yours because if they are anywhere close to what I'm thinking…" The corner of her mouth twitched and a sexy smile spread across her face. "Because I was thinking at least fifty."

Relief slammed into him so hard, he thought he would collapse from joy. "Then I guess we should get busy.

"Absolutely." She ran her fingers through his hair as he worked his way to her breasts. Taking a peaked nipple between his lips, he licked it before he gently sucked.

She arched her back, pushing more of herself into his

mouth. "Yes, Thomas."

Rubbing the opposite nipple with his thumb, he slid his finger between soft folds again. "You're so wet."

Her breathing increased as she began to rock her hips to the rhythm he'd started.

With gentle strokes, he moved his fingers in and out as he felt her vaginal walls tighten.

Her reaction to his touch empowered him. He looked at her with an intent stare as he increased the tempo. "You're beautiful."

"Am I?" She squeaked.

"Yes, Dr. Badass, you are. After tonight, you'll never doubt that again."

The mischievous sparkle in her eye only encouraged him on.

Without a word, he kissed along the scar at her neck, her arm, and down her body until he reached her pussy. His tongue licked her swollen nub, making her gasp.

She grabbed handfuls of the sheets and moaned, "Yes, Thomas. Please, don't stop."

Taking her into his mouth, he sucked her clit, sliding two then three fingers into her.

His cock ached to be touched. Switching hands, he bathed himself in her sweet juices and stroked himself as he continued to taste her.

He increased the pace while he sucked her swollen nub.

She began to tighten around him and grabbed his head, pushing him farther into her. "You're going to... make... me..."

Before he could push her over the edge, he replaced his tongue with his thumb. He grabbed the condom, ripped the package open and rolled it down his shaft.

She scooted back on the bed and he followed her, entering her with one smooth stroke.

Heaven.

Lucy panted as he moved inside her, the pulsation of her climax urging him closer to his. "Yes, Thomas. Yes."

With quick then slow thrusts, Thomas moved inside her.

She wrapped her legs around his waist and pulled him flush. "Come for me, Thomas. I want to feel you come."

It was all the encouragement he needed. He pumped inside her, alternating between fast and slow strokes, driving himself to the edge.

Lucy thrust her hips forward and met him stroke for stroke.

"Damn, Lucy. Yes. I'm gonna… gonna…" He let out a moan as his climax shuddered through his body. His mouth sought hers and kissed her hard.

When the last waves washed over him, he rested his head on her chest. The pounding of her heart echoed in his ear as he soaked in the bliss of falling for her heart, body, and soul.

"Fifty years, huh?" she whispered. Her fingers danced lazily on his back.

"At least." He propped himself on his elbows.

"I could get very used to hearing that for the next fifty years."

Chapter Twenty-Two

"**I**'M NOT DOING it! It's a liability."

"You've got to get this patient out of here."

"What a great thing to hear on my day off. An argument." Lucy smirked despite the crazy of it all. After spending a blissful evening with Thomas, she'd woken to her phone going off at five-thirty this morning.

Evan Watson insisted she come in due to a crisis in the ER.

As much as Lucy hated to leave the warmth of her bed and his arms, she wouldn't tell Evan no.

Turning the corner to the noise, she found Jade and hospitalist Dr. Adam Brady, nose to nose in the middle of the ER.

"You can't admit this kid to the floor." Dr. Adam Brady locked his arms across his chest. "I won't do it."

"Why not?" Jade threw her hands up in frustration. "We've done everything we can. He needs to go upstairs and let the steroids work."

"He's had two racemic epi treatments. He's been on a full course of steroids and he still has active stridor at rest. The epi isn't working yet so he can't go to the ICU, keep him here until this resolves, or transfer him to Billings to see an ENT specialist."

An unresolving croup? That's weird.

Throwing her arms wide, Jade snarled. "His oxygen is good. We need the ER beds. The high school basketball team got food poisoning from some place they stopped at when they were coming back from their tournament in Denver. We're packed. I've got kids throwing up in trashcans in the hallway. You've got to get him up to the floor. He's stable."

The sound of retching from one of the rooms made every one of the basketball members on stretchers in the hallway turn a deeper shade of green.

"I'm not going in there, again. I have no idea what that kid ate, but it's not from this world." Nurse Dave shook his head as he came out of a room. "I'm gonna have to scrub with Lysol when I get home."

Dr. Tom Reynolds chuckled. "That kid have an IV?"

"Yep."

"Try some Zofran." He grabbed the iPad and tapped the screen. "Do the same for the kids in rooms seven and nine."

Dr. Brady drummed his fingers on the counter as he stood his ground against Jade. "That kid's not stable if he's had proper treatment and *still* has stridor. Something else is going on."

Lucy laid her stethoscope on the counter and tucked her phone into her hoodie pocket, then laid the sweatshirt on the back of a chair. "Good morning, Miss Phillips. Dr. Brady."

Both glared in her direction, but as soon as they saw her,

Adam's glare turned into a look of relief. "Lucy."

"She prefers you call her *Dr. Davidson*," Jade snarled.

Ignoring Jade's unprofessional comment, Lucy focused on Adam. "What can I do for you, Dr. Brady?"

Adam shoved his hands into his lab coat. "We have a situation. The child in room five was here five days ago for croup then again early Saturday morning, same complaint. According to the notes, he got a couple of treatments, his first dose of steroids, resolved, and was sent home."

"He'd been back once before tonight, he got a couple of treatments, for the most part, got better, and was sent home. Now he's back." Jade typed at the computer next to the patient's room.

"What do you mean, for the most part? Did he have stridor when he was home?"

Jade's arrogance waned slightly. "I don't know. I was just visiting Thomas when the kid was here last time."

Visiting? Early Saturday morning? That would have been right after the hike. Lucy shoved her questions away for now. "What's his pulse ox?"

"Last I checked, it was in the high nineties," Jade called out as she grabbed another bag of IV fluids, replacing the bag of the kid's IV closest to the desk.

"You said he's had a full course of steroids?" Lucy's brain began working overtime. "When was the last dose?"

Jade grabbed an iPad and tapped the screen. "The father says it was yesterday. Hallway bed C is on bag two of fluids, Dr. Reynolds."

"How old is the child?" Lucy tapped her forehead as she

tried to decipher the patient's situation.

"Four."

"I can't figure out what's going on with this kid." The low voice of Dr. Evan Watson made the hair on the back of her neck stand up. "A kid shouldn't be coming back to the ER three times in a week for croup. Not unless he's got something else going on."

Nothing like solving a problem with the boss looking over your shoulder.

Going down her list of differentials, this was a time when Lucy wished either of her brothers, Edmund or Peter where here. Although she had trained in general ER medicine at a very busy medical center, they'd been through an internal medicine / pediatric or med / peds program. They had a lot more training when it came to kids. "It could be a flu or pneumonia, but that's not going to give him stridor."

"Exactly." Adam joined in. "I've looked at this a few different ways, but nothing's on his films. No structural anomaly. No history of surgeries as a baby. They are smart enough to bring all vaccine records and seem to be very attentive parents. I have no doubt they got the medication."

"They for sure got the medication. I was at the pharmacy when they picked it up. Handed Carol the money, myself."

Evan shot her a smirk. "Did you get two lip balms? They are—"

"Two for four dollars," several of the staff said in unison.

Nurse Dave walked out of the room he swore he'd never go back into, stripped his gloves and washed his hands. "Zofran seems to be working. Now if we can get this kid less green, I think he'll be okay."

Tom Reynolds gave a thumbs-up and entered another room.

Lucy massaged her temples. "Okay. What's been done for this kid so far?"

Jade counted off on her fingers. "Like I said, treatments, observed, loading dose of steroids. Standard protocol."

The snark in her voice was palpable. "Miss Phillips."

"Mrs. Phillips."

Wow. She's in rare form this morning. "Mrs. Phillips. I'm asking a simple question for the care of the patient. Please do your best to stay professional."

A healthy color of scarlet washed across Jade's face as her forehead furrowed as if she smelled something foul. "What are you doing here? Isn't this your day off?"

"It was, but a director's work is never done." She motioned for the chart and pulled up the x-rays on the monitor.

As the medical team members tag-teamed the status of the patient, Lucy had to fight to concentrate. Extreme fatigue settled deep in her bones, threatening to bring her to her knees, but it had been worth getting very little sleep.

Goodness, Thomas had one talented tongue and one responsively amazing body. He was certainly someone she could see spending a whole lot more time with.

At least fifty more years.

If her previous boyfriends had said the same thing to her, she would have run the other direction, but with Thomas it seemed obvious. Easy. And that scared her more than the three words he told her over and over again last night.

When I call back home, they are going to wonder what in the heck happened to me here.

"Dr. Davidson? Any ideas?" Evan asked as he sipped his coffee.

Focus!

"Sorry, I haven't had any coffee this morning." She scanned the notes and came up with no new ideas. "Well, I'd suspect an abscess, but you can't see anything. We could do a CT of his neck, but we'd still need to transport him since I don't feel comfortable aspirating one if it's there"

"Neither do I." Dr. Brady answered as he cleaned his glasses on his lab coat.

"You wrote that the mom's here this time? Not the dad... wait, and the dad."

Crossing her arms across her chest, Jade shrugged. "Yeah, so?"

"And dad has only been here before, right?"

"And?"

That piqued her hopes of solving this sooner rather than later. "Did the mom shed some light on anything? Any new information, any exposure to illnesses?"

Jade shrugged. "I don't know. She only speaks Spanish. Dad does all the talking."

"Maybe the mom might have more to this story. This croup should have resolved by now, especially in a kid this age."

"Dad's been translating. Giving us the information we need." Nodding, Adam stuffed his stethoscope in his pocket. "He's doing okay, but I agree. There's something more to the story."

Jade locked her arms across her chest. "Then the dad should translate better. I'm not gonna go learn another language so I can treat someone who doesn't bother to learn English."

"Quit being to defensive, Jade. I didn't say you did anything wrong." Lucy's fists balled at her side. "You don't have to learn another language. Use the AT&T translator line."

"Why? The dad's here."

Thanks for listening. "I'll go talk to them but for now."

"Great, I'll tell the floor we're sending him—"

Without turning around, Lucy answered as she grabbed her stethoscope off the counter. "We're not sending him anywhere until I examine him, Jade."

She had no doubt Jade was mentally flipping her off right now.

Lucy popped back a mint before entering the room.

"Good morning. *Buenos dias.*"

The tired, tear-stained faces of the parents looked back at her.

The mother's shoulders slumped as she stroked the child's hair. "He no better, *Doctora.*"

Taking her stethoscope, she listened to the child's lungs. They were slightly diminished, but nothing that would indicate croup.

His red cheeks indicated he still had a fever, but what worried her most was his drooling. "Does it hurt to swallow? *Duele cuando tragas?*"

He weakly nodded and held his finger up with the pulse

oximeter on it. The red light illuminated the end of his finger, until he flipped it off. "*No quiero! Dejenme en paz!*"

"Sweet boy, I know, but you have to." Lucy picked it up and put it back on as she gave him a stern look. "*Sí.* Yes."

He stuck his tongue out at her, but left the monitor on.

His honesty made her laugh. "Fair enough."

As his mother calmed her son with a song, the father paced in the small room.

Lucy watched his pulse rate and oxygen levels on the monitor. "One-ten and ninety-four percent."

Nothing came to mind of what could be wrong with this child, but obviously something had him in its grip. "Give me a moment. *Denme un momento por favor.*"

A flash of yellow caught her attention.

In his hand, he held his precious car. The *broken*, plastic car.

Oh no. An excited panic hit her square in the gut.

Immediately, Lucy asked, "What day did you get that toy? *Cuando compraste tu juguete?*"

"*El lunes pasado en burgers.*" The father verified with the mother. "Yes, hamburger place, Monday."

"When did it break? *Cuando se rompió?*"

The parents looked at each other and shook their heads. "*No sé.*"

"You don't know."

The father's eyes went wide. "Wait. Wait. *No sabemos, no nos dimos cuenta, quizas el domingo*"

"You got it Sunday? *Domingo?*"

"*Sí, sí. Domingo.*" The mother's lips thinned. Her tears

falling down her face. "*Por qué?*"

"I need to see the car." Lucy pointed, but the child held it against his chest.

The mother coaxed. "No, no *hijo*. Give it."

"I'll give it right back." When the child, refused, she pried the toy from the child, who immediately cried a husky cry.

Dr. Brady and Jade walked in.

"Any luck?" Adam asked.

"Maybe." Lucy pointed to the missing section of the car. "Where is this piece? *¿Saben donde esta la pieza que falta?*"

The parents shook their heads, obviously confused.

"Where is this piece?" She crouched down and handed the car back to the child. "*¿Hijo, sabes donde está la pieza?*"

For a moment, she held her breath, hoping the child would tell her something.

Tentatively, he reached up and tapped his throat. "*Aquí.*"

"Holy crap!" Jade slapped her hand over her mouth as if the words unexpectedly fell out.

Both parents' eyes went wide and they each rapid fired questions at Lucy.

After she answered as many as she could field, she motioned to Adam and Jade to meet her outside.

"*Un momento, por favor.*" Lucy calmed the parents before meeting the rest at the desk. "I need to see that kid's x-rays from Monday and I need another set right now."

"On it." Poppy nodded as her fingers sailed over the keyboard.

"What? What have we got?" Evan asked as he handed a

to-go coffee to Lucy.

"I think he's got a piece of his Hot Wheels stuck in this throat."

Shaking her head, Jade leaned against the desk. "Hot Wheels are metal. That would have shown up on x-ray. I don't think that kid understands what you mean."

"It's a cheap knockoff from a kid's fast food meal. A plastic car, Jade, and there's a piece missing."

Adam looked at the x-ray again. "That's not going to show up. The only way we can know is to scope him and we don't have that capability here."

"Plus, we can't just send him anywhere if we don't have proof," Jade added, obviously unimpressed with the child's diagnosis.

"We don't need proof of a foreign body. We have a kid who's not clearing after aggressive treatment for croup who may have swallowed a piece of his plastic car. This is beyond what we can provide." Lucy looked around the computer. "Poppy, what's the closest hospital that has an ENT specialist?"

Immediately, Poppy answered, "Probably St. Vincent's in Billings."

"A children's hospital?"

"No, but their specialists do see pediatric patients." Evan blew out a long breath. "You're talking Denver, Salt Lake City, or Boise. We'd have to get Jonah Clark and fly him out."

"Good grief. Which is the closest?" Lucy pictured the map of the state in her head and the towns she drove through to get here.

"They are all at least eight hours away, but Billings is two."

"Do we have someone who can take him?"

Poppy picked up the receiver. "I can call the fire house, see which paramedics are on call and if Jonah can take him."

Bracing her hands against the counter, Lucy shuffled the possibilities, but they became fewer when Poppy informed them a strong storm heading their way grounded any helicopter flights out.

Pressing on the knots in her neck, Lucy sighed. "I need whoever is on call for ENT at St. Vincent's in Billings. I need that other set of neck X-rays, right now. He needs an IV, NPO, and, as soon as I see those, we can make some plans."

"You sure they have pediatric capabilities there?" Poppy nodded and began dialing the phone.

"Yep. That blue binder next to the desk should have all the specialties and hospitals within a three hundred mile radius."

Poppy grabbed the book and opened it. "Cool, who made this?"

"I did. The first week I was here." She pointed to Dave as soon as she saw him. "Mr. Dave. Room five needs your excellent pediatric IV skills, sir."

"Is he throwing up?" The nurse cringed.

"Nope."

"I'm on it."

Within thirty minutes, the child had an IV, a dose of

Motrin, and a new set of films. At the moment, he was resting in his father's arms, still playing with the toy car.

"You can't see it straight on as well, but you can see it laterally right there." Lucy's finger traced along an area in the middle of the throat. "It's faint, but if you know what you're looking for, it's there."

"You sure that's not artifact?" Evan squinted as Adam did the same.

Jade appeared to busy herself with the sick members of the basketball team and came no closer than ten feet of wherever Lucy stood.

"I thought so too, but I compared it to the films from earlier in the week." Setting the two films side by side, Lucy pointed back and forth. "Right there."

"I'll be damned." Adam watched, slack-jawed.

"Great catch, Lucy." Evan gave her a pat on the back as his phone beeped. "Let's get this kid to Billings."

"Do you need to talk to the hospital administrator for hospital to hospital transfer, Evan?" He gave her a curious look. "No, Lucy. It's fine if you can do it. I have a meeting with Dr. McAvoy."

"Thomas? I mean, Dr. McAvoy?" Lucy tried not to sound interested, but what would Evan and Thomas need to discuss.

Unless... oh, no.

She shook the idea away. Thomas told her he had no interest in the director job and she'd believe him, for now.

After arranging the transfer, she talked to the ear, nose, and throat specialist on call as the paramedics Amanda

Carter and Chris Douglas loaded the kid up and got him ready for his adventure to Billings.

Walking them out to the ambulance, she explained again to the parents why they were transferring him and who would greet them there. Happily, she discovered one of the social workers spoke fluent Spanish and would be there to meet them when they arrived.

Several family members arrived as they walked out the back door. The woman Lucy had seen with the mother the day before offered to drive the parents behind the ambulance.

When Chris opened the back doors of the truck, the child's eyes went wide and he pointed excitedly. "Vroom. Vroom!"

The mother hugged Lucy without an invitation and when she was done, the father shook her hand. "Bless you. Bless you."

Tears of relief ran down her face. "I'm glad to help."

This was what she hoped to accomplish coming to Marietta and now that it happened, she couldn't contain her excitement.

Walking back into the ER, the entire staff stood and applauded, including Evan and Denver before they excused themselves for a full afternoon of meetings.

If they'd told her she'd won the lottery, Lucy wouldn't have felt as good as she did right now. She couldn't wait to get back and tell Thomas about her morning. She quickly completed her charting, made sure every member of the basketball team had been treated before sitting in the silence of the call room.

Tears of joy ran down her face or was that relief? She buried her face in her hands, allowing her to purse all the frustration, the worry, the sadness, the joy that had so consumed her for the past several weeks.

Either way, the emotional purge lifted the pressure from her worried soul, and even in this little corner of the world, Lucy had made it her own.

She'd saved a child's life, the same skill someone had done for her twenty-years ago and it felt damned good.

Chapter Twenty-Three

WHEN LUCY WALKED back into the ER, she immediately found Jade and called her into the office.

Jade plopped down in the chair in front of Lucy's desk. "Yes?"

"You going to come in and finish these charts?"

"I haven't gotten McMasters to come in yet."

"Do you think you can?" Lucy could almost see the speech bubble over Jade's head saying I don't need your help.

Then Jade did something unexpected. "I can't do it. Not without a miracle. Not without... help."

Lucy drummed her fingers on the desk as her mind raced with solutions. "What if I can?"

"What? Now you perform miracles too?"

"It's possible."

Jade rested her hands on the desk. "Tell you what, you get him to agree to come in and take care of this mess, I'll agree."

"You're telling me that you're willing to commit insurance fraud instead of clearing your name?"

"Lucy, despite what you think of me, I didn't do anything wrong. I promise you, I did everything I was supposed to."

"Then explain to me what's going on." Lucy held up the file holder.

Looking away, Jade shook her head. "I honestly don't know, but I do know nothing I say will convince you I didn't do anything wrong."

A yawn took over Lucy's frustration.

"Thomas keeping you up late?"

"I know you and Thomas are longtime friends, but that's wildly inappropriate. Please stay out of my personal life and stop changing the subject. I'm trying to help you."

A curious look replaced Jade's defiance "I can't figure you out. You seem to want me gone and then you're trying to help me. Why?"

"There's really nothing confusing about me. I work my ass off. I expect no less from the people I work with."

"Are we done here?"

Before Lucy could begin to answer Jade had her hand on the door handle. "And Jade."

Her shoulders sank. "What, Lucy?"

"By Friday, I want you here in my office to finalize these charts so we can send them to insurance."

Spinning on her heels, Jade's eyes were wide with anger. "That's great. I'll be here and Dr. McMasters will be?"

"Here." *Although I have no idea how.*

Waving her off, Jade laughed. "Oh, okay, well, when you get him to come in, let me know."

"You need to take care of this."

"And what if I don't. What if I don't do what you say?"

"You're fired." Lucy expected an explosion, but Jade

simply walked out of her office without a word. She didn't even throw the door open as she left.

"Now all I have to do is figure out how to get Dr. McMasters in here," Lucy mumbled as she turned off the light and began to gather her things, but her exhausted body simply wouldn't get out of the chair after she sat down again.

She sat in the silence of the room only lit up by the sunshine pouring in from outside.

The back door whooshed open and two familiar voices came in.

"I think this is a great idea, Thomas," Evan exclaimed. "I don't know why we didn't think of it before."

Lucy leaned forward as they stood outside the office, hoping to surprise Thomas. As she reached for the door, Thomas said, "I appreciate you bringing me on full-time. This director's position is a good happy medium."

"Agreed." Evan asked, "You told Lucy, yet?"

Thomas coughed several times. "No, I had the contract last night, but haven't told her yet. Wanted to surprise her over breakfast, but she got called in. Wonder where she is?"

Their voices faded down the hall, but Lucy froze as her heart shattered.

What did they just say? Director.

She sank into the chair next to her as her legs gave way, her body weighed down by the overwhelming blanket of betrayal.

He lied to me.

She cursed herself for thinking getting through a broken heart would be so easy.

No broken bone feels this bad.

Chapter Twenty-Four

H E WAITED FOR her to come back. Thomas looked at
the contract again.

Was he making the right decision staying here? Would
she want him after he told her what he'd done?

He looked out the window at the mountains. The snow
had slowly begun to melt and patches of green replaced the
white.

The winter still bothered him as his chest rattled with a
cold, but Thomas couldn't imagine a life without Lucy. If
she was going to be the clinical director of the ER, he had to
stay here. For the first time, he wasn't worried about setting
down roots.

Just like his parents had done so many years ago, he'd
finally found where he belonged.

The restlessness had all but calmed because of a fiery
redhead who literally knew how to kick ass.

Quick footsteps and the buzz of the digital door lock
caught his attention. He threw the door open and saw hers
begin to close.

Taking a deep breath, he approached her room, paper in
hand.

Before he could knock, her door flew open. "What?"

Her fury wasn't what he expected. "Congratulations on the catch."

"I got lucky." She turned and let the door begin to close.

He stuck his foot in the way of the door before it locked behind her. "Lucy, what's wrong? You did an amazing thing today."

"Turns out he'd swallowed a piece of a toy. It was lodged in his throat." Fat tears ran down her face. "We missed it. We all missed it."

"But you caught it, right?"

"Yes, he's fine. He's on his way to Billings. The ENT staff is waiting to take him to surgery. Why didn't you tell me you were taking my job?"

She'd said everything so fast it took him a moment to process it all. "That's good. Wait. What?"

"You and Evan walked by the office earlier." She clenched her fists at her sides. "Do you know how long I've worked for a position like this? How little sleep I've gotten? How long I've waited."

"Lucy, wait. Wait." He held up his contract, but she slapped it away.

"You lied to me."

"When?"

"You said you had no desire to be the ER Director.

He handed her a box of Kleenex when she wiped her nose with the back of her hand. "I don't."

"Ugh, you're confusing."

He reached for her, but she put her hands up, warning

him to stay back. Considering what she did to Junior, he had no doubt she'd make good on her threat. "Lucy."

"What? What are you going to lie to me about now?"

"I didn't lie. Things changed. I changed." He waited for her emotions to soften before saying anything. Even then, he chose his words carefully. "Lucy."

"Stop saying my name. Just spit it out."

"I love you."

She shook her head as though she struggled to believe him. "How can you?"

"How can I? Why wouldn't I?" Clenching his fists at his sides, he tried to find the right words, but she deserved the truth, no matter how weak it made him look. "Lucy, I can't be the ER director and I was never considered for the position anyway."

"What? Why?" Concern replaced fury, which made him only love her more. "Thomas, are you okay?"

How he hated what he was about to do. He hoped his confession wouldn't make him less of a man in her eyes.

Removing his shirt, his chest tightened from angst. "I have to tell you something."

"As impressive as you are, I don't think this is the time." She sniffled and stepped forward.

"I love your sense of humor." He turned his back to her. "The scars to my back. That's from when Jade's ex-husband stabbed me. Punctured a lung."

"Yes, you've told me. Showed me."

Facing her, he ran his finger along his left flank. "He got me again here. These two spots here, they're where my chest tubes where."

Lucy's eyebrows furrowed as she approached him. Her fingers tracing along the scars. "You must have been in so much pain."

The tenderness of her touch made him shiver from delight. "He had knocked me to the ground, had me by the hair and was about to cut my throat when she shot him."

"Why are you telling me this, again?" Her eyes, her hands roamed his beaten body without pause.

Every nerve ending was on high alert to her touch. "My pulmonologist suggested I quit ER after I was cleared from rehab."

"What? Why? You're a tremendous physician. Why would he tell you—"

"Because of the patient load, the constant exposure to respiratory illnesses. Said I would do better being behind a desk for a year, but I didn't want to listen. I figured if I came here, I'd be in a smaller unit, get some good air in my lungs and be on my way." He slouched on the end of the bed. "But turns out, I'm still tired in a smaller unit. Not up to where I was before."

"Maybe you simply need more time to recover."

"It's been close to two years, Lucy. I've recovered as much as I can."

She knelt in front of him, resting her hand on his knee. "I'm sorry to hear that, Thomas."

"I'm not." Taking her hand, he interlaced her fingers with his. "Because now I get to work with you."

"What do you mean?"

"I'm in charge of getting the hospital ready for JCHAO."

"What?" She tried to pull her hand away.

"All those files in your office? That's my job now, which leaves you in charge of the ER." He waited for her to say something. "I'm good with details. Evan said I can still work in the unit a shift or two when needed, but working daylight hours and getting out of the unit for the most part will help me."

"I didn't ask you to do that."

"You need help, Lucy. You can't do it all yourself." He'd expected her to smile and pull him into her arms, beg him to make love to her, but not anger.

"I don't need your help. I don't need anyone's—" She pulled her hand out of his grasp and backed away. "Ugh, I hate how I sound right now."

"Dammit, Lucy. Why are you so stubborn? You can't do it all. You can't work sixty hours in the ER and do one hundred hours of paperwork a week. No one can."

Fat tears ran down her face. "I needed to prove I can do this job without anyone. Without being anyone's sister or daughter or some girl who survived a crash. Do you know how long I've tried to break out of that mold and now I'm here and… and… I find I can't do it all by myself."

"You think you should be able to?" Cautiously, he approached her.

"Why not? My siblings do."

"I bet their lives aren't as easy as you think." He moved her hair away from her neck. "You're my Lucy. The kick ass, Kung Fu ER doctor who runs the unit with an iron fist."

He waved his arms around in an attempt to look like he knew anything about martial arts.

She sniffled and laughed. "You look like you're having a seizure."

Taking her hands in his, he kissed her wrists. "Lucy, I've moved a long time and I've never wanted to stay anywhere. But you've given me a place to settle. A place I want to stay. Build a life with, because I can't imagine being anywhere you aren't."

"That's the sweetest or creepiest thing you could say to me right now."

"Which one is it?"

"I haven't decided." Grabbing him by the shirt, she closed the gap between them. "Kiss me first and I'll decide."

He leaned down to kiss her, but stopped short. "Does this mean you're happy about my job? Being the QA director?"

"Of course I am." She fiddled with the buttons on his shirt, loosening the top couple. "I'm glad you found your place in the world."

"But?" The tenderness of her touch drove him mental. He wanted to throw her on the bed and make love to her all afternoon.

She let out a long breath as if trying to find the right words. "I can't promise I'll be easy to work with. I'm stubborn and really, really ODD at times. That I'll still try and do it all on my own."

"I wouldn't expect anything less from you."

"But there is one problem with this plan." Her fingers

danced tentatively over his skin then unbuttoning his shirt. "If we're going to be working together every day, how am I going to keep my hands to myself? How am I going to get anything done with you looking as good as you do?"

"Don't worry. When I start talking about coding and billing errors, that should make you want to keep your hands to yourself." He pulled her flush, relishing the feel of her next to him.

"My own hot nerd." Her hands slid under his shirt and pushed it off his shoulders. A look of lustful determination on her face as she raked her eyes over him.

His cock stood at attention as she ran her hands down his hips, then grabbing his butt. "I would have given anything for a girl like you to look at me like that when I was in high school."

Resting her head on his chest, her fingers danced up and down his spine. "If no girl was smart enough to snatch you up back then, it's my gain. Their loss."

"We should probably have a safe word while we work." He buried his nose in her hair, soaking in the ginger and lemon scent. "We can get a small stack of those files caught up in a day."

"And how do you plan to do that?"

He whispered in her ear. "It's all on the computer. I can organize every printed file put it in digital folders where you can find it anytime you want."

"Keep talking." Her arms wrapped around him as her breathing quickened.

A feeling he'd never get enough of. "Once a computer

geek, always a computer geek."

Her head popped back, almost hitting him in the chin. "Wait, what did you say?"

"Once a computer geek, always a computer geek."

"Oh, my gosh! I've figured it out. Those charts on my desk. Can you help me right now?" Before she could escape from his arms, he kissed the base of her neck.

"You sure you want to take care of it *right now*?"

She sighed. "In an hour?"

"Make it two."

"WHAT'S THE MEANING of this?" Dr. McMasters hobbled in, his serpentine cane clutched in his hand. "Getting me down here on a Friday afternoon. I don't have time for this."

"Thank you for coming, Dr. McMasters." Lucy held a chair out for him as he plopped down.

Jade sat on the opposite side of the table. She wrung her hands in her lap. "I'll be damned. You really did get him here."

"This better be worth it, I'm in the middle of a binge watch of…" He grumbled something under his breath, then noticed the files. He opened one and closed it, shoving it across the table. "I'm not doing this."

"Actually, yes, you are." Lucy sat next to him as Thomas entered the room. "Dr. McAvoy and I have done some digging. The last week you worked here, more than half your patients received narcotics of different sorts. Mostly pills, but some orders for Demerol and Phenergan."

"And? What? People come in pain."

"They do." Thomas added, "But your patients had an extraordinary high narcotics rate, higher than any other doctor at the time."

Dr. McMasters remained stone-faced. His finger tapped on the head of his cane. "What do you want me to say?"

"I don't think you have to say anything." Lucy shrugged. "That day at the pharmacy, when you were talking to Carol Bingley."

"So?"

"She mentioned you'd run short of your medications at home a few months before. The insurance company was dragging their feet with coverage. You didn't want to be in pain, so you wrote orders on patients after they left and pocketed the medication."

The man's lip twitched and he opened a file. "Why are you talking to me? She saw the patient. Why aren't you asking her about this? She's probably stealing for her brother."

"You mean, mean old man!" Jade slammed her hand on the table. "I would never do such a thing."

Lucy drummed her fingers on the table. "Dr. McMasters, there's no need to lash out at Jade. She's gone through and signed off on the orders you gave and there are about a dozen charts that were changed after the patient left. Specifically to obtain narcotics."

"Changed after the patient left?" Shaking her head, Jade adjusted in her seat. "As much as I'd like to believe this, Dr.

McMasters would have a hard time faking anything on the computer. He can't use them."

The man beamed as though he'd won the Super Bowl. "She said it."

"Really? The entire time you were trying to train him, Jade, he was memorizing your passwords." Lucy raised an eyebrow. "All these charts that I showed you with the narcotics orders? You didn't write them or enter them to get them out of the Pixis. He did."

Thomas laid a piece of paper on the table between Jade and Dr. McMasters. "This column is the time the patient was checked in to the unit. This column is when the patient checked out per written documentation and this is the time the medications were ordered and taken out of the dispenser.

As much as Lucy initially hated needing help, Thomas had been brilliant when it came to charting and organization. With his brilliance, it took less than half a day to figure out what happened with the files.

Jade's hands shook. "Why would you do that?"

The man's mouth blanched from him thinning them so hard.

"I worked with you for over a year. Why would you set me up this way?"

"Because my insurance kept screwing me over on my pain medication. I was about to retire. Ever sit around with rheumatoid arthritis? It's painful, all day. Every day." He held up his hands, his swollen knuckles kept him from closing them all the way. "I couldn't go without so I figured who would it hurt?"

"Who could it hurt? I could have lost my job! They thought I'd stolen drugs from the hospital." Jade buried her face in her hands. "Oh, my gosh. I trusted you."

Without a hint of compassion, Dr. McMasters replied, "That was your first mistake. Don't trust anyone."

"Okay, y'all have work to do." Lucy turned to Thomas. "Can you take it from here? I'm going to check the unit."

"That's why they pay me the big bucks."

"Yes, yes it is."

A few hours later, they were done, and Dr. McMasters left, grumbling every curse word under the sun as he headed out the ambulance entrance.

"Thank you, Lucy." Jade picked up her purse. "I can't believe you did that."

"After we talked last week, I realized you and I aren't that different. I know what it's like to try and do it all on your own. To refuse to let anyone help you. Think you don't need anyone." Reaching across the table, Lucy gave Thomas's hand a squeeze. "It's not the easiest thing to admit that it's not a one person job."

"No, no it's not." Jade's eyes darted back and forth between Lucy and Thomas. "And you're right, I couldn't have done this without your help. I hate saying this again, but thank you."

"I know you hate saying that. You're welcome. Truce?" Lucy extended her hand to shake. "We don't have to like each other, but can we be professional and work together?"

She turned to Thomas. "Still whistling?"

He nodded. "Yep. Gonna be for awhile."

A sweet sadness washed across Jade's face. "I'm glad for you."

"Whistling?" Lucy's forehead furrowed.

"I'll tell you later." Thomas winked.

"Truce. We can work together." Jade responded in kind, taking Lucy's hand. A phone beeped. Jade picked it up and smiled. "It's Maddie Cash. She's meeting me today. Helping me make some decisions. Tough choices."

"Junior still giving you trouble?" Thomas stood and gave Jade a hug before she left.

"It's nothing I can't handle."

"You sure?"

She sighed. "Well, if I can't, I know who to ask for help."

Lucy and Thomas watched her drive away before walking back to the Graff. Spring was in full force. The sun light up a cloudless blue sky.

As they walked toward the hotel, relishing the warmth of the sun on their faces, Thomas asked, "Are you going to turn him in to the state medical board?"

Lucy shook her head and grabbed his hand. "No, he's retired. He's not interested in practicing medicine ever again."

"Lucy, you can't—"

"However, we are going to give Denver and Evan a rundown of what happened. Let them have the final say."

He held up their hands as they walked into the lobby of the hotel. "I thought you didn't want any show of affection at work or anywhere else."

Lucy shrugged as the elevator doors closed behind them.

"Meh, Carol knows I bought condoms. The entire town probably already knows we're having sex."

"It's a helluva lot more than sex." Thomas leaned down, kissed her cheek, whispering against her skin, "We shared some hot chocolate."

She shuddered when the heat from his breath tickled her neck. "You're impossible to resist. You know that?"

The ding from the doors opened and they walked into the hallway, still hand in hand.

"That's because you love me."

For the first time, Lucy had no reservations or worries hearing those words. "You're right, Dr. McAvoy. I absolutely do."

The End

The Marietta Medical Series

Book 1: *Resisting the Doctor*

Book 2: *Challenging the Doctor*

Book 3: Coming soon!

Available now at your favorite online retailer!

About the Author

Native Texan Patricia W. Fischer is a natural born storyteller. Ever since she listened to her great-grandmother tell stories about her upbringing the early 1900's, Patricia has been hooked on hearing of great adventures and love winning in the end.

On her way to becoming an award-winning writer, she became a percussionist, actress, singer, waitress, bartender, pre-cook, and finally a trauma nurse before she realized she needed to get her butt to a journalism class.

After earning her journalism degree from Washington University, Patricia has been writing for multiple publications on numerous subjects including women's health, foster/adoption advocacy, ovarian cancer education, and entertainment features.

These days she spends her days with her family, two dogs, and a few fish while she creates a good story with a touch of reality, a dash of laughter, and a whole lot of love.

Visit her at PatriciaWFischer.com.

Thank you for reading

Resisting the Doctor

If you enjoyed this book, you can find more from all our great authors at TulePublishing.com, or from your favorite online retailer.

TULE
PUBLISHING

CPSIA information can be obtained
at www.ICGtesting.com
Printed in the USA
BVHW031824010819
554900BV00001B/73/P